Home for Christmas
By Kate Davies

She left everything familiar behind—but love found her anyway.

Sophia is determined to spend Christmas on her own terms this year. Her daughter will be spending the holidays with her boyfriend's family, and Sophia has no intention of staying home alone with her memories.

She knows Ethan would be more than happy to keep her company. But he's her business partner—and her late husband's best friend. It's past time to stop leaning on him and learn to stand on her own two feet. A cruise to the Caribbean might be just the ticket to discovering who she is now, and what she really wants.

Ethan is stunned to discover that Sophia has decided to go on a cruise for Christmas—alone. He'd thought something more was finally developing between the two of them. If she's ready to move on after the loss of her husband, he'll be damned if he lets her move on without him!

On the spur of the moment, Ethan books a stateroom, determined to prove to Sophia that what they have goes far beyond friendship. The romantic atmosphere of the cruise sparks a passion the two had only dreamed of before—but can their fledgling relationship survive beyond the vacation of a lifetime?

Look What Santa Brought
By Annmarie McKenna

He is looking for the love of his life, she is looking for a little refuge.

Scott Wyatt knows what he wants for Christmas and it comes in a beautiful-voiced, make his heart race, more than tempting package. If only he could see her.

Tara Patrick needs a man to make her ex see the light. But her best friend's gorgeous brother offers himself for the job, she has to say no. How could she possibly use the blind man who makes her heart flutter and not get hurt in the process?

Staring at the business opportunity of a lifetime, Tara finds herself living as close to Scott as one can without sharing a bed. Tara's ex isn't happy and he sets out to prove he won't lose her. But when darkness falls, which man has the advantage, because Scott isn't willing to let Tara go either.

Love Me, Still
By Maya Banks

Forgiveness is the most difficult thing to give but the most cherished thing to receive.

Beloved mate to two wolves, Heather lived an idyllic life until hunters destroyed the pack's peaceful existence.

Believing their mate betrayed them and was responsible for their father's death, Cael and Riyu cut Heather from their lives. But when they realize their terrible mistake, can they ever gain her forgiveness and win back her love?

Miracle at Midnight
By Stacia Wolf

Can a heart encased in stone discover the true meaning of love?

Comtesse Amara de la Cortese isn't a very nice person. In 1507, she's a hard-hearted ruler who thinks nothing of imprisoning beggars and ordering their children sold. Enter one saint—Saint Nicholas—whose quest is to protect the young. He imprisons her in stone, but he believes in redemption. Once every fifty years, he grants her forty-eight hours of freedom to answer one apparently simple question. Ten chances. The same question. *What is the true meaning of love?*

Sounds simple? Amara, whose heart is stunted by a loveless past, fails each time. On her very last shot at lifting the curse, she finds herself in present-day Manhattan. She meets six-year-old Samantha, who totally believes her fantastic story, and her doctor dad, Nick, who totally doesn't.

Despite the threat hanging over her head, Amara is determined to enjoy her last bout of freedom. With Nick and Sami, she explores New York's unique style of Christmas. She also finds herself falling in love.

All too soon, time runs out, in a way none of them imagined. Will Amara find the answer? Or is she doomed to forever have a heart of stone?

Second Chance Christmas
By Mackenzie McKade

They say cowboys don't cry... Apparently they don't forgive and forget either.

After four years, Lori Dayton is returning to Safford, Arizona to spend Christmas with her family and face her past. She has reservations about seeing Dean Wilcox again. But time hasn't changed her. She still loves Dean more than ever.

Time heals all things... Yeah right! Lori still heats Dean's blood like no other woman. Even after all she's done, he can't resist the urge to take her in his arms, feel her body pressed to his. He wants her naked against him, just like before.

Can he forgive her, as well as himself, for that dreadful night when they lost so much?

The Perfect Gift

A Samhain Publishing, Ltd. publication.

Samhain Publishing, Ltd.
512 Forest Lake Drive
Warner Robins, GA 31093
www.samhainpublishing.com

The Perfect Gift
Print ISBN: 1-59998-661-2
Home for Christmas Copyright © 2007 by Kate Davies
Look What Santa Brought Copyright © 2007 by Annmarie McKenna
Love Me, Still Copyright © 2007 by Maya Banks
Miracle at Midnight Copyright © 2007 by Stacia Wolf
Second Chance Christmas Copyright © 2007 by Mackenzie McKade

Editing by Jessica Bimberg
Cover by Scott Carpenter

First Samhain Publishing, Ltd. electronic publication: December 2007
First Samhain Publishing, Ltd. print publication: September2007

Contents

Home for Christmas

Kate Davies

Dedication

For Patricia Helen. Thanks for being my second mom, my mom's best friend, and an all-around wonderful person. Though you probably won't recognize it now that I've gotten through with it, this story was sparked by your idea, and I'm forever grateful.

Chapter One

"Surprise!" Samantha kissed her mom on the cheek as she bounced into the house, arms loaded with packages. "Bet you didn't expect to see me today!"

"You'd be right," Sophia said, a smile tugging at her mouth despite herself. "What are you doing here?"

"Presents, of course."

Sophia quirked one brow. "Giving or getting?"

Sam stuck her tongue out. "Both."

"Well, at least you're honest," Sophia said, a hint of laughter in her voice. "Aren't you and Robert supposed to be on your way to his parents' house by now?"

"We're heading out after this. His parents aren't expecting us until dinner. He sends his love, by the way." Samantha smiled, her cold-chapped face glowing even brighter. "He's busy getting the car packed."

"So you two are all ready to hit the road, huh?" Sophia gave Samantha her best concerned-Mom look. "Make sure you drive carefully, and if the weather turns bad don't hesitate to stop."

Samantha rolled her eyes. "Mom, we're both safe drivers. We'll be there by dark. Besides, the big snowstorm isn't supposed to hit until tomorrow."

"I'm your mother. It's my job to worry."

"Yeah, I know."

Sophia put her arms out for the presents. "Here, let me take those."

"Nah." Sam sidestepped her and headed straight for the living room. "I'll just stick them under the..."

Sophia froze, waiting for her reaction.

She wasn't disappointed.

Samantha stomped back into the hall, eyes wide. "Where's the tree?"

"I, uh..."

"Mom, it's five days until Christmas! You always have the tree up way before this!"

Sophia's voice was low. "Not this year."

"Why didn't Ethan help you?"

"I didn't ask."

"I don't believe this." Sam looked around, noticing her surroundings for the first time. "You don't have any decorations up either."

"Not this year," Sophia repeated.

Samantha looked down at the wrapped gifts she was still carrying. "Well, I have to put these somewhere," she muttered.

"Kitchen," Sophia ordered, finally taking control of the situation. Or at least as close to control as she could get.

Samantha followed her to the back of the house, the little gasps and exclamations as she passed each undecorated area grating on Sophia's already jangled nerves.

Once inside the kitchen, Samantha dropped her packages on the table and sat down. The shock had worn away, leaving her with a bewildered expression that tugged at Sophia's mommy-guilt.

Sophia debated sitting across from her, but long experience told her that she'd be better off keeping busy for this discussion. She headed for the stove, turned on the burner under the teakettle and pulled two mugs out of the cabinet.

Samantha wrinkled her nose. "Not even the Christmas mugs?"

Biting back a sigh, Sophia rummaged through the cabinets for the tea canister. Her back still to Samantha, she asked, "Lemon or peppermint?"

The chair scraped along the linoleum as Samantha stood. She walked over to the counter, forcing Sophia to meet her gaze. "Mom, what's going on?"

Sophia shook her head. "I just—couldn't. Not this year."

"But why?" Sam's brow furrowed. "I'd understand if we were talking about last year, but..."

Sophia closed her eyes for a moment. How could she find the words to explain? She almost didn't understand it herself. "Last year was..." She stopped. "We were all in a sort of fog, weren't we? The first Christmas without your father."

They'd all tried, Sophia and Samantha and even Ethan, to keep the traditions alive. They'd decorated and baked cookies and had the traditional Christmas Eve dinner.

And Sophia had hated every minute of it.

"The thought of going through that again... I just couldn't."

"Oh, Mom." Samantha reached out and wrapped her arms around her mother. "I know it's hard. I miss him so much, too. But it's been almost two years."

Sophia closed her eyes and swallowed. Even after two years, she couldn't believe Dan was gone. He'd been her partner, her lover, her best friend since they were in high school. Now she was a widow in her mid-forties, with a grown daughter and an empty house.

"But don't you think you'll feel better if you, I don't know, decorate and stuff?"

Sophia gave her beautiful, sweet daughter a squeeze and stepped back, shaking her head with a smile. What Samantha really meant was *she'd* feel better knowing the house was decorated. "I won't deny that it feels a little strange," she admitted.

"So let me help you put some stuff out! It's not too late." Samantha bounced up and down. "I'll call Robert and let him know. Then you can call Ethan and have him bring a tree by."

"No."

Samantha crossed her arms over her chest. "What do you mean, no?"

"I mean that there's no point in decorating the house when no one's going to be here to celebrate."

Samantha's mouth drooped a little at the corners. "You said you were okay with me spending Christmas with Robert's family."

"Oh, honey, I am." Sophia hugged her. "I admit, I had a hard time with it at first, but you two are getting pretty serious, right?"

"Well..."

Sophia raised an eyebrow. "I'd say that looking at rings is a damn big step, if you ask me."

"We were just talking hypothetically," Samantha protested.

Sophia smiled. "In any case, you're an adult now. I can't expect you to give up your life to babysit me."

"Even if I do go, you won't be alone." Samantha plucked the tea canister out of her mother's hands and fished out a packet of apple spice tea. "You have Ethan."

"No, I don't." Sophia poured hot water into Samantha's mug. "I can't expect him to give up his life babysitting me, either."

"Mom!" Samantha fisted her hands on her hips. "He's your friend, not your babysitter."

"I know." Sophia filled her own mug, then sat at the table and waited for Samantha to join her. "And as a friend, I can't keep leaning on him for everything."

"You know he doesn't mind."

That was true. He'd been a godsend since Dan's death, sharing his time, expertise and friendship with her without a complaint.

"He's done a lot. But this is something I need to do by myself. *For* myself."

"What are you talking about?"

Sophia smiled. "I've given it a lot of thought, and realized that I needed to do something different this year, something I've always wanted to do."

Samantha wrinkled her nose. "Sit around an undecorated house feeling sorry for yourself?"

"Of course not." Sophia chose a tea bag and set it in her cup. "Take a cruise to the Caribbean. I'll be heading for the airport in less than an hour."

Seconds ticked by as Samantha's mouth gaped open and shut, like a beached carp. When the explosion came, it was as big as Sophia anticipated. Her daughter was a drama teacher, after all.

"You *what?*"

Sophia calmly spread the brochure out on the table, though inside her stomach was swooping and diving. "I'm flying out tonight for Florida, then boarding the ship tomorrow morning."

"But—I—you—"

Sophia reached over and patted Samantha's hand. "I'll be back by New Year's, honey. We can talk all about it then."

"I don't believe this."

An unexpected flare of anger caught Sophia by surprise. "Why? What's so unreasonable about wanting to do something fun and different for the holidays?"

"What about tradition? What about being home?"

"Tradition doesn't hold a lot of appeal this year." With a soft smile, Sophia silently urged her daughter to understand. "I look around this time of year and all I can see is the pain we went through last year trying to keep everything the way it was when your father was alive. The absolute last thing I wanted was to sit around, alone, with my memories."

Samantha shoved a hand through her hair. "I can stay home. I'll call Robert and explain. I'm sure his parents will understand."

"Absolutely not." Sophia took a sip of her tea. "I know you've been looking forward to this for a long time, and I won't take that away from you just to have company at a pity party. Besides, I'm not willing to give up my trip, either."

"But, Mom..."

Sophia held up a hand. "I want to do this, Samantha. I'm excited about going. This isn't a consolation prize, a way to make myself feel better about being abandoned or some such nonsense. With your father gone, and you spreading your wings, it's time to make some new traditions."

Samantha sat back, all of her arguments temporarily shot down. Sophia could see her brain calculating, though, and it made her smile inwardly. She was so like her father.

"What does Ethan say about it?"

Sophia resisted the urge to roll her eyes. "Nothing," she said. "It's none of his concern."

"You mean you're too scared to tell him," Samantha guessed.

"Oh, honey, don't be ridiculous." Sophia laughed lightly. "He's a friend who's helped me out a lot, both with the business and getting back on my feet in general. But that's all." At least, that's all she felt confident enough to ask for.

"So why not get his opinion? As a *friend*."

"Why should I? It's my decision, my choice. I don't need permission from him, or anyone else." Though she smiled, she knew Samantha could hear the steel in her words, as well as the pointed reminder.

Samantha, though, was undaunted. "Maybe not, but why not even talk to him about it?"

Because I'm afraid he'd try to talk me out of it. Sophia gritted her teeth. "It's a done deal, sweetie."

"He was Dad's best friend and business partner. He would know better than anyone else what Dad would have wanted."

Oh, that was a low blow, but Sophia turned it aside. Samantha was hurting right now, and Sophia didn't blame her. Life had changed so much in the past couple of years, was it any wonder she wanted to hang onto traditions, even when she wouldn't be there herself to experience them?

Softly, Sophia said, "Actually, *I* would know better than anyone else what Dan would have wanted. Your father would have wanted me to be happy. This will make Christmas bearable—even enjoyable—for me this year. I hope you can understand that."

Samantha looked away. "Okay, I guess I do understand."

"Thank you, sweetie."

"So were you even going to tell me? I mean, if I hadn't stopped by." Samantha crossed her arms over her chest. "Or were you planning to just sneak away without a word?"

"Not exactly." Sophia winced. "I was going to call you from the airport."

"After it was too late for me to do anything about it."

Sophia didn't say anything, but she knew her smile acknowledged the truth.

"And Ethan?"

"I'll send him a postcard."

"Mom!"

"It's what I'd do for any other friend."

"Ethan is more than just a friend, Mom, and you know it," Samantha said. "He was Dad's best friend. He's practically family."

Yes. And that's why Sophia needed to do this. She wasn't sure anymore if what she felt for Ethan was based on their long-term friendship, or something more. In the same way, she had no idea how, exactly, Ethan felt about her. Over the past few months she'd caught a few glances, a flash of emotion on his face when he thought she wasn't looking. They gave her hope.

And scared the crap out of her, too.

So yes, he was practically family. But the feelings she had for him were not in any way sisterly.

She couldn't keep pretending he was only a buddy. And just assuming they would spend the holidays together—like neither of them had anything better to do—felt wrong, somehow.

Not that she wouldn't miss him terribly.

With a brisk smile to mask the threatening tears, Sophia stood. "Now, why don't you come help me get my suitcases out to the foyer? The courtesy van from the airport should be here anytime."

❄❄❄

Ethan hefted the evergreen wreath out of the back of the SUV, grimacing a little at the unexpected weight. The guy at the tree lot had tossed it in there like it was made of tissue paper. How in the heck was this monstrosity supposed to stay put? He'd lay even money that it would fall right off the door hanger from the sheer bulk of it.

Oh, well. It still looked nice, and Sophia would be able to figure out what to do with it. She was a genius at those things.

A smile softened the line of his mouth. He could just see her, soft wavy brown hair bundled up on top of her head, little bits of it curling down around her face like she'd completely forgotten it was up there. Her hazel eyes would light up with surprise when she saw the wreath, and she'd say—

"What are you doing here?"

Ethan looked up. He wasn't even to the porch yet, still wrestling the decoration up her walkway, but she'd already opened the door.

"Merry Christmas." He heaved the wreath another foot or two. "Brought you an early present."

"Uh, thank you." Her eyes darted from side to side. "You really shouldn't have."

Concentrating on the wreath, Ethan almost missed the tone of her voice. She sounded—upset. Distracted. Not at all like the sweet, positive Sophia he knew.

"You okay?" Finally at the porch, he leaned the wreath against the railing and climbed the steps. He brushed a curl away from her face. "You don't seem like yourself."

"I, uh—"

A thud resounded from inside the door, and Sophia's daughter poked her head out. "That's the last of them—hey!" She rushed over to give him a hug. "I'm so glad you're here!"

"Thanks," he said. "What are you doing here? I thought you were on your way across state with lover boy."

She smacked him on the shoulder, just as she did every time he called Robert that. "We're heading out in a few minutes. In fact, I have to get going. Maybe you can talk some sense into Mom."

"What?" His head swiveled from daughter to mother. "What are you talking about?"

Samantha glared at her mother. "You haven't told him yet?"

"Samantha," Sophia said, shooting her a look that was full of warning.

Sam let out a huge gust of a sigh, then gave her mom a hug. "Can't say I didn't try."

"I love you. Be safe," Sophia said.

"You too," Samantha said, which made no sense. How much trouble could Sophia get into here at home?

Especially when he'd be keeping an eye on things, like always?

Sam gave him another hug, pausing long enough to whisper "call my cell" in his ear when Sophia wasn't looking. Then she was off the porch and in her car before he could ask her why the hell she was acting like a double agent.

Shaking his head, he turned back to Sophia. "Tell me what?"

"Hmm?" She was fussing with the red velvet bow at the top of the wreath.

"Sophia." He waited until she looked up. "Samantha asked if you'd told me yet. Told me what?"

"Oh, nothing." She bit her lip. Then, squaring her shoulders, she said, "No, that's not true. Samantha is mad at me for making some plans for the holidays."

"She's going to be gone, anyway. Why would she have any say in it?"

"Exactly what I said!" Sophia smiled at him. "I knew you'd understand."

She'd been smiling at him for over a decade now, since he and Dan started their property management business together. It was only in the last six months or so that it had started knocking him on his ass.

Even now, his breath hitched when she turned the full wattage of her smile on him.

He cleared his throat. "So what kind of plans?"

"Oh, you know." She waved one hand, as if that explained everything. "Just wanted to do something...different this year."

Ethan nodded. Last Christmas had been hellish for all concerned.

"So I—"

A honking horn interrupted whatever she was going to say. A flash of—was it relief?—washed across Sophia's face.

"There's my ride!"

Ethan turned, confused, to see the airport courtesy van idling in the driveway behind his SUV. "Your ride?"

By the time he looked back, Sophia was already locking the front door, several suitcases piled around her feet. "With the new check-in procedures, I want to be sure to get there in plenty of time."

"Check in? Get where? Where are you going?"

She hesitated. "On an adventure," she said finally.

"And adven— Sophia, have you lost your mind?"

"Probably," she said, a dimple appearing in her left cheek. "Don't worry. I'll tell you all about it when I get back."

"Get back from where?" He couldn't seem to do much more than repeat what she'd just said, but damned if she hadn't completely pulled the rug out from under him. "What about Christmas?"

Her gaze softened and she placed one gloved hand on his cheek. "I'm sorry to do this in this way," she said. "I know it's not very fair of me."

The driver beeped his horn again. Didn't the jerk understand this was important?

Sophia was busy gathering her suitcases, though it was obvious she wouldn't be able to carry all of them in one trip. With a mounting sense of dread, Ethan picked up the last two and followed her to the van.

The driver got out to stow the bags. Sophia started to climb into the van, but Ethan stopped her with a hand on her arm.

"Can't you at least tell me where you're going?"

She shook her head, tears shining in her eyes. "I'm sorry, I can't. This is something I have to do on my own."

Ethan just stared at her. It was as if she'd turned into a stranger overnight. Who was this woman, and what had she done with his Sophia?

She leaned down and kissed him on the cheek. "I'll explain everything when I get back." Then she vanished into the van.

He watched in disbelief as the van pulled out of the driveway and trundled down the road. His Sophia. Who was he kidding? She was as much a mystery to him now as she'd ever been. Probably more.

Eyes narrowed, he grabbed his cell phone and dialed Samantha.

She answered in one ring.

"Okay, kiddo, I think it's time someone told me what the hell is going on."

Chapter Two

"Champagne?"

Sophia looked up and smiled at the formally-dressed waiter standing by her elbow. "Thanks," she said, lifting a flute off his silver tray. He nodded and moved on to the couple next to her.

She turned sideways, leaning one arm on the railing of the ship. The deck was crowded, people stacked three- and four-deep all around the ship. She'd staked out a place on the port side of the ship early on, not wanting to miss a single experience. If she was going to do something so completely different for the holidays, she was going to do it right.

She winced as she thought about all she'd done wrong so far. She'd handled the situation with Ethan badly, rushing off without an explanation. She could still see him standing in her driveway, his expression perplexed—and hurt.

Knowing she'd hurt Ethan twisted her stomach in ways she didn't want to contemplate. There'd be a lot of damage control to be done when she got home.

But she was here to enjoy herself. Time enough to think of her relationship with Ethan when she got home.

She looked around, taking a sip of her champagne. As far as she could tell, she was the only singleton on board. Everywhere she looked, couples walked hand in hand, or stood at the railing, arms around each other. Entire families clustered together, from grandparents to grandchildren, chattering excitedly about the adventure ahead.

Sophia leaned on the railing and rested her chin in her hand. She'd planned this trip to make a break with tradition, find a way to enjoy the holidays on her own terms. But moments like these made her wonder if she'd done the right thing.

Had she just brought her loneliness along with her for the ride?

"This is so exciting," the woman next to her said, disrupting Sophia's maudlin thoughts. "Is this your first Christmas cruise?"

"My first cruise, period," Sophia admitted.

"First time for everything," the woman's husband replied, holding out a hand to Sophia. "Rick Zimmerman. Nice to meet you."

Sophia introduced herself to him and his wife Deborah, who were taking the cruise to celebrate their thirty-fifth wedding anniversary.

"We got married right before Christmas," Deborah said. "It makes it easy to remember our anniversary, but harder to focus on just the two of us, what with all the holiday craziness."

"That's why we decided to take this cruise," Rick added.

Sophia nodded and took another sip of her champagne. Deborah continued to chatter away, a cheerful litany of their comical struggles to get to the ship on time. Sophia listened politely with one ear, even though her attention was mostly focused on the activity far below. In the distance, a crew member called out orders, muffled by the sounds of the crowd. The increased activity hinted that they were getting closer to departure.

The crowd around them continued to grow as late-arriving travelers attempted to get close enough to the railing to participate in the traditional send-off. Sophia held her champagne close to her chest so it wouldn't spill, juggling her handful of streamers at the same time.

Deborah gestured at the tiny space between them. "Are you trying to save room for someone? We can scoot over if you'd like."

Rick nodded and took a step to the side. "We can always squeeze in one more."

Sophia shook her head. "Thanks, but it won't be necessary. I'm on my own."

She watched as something uncomfortably close to pity flashed across their faces.

"Good for you." Deborah patted Sophia's arm. "Very brave of you."

Brave? Sophia fought back the urge to grimace.

"And you'll have to join us for dinner tonight. Can't have you eating alone."

"Thanks," she said, though she wasn't quite sure she was ready to be anyone's project on this cruise.

"Maybe you'll meet someone special," Deborah said, eyes sparkling. "Wouldn't that be romantic? A shipboard love affair!"

Sophia shook her head with a smile. "I'm not really looking to meet someone," she said.

"Good."

All three of them turned around at the interruption.

"Ethan," Sophia whispered. Her knees turned wobbly and she had to lean against the railing to stay upright. "What are you doing here?"

"Same thing you are," he said. "Spending the holidays on a cruise."

He was still wearing the same outfit he'd had on back home when she'd left him in the driveway. The cable-knit sweater and jeans were much warmer than he would need in the Caribbean.

"I—I don't understand," she stammered.

"Mind if I join you?"

Sophia shook her head. Deborah and Rick moved over, giving Ethan just enough room to slide into the spot next to Sophia.

His arm brushed against hers, sending a shiver of awareness through her body. He leaned one hand on the railing and put the other around her shoulders. "Surprised?"

"Uh, yeah," she said.

"So was I," he murmured, his mouth a mere breath away from her ear.

She started to say something—anything—but a loud blast from the ship's horn startled her back into silence.

Ethan lifted the champagne glass out of her suddenly nerveless fingers and took a sip. Then he held it to her lips. "To new adventures."

She drank the rest of the champagne in one gulp. Somehow, she had a feeling she was going to need it.

❄❄❄

He'd either made the best move of his life, or the biggest mistake. At this point, it was a toss-up.

His carry-on bag was still slung over his shoulder, evidence that he hadn't even bothered to see his room before traversing the deck looking for Sophia. On the limited schedule he'd had to work with—due to Sophia's stubborn insistence on keeping her destination a secret, and the difficulty of finding a travel agent willing to help him on his wild goose chase so close to Christmas—he'd barely had time to throw a few outfits in his suitcase and an overnight kit in his carry-on.

Shopping for something to wear for the rest of the seven-day cruise would be a high priority.

Tomorrow.

Today, he had more important issues to handle.

Like how he was going to explain why he'd shown up aboard this ship.

Ethan wasn't known for throwing caution to the wind. He was the steady one, the responsible one, the person you could count on to do the expected. But the idea of spending the holidays away from Sophia had been like a fist in the gut. And so he'd acted on instinct.

He just hoped he hadn't made a damn fool out of himself in the process.

Sophia stood at the railing, gaze fixed on the rapidly disappearing coastline. The rest of the revelers had long since wandered away, probably exploring the ship or heading back to their rooms to change for dinner. Ethan stood a foot or two away, just watching her.

God, she was beautiful.

He'd always thought she was beautiful, of course. It was an empirical fact, something everyone with eyes could agree on. But she was off-limits. His partner's wife.

Until Dan was gone, and Ethan's world shifted on its axis.

It was tough enough to keep the company going without his best friend and business partner. He and Dan had built their property management firm from the ground up, both putting in the long hours and hard work needed to grow a new business. They'd had a great partnership. Dan had been the visionary, the one with the enthusiasm and gung-ho attitude that pushed them forward. Ethan had been the detail-man, keeping everything running smoothly in all aspects of the business.

When Dan had gotten sick, Ethan had shouldered the extra work without a complaint. Even on his worst days, Dan had contributed to the business, if only by a suggestion or solution to a problem. They'd been a team.

Then Dan died. The first several months Ethan had been on autopilot, with only the knowledge that the business—and Sophia—needed him keeping him focused.

A few months later, Sophia started coming into the office to work. The business was her legacy from Dan, she'd said, and it was high time she started treating it that way.

Over time, their partnership had grown strong. It was different than the working relationship he'd had with Dan, but it was good.

And then one day, he looked over at her, sitting at Dan's former desk, going over paperwork. Her head was down, a section of her thick, rich hair swooping over one eye as she tallied up a row of figures. Without warning, she'd looked up at him and smiled.

Just like that, she'd stopped being Dan's widow, and became simply Sophia.

But there was nothing simple about his feelings for her.

He had refused to take a step while she was still grieving. It just felt wrong to expect her to be ready on his timetable.

He'd lost his best friend, but she'd lost her husband.

And when the first anniversary of Dan's death came and went, Ethan had started watching for a sign that Sophia might be ready to move on.

There, in her driveway, watching the airport van drive away, he'd gotten one hell of a big sign—and he knew that if he didn't get his ass in gear, she'd be moving on without him.

So he'd called Sam on the way back to his apartment to pack. She had been happy to assist him in his quest to save Sophia from her "temporary insanity", as Sam had called it, and filled him in on all the specifics.

And here he was, on board a cruise ship with the woman of his dreams, praying it didn't turn into a major nightmare.

"I should be furious with you," Sophia said suddenly, turning away from the railing. "Pulling a stunt like this."

He took heart from the inclusion of the word *should*. "A stunt?"

She folded her arms over her chest. "I'm not a child, Ethan."

That was for damn sure.

"And I don't remember inviting you along," she continued.

"You didn't." He stuffed his hands in his pockets to keep from reaching for her. "I just—had to come."

She looked at him for a long time, her eyes focused and intent. "Did Sam convince you I needed a babysitter?"

His eyes narrowed. "Are you kidding? You don't need a babysitter."

"Why else would you be here?"

He threw up his hands in frustration. "Because I couldn't stand the thought of being away from you at Christmas."

She fisted her hands on her hips. "I wasn't particularly looking forward to that part, either."

He wanted to ask why she'd done it, then, but he held back. "So here I am. Are you going to hold it against me for the whole cruise?"

"I should." She glared at him. Then she seemed to soften. "Did you manage to bring anything appropriate to wear?"

He glanced down at his clothes. "I was in a bit of a hurry."

Sophia shook her head. "Well, you'd better get settled and changed. Dinner's in an hour."

"I don't have a lot of options," he admitted. "But I do have another bag in the room. I think."

"You think?"

"I haven't actually seen the room yet. I'm hoping that my suitcase showed up."

"I can't believe you were in such a hurry you didn't even check out your room first..." Her voice trailed off, and she flicked a quick glance at him before looking away. "I, uh, couldn't wait to see my room when I got on board."

Left unspoken was the fact that he'd skipped the room tour in his haste to find her.

She gestured toward the interior of the ship. "You'd better get going, then. Good luck finding it, though. I get completely turned around on here."

"I'll muddle my way through," he said. "Walk with me partway?"

She nodded and fell into place beside him as they walked, a spot he thought worked very well. "So, where are you staying?"

He gave her the location, which made her gasp.

"That's one of the best rooms on the ship!"

"You can tell by the number?"

Sophia gave him one of her patented *looks*. "I spent months reading up on this cruise. I can tell what type of room anyone has, just by the floor and room number."

Ethan shrugged. "Well, when you're buying last minute, you take what you can get." In this case, what he could get was a two-room suite with a balcony.

"It must have cost you..." Sophia turned to him, mouth agape. "Ethan, how in the world could you afford this?"

"I couldn't afford not to."

"And it's not just the expense. What about the time away from work?"

"I'm the boss, Sophia. Or at least, the co-boss. I'm hoping my partner doesn't hold it against me." He glanced over at her. "You didn't exactly fill out a vacation request, you know."

Sophia cringed. "Actually, if you had gone into work today, you would have found the paperwork on your desk."

Ethan laughed. "Only you, Sophia." He slung an arm companionably around her shoulders. "It's no big deal. You know how things slow down around the holidays. There's no need for either of us to be there. Really, it's the perfect time to be gone."

He stopped at the bottom of the staircase and pulled her to one side, letting other passengers go by. "I understand that you needed to get away. I was there last year. I remember how awful the holidays were, for everyone." He didn't add that the hole caused by Dan's absence had been palpable.

He didn't have to.

"And if you still want to be alone for the holidays, I'll respect that." He waved an arm at the bustling crowd. "It's a damn big boat, Sophia. We don't have to spend a single minute together."

"You would come all this way, spend who knows how much money, only to *avoid* me?"

He shook his head. "Wouldn't be my first choice, but it seems only fair. I know my showing up was a bit of a shock for you." He smiled. "Sort of like what you did to me, but in reverse."

"Ethan, I'm sorry."

"Don't apologize," he said. "You have every right to do whatever you want and go wherever you want, with or without input from me or anyone else. I'm not here because I thought you needed looking after. I'm here because I want to be where you are, even if you need to spend most of your time alone. You're as close as I've got to family, Sophia. Christmas just wouldn't be right without you nearby."

Then, before he said too much, he squeezed her arm and hitched his overnight bag higher on his shoulder. "Will I see you at dinner?"

She nodded. "Why don't you stop by my room on the way?" She scribbled the room number on a piece of paper she dug out of her purse. "We can find a table together."

"Sounds wonderful." He smiled and turned away. Over his shoulder, he said, "Looking forward to it."

Then he took the stairs two at a time. She had no idea just how much he was looking forward to dinner—and beyond.

❄❄❄

It took her three tries to latch her necklace.

Sophia swore under her breath and placed her hands on the tiny dressing table, leaning forward until her forehead rested against the mirror. Dinner was in fifteen minutes and she wasn't anywhere near ready.

It had taken her almost an hour to choose an outfit, trying on and discarding almost every variation of clothing in her holiday wardrobe other than her formal gown for the Christmas Eve party. She'd had such a fun time buying the clothes for this cruise, packing her suitcases with such care. Everything had been perfect.

Until tonight. Until she knew that Ethan would be there.

Even the thought of him sent the butterflies in her stomach swooping around like demented barn swallows.

Willing her hands to stop shaking, she went to work on her earrings. Barely managing to get them on without stabbing herself in the ear, she grabbed a brush and started attacking her hair.

Making a face, she forced herself to put the brush down. She was acting like a teenager getting ready for her first date. It was just dinner with Ethan and who knew how many other hundreds of people.

Deep down, though, she knew that this was more like a first date than she wanted to admit. Frowning at her reflection, she started pinning up her hair. She could at least look put together, even if inside her emotions were tumbling all over the place.

She still couldn't believe he was here, on board the ship. Her first glimpse of him had told her more about her own feelings than she had acknowledged up until that point. Because as much as she pretended to be angry with him for intruding on her act of independence, the first emotion she'd felt when she saw him was pure, unadulterated relief.

Followed very closely by a hefty dose of lust.

Sophia pressed a hand to her middle, trying to hold back the attack of nerves that threatened to overtake her. She was in her mid-forties, for heaven's sake. She was a widow with a grown daughter. She wasn't supposed to be panting after good old reliable Ethan.

But "supposed to" had all but disappeared from her vocabulary over the past few weeks as she'd planned her trip. She'd made a conscious choice to grab hold of what she wanted, to make it happen.

What she wanted, she had to admit, was Ethan. The fact that he was here was a hint that he might not object to being grabbed.

What if she was misreading the situation? What if he really was only here out of some misplaced sense of obligation to her—or, worse, to her late husband?

Oh, God, if he was here to keep an eye on her because he felt it was what Dan would have wanted...

No. She wouldn't think like that. She couldn't.

A knock at the door pulled her attention away from the swirling turmoil of her thoughts. "Just a minute," she called, picking her wrap up from the bed where she'd discarded it. Then she opened the door.

Ethan was standing there, looking at her with a combination of intensity and something she couldn't quite name. "You look beautiful."

"So do you," she replied, then laughed. "Or, well, handsome."

"Thanks." He smiled. "Either works for me."

He wore a long-sleeved, cranberry-colored knit shirt with black slacks, maybe a bit too warm for the humid night, but the combination of casual and pulled together just looked right on him. His hair, still a little damp from the shower, curled a bit at the temples. A rush of desire, so strong she could almost touch it, washed through her.

He smiled, a slow, lazy grin that warmed her from the inside out. "Ready to go?"

"Sure," she said, slipping past him through the doorway. It was a tight fit, and her shoulder brushed against his chest as she exited the room.

Even that little touch made her a bit weak in the knees, and he put a hand on her elbow to steady her. "I've heard it takes a while to get your sea legs," he murmured.

She smiled weakly and closed the door behind her. The seismic shift in their relationship was so big, she wasn't sure if she'd ever find her balance again.

❄❄❄

Ethan pushed back from the table, surveying the remains of their dinner. "I don't think I'll ever eat again," he groaned.

"I don't know how people do this three times a day for a week," Sophia agreed. She glanced ruefully at her dessert plate, the chocolate torte mostly untouched. "If I'd known this was coming, I would have saved some room."

"They have a dessert bar at midnight," another diner tossed in helpfully. "You can get another one then."

Sophia looked at Ethan, her eyes huge. "Dessert at midnight? At this rate, I won't be able to fit into my Christmas party gown."

"I doubt that," Ethan said. "You always look amazing, no matter what you wear."

"He's a keeper," the silver-haired woman at the end of the table announced with a wink. "Better hold on to him, honey. Heck, if I was twenty years younger I'd go after him myself."

"Oh, he's not my—" Sophia clamped her mouth shut. She glanced at Ethan, her cheeks pink.

At that point, Ethan knew he'd reached his small-talk limit. He stood and held out a hand to her. "It's been nice meeting you all," he said to the rest of the table. "Sophia, would you like to take a walk on deck with me?"

Amid sighs of approval from the women and teasing laughter from the men, Sophia took his hand. "Good night, everyone," she said.

Forcing himself to a slow and respectable pace, Ethan led her through the maze of tables to the doorway. From there, it was a short walk to the deck, where a soft, warm breeze greeted them.

Sophia turned her hand in his, lacing their fingers together, and drew him over to the railing. She stood looking out at the water, silver moonlight capping the edges of the waves. She kept her gaze fixed firmly on the water far below.

He'd been patient for a year. He could wait a little longer.

"I don't know what's happening," she said finally, her voice barely above a whisper. He had to lean in to hear her over the shush of the boat cutting through the water. "Why are you here, Ethan?"

He turned so they were facing each other, less than a foot of space between them. The deck was almost deserted, only a few other passengers wandering along the darkened walkway.

Ethan took a step forward and cupped his hand around her neck. "This is why," he murmured before leaning down to kiss her.

The first touch of their lips was like an electric current traveling through his body. Dimly, he heard a sharp intake of breath from Sophia and knew she felt it, too. Then he touched the tip of his tongue to her lips. There was a moment's hesitation before she opened to him and he swept his tongue inside.

She tasted of chocolate and champagne and sweet, delicious Sophia, and he couldn't get enough. One hand held her head steady, the other stroked down to the small of her back, wordlessly urging her forward as the kiss intensified.

Her breasts pillowed against his chest as she leaned into him, her curves fitting against him as if the two of them were a matched set. Her softly rounded stomach cradled his erection, straining painfully at the fly of his pants. He knew as soon as she noticed it, too, because her eyes flew open. "Ethan," she breathed, her chest rising and falling with each breath.

He smiled at her and took in the startled look in her eyes, the damp, rosy bow of her mouth, the slim column of her neck—so tempting. Bending his head, he pressed an openmouthed kiss to the pulse thrumming at the base of her neck, drawing a contented hum from Sophia as she melted against him.

Straightening, Ethan twisted a curl of her hair around his finger. "Sophia," he said.

Her eyes were half-closed, her face soft and flushed. "What?"

Ethan took a breath. "Will you come back to my room?"

Chapter Three

Oh God.

Sophia stood with her back pressed against the door, hands clasped in front of her.

Fresh flowers spilled out of a crystal vase on the table just inside the door. A couch and easy chairs formed a cozy sitting area across from the sliding door to the private balcony. There was even a dining table and a...

"Is that a grand piano?"

Ethan shrugged out of his jacket and held out a hand for her wrap. "Baby grand, I think. Makes even 'Chopsticks' sound impressive. Which is good, considering that's the extent of my piano-playing ability."

She laughed a little breathlessly and pried herself away from the door, taking a few steps into the wood-floored foyer.

"Take a look around," Ethan said. "It's pretty cool."

Sophia walked over to the flowers and leaned down, breathing in the rich scent. "Wow."

"I know," Ethan deadpanned. "It's nice being one of the beautiful people." He dropped down on the leather couch. "For the next six days, at least."

Despite her best intentions, Sophia couldn't help gawking at the suite. It was just so—over the top. In addition to the baby grand, there was a wet bar behind the dining area, with a full-size fridge and padded bar stools in the same leather as the couch and love seat. A plasma-screen TV hung on the wall opposite the sitting area. "This is amazing," she said, turning in a slow circle in the middle of the room.

"Good to know I've impressed you," he said. He patted the cushion next to him and waited for her to sit. "Or at least my ability to use a credit card."

"I know it's none of my business," Sophia started, but he shook his head.

"Not true," Ethan said. "Nothing is off-limits where you're concerned, Sophia."

She swallowed. "Okay. I was just wondering—how in the world are you going to pay for this? It's got to be costing you an arm and a leg."

"Don't worry. I've got a spare of each." When his joke fell flat, Ethan turned sideways on the couch, one leg bent up on the cushion, almost touching hers. "Some things are more important than money."

This time, she kissed him.

Unlike the first kiss, this one was full of heat right from the start. No tentativeness, no hesitation. Their tongues tangled and stroked together as if they'd been doing it for years. Within moments, the two of them were entwined on the couch, Ethan's hardness cradled between her thighs.

When he lifted his head, they were both breathing hard. "God, you're amazing," he murmured.

She closed her eyes and swallowed.

Immediately, he sat up, giving her space to move as well. When she was sitting again, he took her hand. "Sophia, what's wrong?"

"I, um—" She looked away. "I'm fine."

"Truth, Soph. Is this moving too fast for you?"

"No. Yes. I don't know." She shoved a hand through her hair, dislodging what was left of the pins anchoring her updo in place. "I'm here because I want to be here. Please don't doubt that."

Just saying the words aloud made her blush furiously. But all she saw on his face was caring and concern, which made it easier for her to continue. Taking a breath, she said, "I guess I'm afraid."

To her surprise, he nodded. "I know what you mean."

Her mouth dropped open. Ethan? Afraid?

He smiled at her self-deprecatingly. "I've been dreaming about this for so long, I'm terrified of disappointing you."

"Disappointing me?" She shook her head. "Ethan, that's not possible."

"Sure it is." He shifted so their knees touched. "It's always nerve-wracking to be with someone intimately for the first time. Especially when you want it to be perfect."

"That's just it!" Sophia tugged her hand from his and started pacing around the room. "I don't have near your experience. I can barely remember what it's like to be with someone new."

"Of course you don't." He shrugged. "Maybe it's time to acknowledge the elephant in the room."

She glanced at him quizzically.

"Sophia, you were with Dan for over twenty years," he said, his voice quiet.

"It's not just Dan," she said. "Even before that, I've only ever been with two other men. And since Dan died... Well, you know there hasn't been anybody."

"It's an honor to be in such select company." Ethan watched her from the couch.

"But what if you're disappointed?" She threw her hands in the air. "What if I can't live up to your expectations?"

"You've already surpassed them," he said.

She blinked back sudden tears. "How do you always know the right thing to say?"

He stood and walked across the room to her. "Pure, blind luck."

Sophia clenched her hands at her sides. "Do you really mean it?"

"I never say something I don't mean," he said.

She stretched up and pressed a soft kiss to his lips. "Take me to bed," she murmured against his mouth.

He pulled back. "Are you sure?"

"I never say something I don't mean, either," she said.

The smile that lit his face was blinding. "Thank God." He nuzzled her neck. "I wasn't looking forward to groveling."

Sophia chuckled, grateful that his sense of humor had dissipated some of the tension that hung over the room. "Oh, I don't know," she teased. "A little groveling never hurt anyone."

With a shout of laughter, Ethan stepped back. "How about a display of raw masculinity?"

Before she could ask what in the world he was talking about, Ethan scooped her off her feet and swung her into his arms. With a shriek, she wrapped her arms around his neck and held on.

"See, I figure you'll be so busy being impressed with my strength and power, you can forget about the rest."

Sophia tucked her head into the curve of his shoulder. "You'll need every ounce of that strength to lift me."

He stopped dead in the middle of the hallway, right outside the door to the bedroom. "You're kidding, right? Sophia, you're absolutely perfect. Curves in all the right places, a body to make a man weep."

"Now you're exaggerating."

In response, Ethan lowered her to the ground, pressing her close so her body brushed against his every inch of the way.

Once she was on her feet, he stepped back. He cupped a hand under one breast and stroked her nipple through the thin fabric of her dress. Immediately, it tightened, budding visibly.

"Perfect," he repeated, before swooping down for another kiss.

One led to two led to many, until Sophia lost count. She also lost track of where she was until her legs bumped up against something solid. Breaking the kiss, she turned slightly to discover that he'd walked her right up to the bed.

"Perfect," he said again, a devilish twist to his smile. Then he picked her up by the waist and tossed her onto the bed.

She lay there on top of the covers, breathless and laughing, as she gazed up at him. He popped the button on the collar of his knit shirt and stripped it off, breaking eye contact only when the shirt was over his face. The laughter faded as she took in the sight of his torso, sleek muscles lightly dusted with hair.

"My, what big eyes you have, my dear," he teased, toeing off his shoes and kicking them under the bed.

"Hey, you're the one putting on the show."

"Yeah, what's up with that?" He leaned down and kissed her, toying with the bodice of her dress. "You'd better get working, girl. You've got some catching up to do."

"Oh, I don't know," she said with a grin. "I'm enjoying being the audience."

In response, Ethan grabbed her hands and pulled her to a sitting position. "All right, you asked for it." He hopped up on the bed behind her and unzipped her dress.

"Ethan!" She clutched the front of her dress before it fell off completely. "What are you doing?"

"Helping you catch up," he said blithely, sliding his hands under the fabric of her dress and stroking the heated skin of her back. "If I'm topless, you should be too. It's only fair."

She looked at him over her shoulder. The patterns he was tracing on her back were sending shivers down her spine. "You want fair?"

He hooked a finger under her bra strap and tugged it down. "Mm-hmm."

With a daring she barely recognized, she slid off the bed. Turning around, she faced him. Then she lowered her hands.

The silky fabric slipped off her to pool at her feet, leaving her in a peach-colored bra and panty set and stockings.

Ethan stilled. "Are those thigh-highs?"

"A woman likes to have her vices," she said. "Pretty lingerie has always been mine."

"Lucky me," he said, his voice almost a growl.

Reveling in the power of his reaction, Sophia reached for the front closure on her bra.

Ethan hopped off the bed and stood in front of her. He shook his head, placing his hand atop hers. "Please. Let me."

Clenching her thighs against a sudden rush of moisture, she nodded. Slowly, she let her hands drop to her sides.

He traced the lacy contours of the demi-bra, leaving a trail of heat in the wake of his calloused fingertip. Closing his hand over the clasp, he flicked the bra open.

The peachy fabric slid apart, exposing her breasts to his hungry gaze. He stepped back and looked his fill.

Sophia gave a little shimmy and let the bra slide down her arms and drop to the floor. At this rate, all her clothing would be in one big puddle at her feet.

Judging by the hot look in Ethan's eyes, he wouldn't object.

"Your turn," she whispered, reaching for the buckle on his belt. She tugged at it, sliding the leather free.

He stood stock-still as she unbuttoned his slacks. Behind the calm exterior, she could sense a building tension, as if he was holding himself back for her sake.

Enough of that. They'd both waited long enough.

Pulling the fly of his pants open, she slid her hands down the back of his pants and cupped his ass.

"Whoa!" Ethan looked at her with barely concealed humor. "That was unexpected."

"Good." She gave those tight cheeks a little squeeze. "I'd hate to be predictable."

"Never," he murmured, pulling her closer.

His hands were all over her now, one tugging at a taut nipple, the other slipping her now-soaked panties off. She stepped out of the scrap of fabric and tilted her hips, cradling him between her naked thighs.

He groaned against her mouth, kissing her with rapidly increasing passion. His thumb strummed across her nipple, gently chafing it. Sophia whimpered.

Frustrated by the layers of fabric still separating them, she tugged at his pants and boxers. Ethan broke the kiss long enough to shuck his remaining clothing off. Then he reached for her again.

She barely had enough time to register the sight of him, gloriously naked, before his hard shaft was pressed against her stomach. His hands slid down her back, cupping her buttocks, pulling her closer. With seemingly little effort, he lifted her off her feet, silently urging her to wrap her legs around him. Then he pivoted and lowered them both to the bed, fully entwined.

Sophia sucked in a breath, reveling in the sensation of his heat and weight atop her, pressing her deeper into the down comforter. She couldn't stop touching him, fingers caressing the silky skin of his back, exploring the tautness and breadth of his arms as the muscles bunched and flexed under her hands. Stretching lower, she sank her fingers into the tight curve of his butt.

Ethan arched up, smiling at her with one eyebrow raised. "Why, Sophia," he drawled. "You surprise me."

Then he reached behind his back, capturing her wrists in his capable hands. Lifting them off his body, he raised her arms up over her head, holding them against the bed with one hand. "My turn."

Slowly, lazily, he kissed his way down her arm, teasing the sensitive skin at the inside of her elbow with his darting tongue. Skimming over her shoulder, he explored her collarbone, covering it with openmouthed kisses until he reached the hollow of her neck. He dipped his tongue inside, tasting the pulse beating rapidly against her skin. "Delicious," he murmured.

His jaw was shadowed with new growth, and the tiny stubble brushed delicately against the upper curve of her breast. Held fast by his hand, all Sophia could do was whimper and writhe under the sensual assault.

Ethan stilled as she squirmed beneath him, the tight buds of her nipples brushing his chest with an erotic rhythm that damn near killed him. Unable to wait any longer, he dipped his head lower and licked one nipple into his mouth.

Sophia arched off the bed, lifting herself closer as he nipped and sucked, swirling his tongue around the areola. He rolled to the side, giving himself better access to her amazing body. Ethan let go with an audible pop, turning his attention to her other breast.

He trailed his tongue to the next budded tip, laving her generous curves. She tasted so good, her skin slightly salty from exertion.

By the end of the night, he wanted her sated, hair damp with perspiration, body limp with exhaustion.

He wanted that for himself, too.

With his free hand, he stroked the downy skin of her stomach before delving lower. Her curls were already soaked, her juices coating his fingers as he explored. He twirled one finger around her clit, making her jump like she'd received an electric shock. Her head whipped back and forth on the comforter, hair tumbling around her face in a rich tangle.

Releasing her wrists, Ethan settled between her thighs. With a smile, he dipped his head and tasted her.

Her hips lifted, almost bucking him off. He cupped her ass with his hands and held her in place while he leisurely explored her.

Ethan teased her clit with his tongue while he slid a finger inside her. Damn, she was tight. Tiny contractions already gripped his finger in a pattern that threatened to make him come. And he wasn't even inside her yet.

He added another finger to the first, sliding them slowly in and out of her tight passage. Ethan could sense her climax approaching, the pulsing contractions increasing in intensity, her wetness growing more pronounced.

Without warning, he thrust three fingers inside and sucked her clit into his mouth. Sophia screamed, arching off the bed, her orgasm rippling over her body.

Breath sobbing in and out of her lungs, she gripped the comforter with both hands and shook with the intense pleasure of it.

Ethan watched her ride it out, his cock achingly hard at the sight. Finally, her climax slowed, leaving her limp and panting.

Sliding his fingers from her body, Ethan scooted up on the bed. Then he stretched across to the nightstand, pulling a small box from the top drawer.

Sophia watched him with dazed eyes, her chest rising and falling as she regained her breath. A slow smile curved her mouth when he nabbed one foil packet and tossed the box back on the nightstand.

"You're such a boy scout," she teased, lifting one hand and running it down the length of his arm. "I like that about you."

"Not so much prepared as hopeful," he said with a grin. He rolled on the condom. "Very, very hopeful."

"Me, too," she murmured, widening her legs to invite him in.

Gritting his teeth, he pressed the broad head of his erection against her, sliding in just a fraction. She shifted her hips to grant him easier access, sighing as he slid forward.

They both groaned as he seated himself fully inside her, and he rested his forehead against hers as he fought for control. The aftershocks of her orgasm still rippled through her, milking him. When he was no longer in danger of coming on the first thrust, he started to move.

Sophia wrapped her legs around him. They moved in easy tandem, in sync as if they'd been doing this for years. Too soon, Ethan was ready to come, but when he slowed his movements in an attempt to hold off the inevitable, Sophia wordlessly urged him on with her body.

Sure enough, the next thrust sent him over the edge, Sophia tumbling after as she cried out his name. Ethan shuddered as the orgasm pulsed through him, his arms trembling as he braced himself above her to keep the bulk of his weight off of her.

With a groan, he collapsed, wrapping his arms around her to carry her with him as he rolled sideways. Still inside her, he held her soft body against his, tucking her head into the curve of his shoulder. Slowly, their ragged breathing returned to normal.

The reality had been light-years beyond his fantasies. Now, he just needed to figure out how to make this a reality beyond the cruise.

Chapter Four

"You know what I love about this overpriced, ostentatious stateroom?"

Sophia blew a handful of bubbles at him. "The two-person jetted tub?"

Ethan felt around under the water for her foot. Lifting it into his lap, he began to massage it. "That's definitely a perk."

She leaned back and closed her eyes, humming a little with pleasure.

"But actually, I was thinking of the concierge service."

She squinted at him. "Really?"

Through the half-open doorway of the bathroom he could see the corner of the dining room table. "Yep."

"Don't leave me in suspense, Ethan. Why the concierge service?" She slid her other foot into his lap, teasing his groin with her toes. He hardened immediately, a common occurrence so far this vacation.

Responding to her silent request, he dug his fingers into the arch of her other foot. "Because we haven't had to leave the room for the past two days."

Sophia grinned and stretched her arms over her head, dripping bubbles on her tousled hair. "That is a plus," she agreed.

Leaning over to look at his watch on the marble surround, Ethan made a face. "Unfortunately, that's about to end."

Pouting, Sophia ducked under the water, resurfacing right in front of him. She caressed his hardened cock, a wicked smile on her face. "Are you sure about that?"

Ethan groaned. "Don't tempt me, woman." He reached for a towel and held it out to her. "Besides, you're the one who signed us up for this shore visit."

She lifted her shoulders, one rosy nipple peeking out above the bubbles. "Can't blame a girl for trying." She grabbed the towel and stood, wrapping it around herself. "But you're right. It seems crazy to go on a Caribbean cruise and hide out in the stateroom the whole trip."

Privately, Ethan wouldn't have minded doing exactly that. But eventually they were going to have to leave their little cocoon and venture out into the real world again. Might as well do it in paradise.

Sophia stepped out of the tub and handed him a towel, moving aside to give him room. She headed into the bedroom. "I'm so glad you thought to have my bags brought here," she called over her shoulder. "This is much more convenient."

Ethan grimaced and turned away. Yeah, it was convenient. It was the whole going back home and facing reality that worried him. What would happen when being together wasn't convenient at all?

❄❄❄

Sophia leaned back and closed her eyes, soaking up the warmth of the sun beating down on her. The sightseeing boat rocked gently as it transported them back to shore. "Do you think we could move company headquarters down here?"

Ethan chuckled quietly beside her. "I don't see why not. Might be hard to manage property from so far away, though."

"Damn." She cracked one eye open. "I could get used to this."

The boat lifted and fell as it rode over the waves. Around them, dozens of other cruise-goers chatted about the tour.

Ethan sat up, propping his elbows on his knees. "Wearing shorts in December is pretty appealing." He leered at her. "Looking at you wearing shorts in December is even more appealing."

Sophia rolled her eyes. "At least you've got appropriate clothing now." They'd stopped at the first shop once they reached shore that morning, loading up on casual warm-weather clothing for Ethan. Most had been sent back to the ship, but he'd kept one outfit to change into right away.

"So, what's been your favorite part of the day so far?" Ethan rested his arm on the back of her chair, tracing patterns on the bare skin of her arm. She shivered as he toyed with the strap of her tank top.

"The stingrays, of course," she said. "A once in a lifetime experience."

"Yeah, I'd have to vote for that, too. They're much bigger than I expected."

"And beautiful. Never thought I'd actually get to swim with stingrays."

"And feed them," he added.

"Samantha would have loved it," Sophia said, a little wistful. "She's so adventurous."

"She got that from her mom," Ethan said with a playful nudge.

The sunburned woman sitting across from them leaned forward. "You actually got in the water with them?" She shuddered. "Too dangerous. You couldn't pay me enough."

"The snorkeling instructors said they're tame," Sophia said. "We didn't have any problems."

Ethan looked at Sophia and smiled. "Besides, some experiences are worth the risk," he said.

Sophia smiled weakly and turned to look at the water rushing by, white foam tossing above the bow of the boat. Was that how he saw the two of them? A once in a lifetime experience?

She wondered just how much she had risked by becoming intimate with him—and how much more of her heart was in danger?

Ethan watched as Sophia toyed with her food, her mind obviously far from the ship's dining room. At some point during their shore excursion, the light had gone out of her eyes, and she'd become strangely reserved.

Maybe she was missing Samantha more than she'd expected. Maybe she was thinking about Dan.

Maybe she was regretting their time together.

He just didn't know, and he was almost afraid to ask.

"Hard to believe Christmas is tomorrow," the man across the table said. "Something about being on board a ship makes the holiday seem a little unreal."

"Are you going to the dance tonight?" His wife grinned at them. "I just love getting all gussied up."

"I'd completely forgotten about the dance!" Sophia glanced at Ethan. "I don't know what our plans are, though."

He gave her a little squeeze. "Plans can be changed. You want to go?"

She bit her lip. "Well, I did get a new dress," she said.

He smiled at the other couple. "I guess we'll see you there."

Their talk would have to wait.

Sophia stood at the bathroom mirror and clasped one of her earrings. The sapphire flashed in the bright glow of the track lighting above the sink.

"You about ready?" Ethan came up behind her and nuzzled her neck. "Mm, you look good enough to eat."

She put on the other earring, watching him in the mirror. "Thank you."

With a smile, he crooked his arm toward her. "Your ball awaits, milady."

She slid her hand into the curve of his elbow, admiring the way he filled out the tux jacket. "I can't believe you brought a tux," she said for the dozenth time. "Can't manage short-sleeved shirts, but a tuxedo? No problem."

"Hey, I may not be prepared for the right weather, but I'm up on my social graces." He escorted her out the door of the suite. "Even I know you need appropriate formal wear for at least one occasion on board."

"Well, I approve," she said.

"A big thumbs up on your dress, too." He looked her up and down. "It's stunning."

The dress had been one of her major coups when shopping for the cruise. It was deceptively simple, a slim column of royal blue satin that draped gracefully at the neck and clung to every curve all the way down to the floor. A subtle slit up the side flashed just a bit of skin. Daring, but not flashy. "Thanks," she said again.

She cast about for something more to say, a problem she'd never had around Ethan. Their relationship had always been easy, comfortable, friendly. But ever since this afternoon their conversations had been short and uncomfortable.

It was her fault, she knew. How could she chat about everyday topics when what she really wanted to do was blurt out that she was in love with him?

"Here we are." Ethan held open the door to the ballroom. The sound of music and people talking spilled out into the wide entryway. He leaned in, his mouth next to her ear. "May I have this dance?"

She shivered, swept with a wild combination of love and lust at having him so near. She nodded, not trusting her voice. A dance would be just fine.

❄❄❄

Whoever invented dancing was a genius, Ethan thought, as he spun around the crowded dance floor with Sophia in his arms. For the first time since they'd gone on the shore trip, Sophia was relaxed, smiling up at him as she clung to him. They moved together as if they'd been partners forever.

He gritted his teeth and spun her around once more. Maybe that was the problem. Maybe the two of them only worked on a physical level. Dancing, making love...

No. They had more than that, damn it.

But would they still have more once they left the ship for good?

Sophia sighed, her head resting against his chest. "I feel like Cinderella," she said.

Ethan pressed a kiss to the top of her head. "You're definite Cinderella material."

"Too bad it has to end."

His heart slammed against his chest. "What do you mean?"

"It always does." She slipped her hand from his long enough to gesture at the elegantly decorated room. "The clock strikes midnight, the magic goes away, and the princess finds herself back in her old life again."

He captured her hand again, slowing to a standstill right in the middle of the dance floor. "Is that what you want?"

She looked him right in the eye. "What I want," she said, her voice low and enticing, "is for you to take me back to the room. Now."

His body responded immediately, but in the back of his mind, he worried. Yes, they were magic in bed together. But it wasn't enough for him anymore. He wanted more.

But for tonight, what Sophia wanted would have to be enough.

Coward.

Sophia cursed herself twelve ways from Sunday as they entered the suite. Why couldn't she say the words? Why did she have to fall back on the one thing she knew was solid between them, instead of taking the chance and telling him what she really wanted?

Deep down, she knew it was fear. She was afraid to tell him how she felt, afraid to hear him say that this was all he wanted.

Afraid to risk her heart again.

She needed to do it. She couldn't keep the truth from him much longer. But tonight, she needed to have this one last chance to be with him, to show him how she felt, even if she couldn't say the words.

Chapter Five

Ethan woke early on Christmas morning.

Sophia was sleeping on her stomach next to him, face turned toward the pillow. Though the sheets were tangled over her body, glimpses of her bare skin revealed that she had slept naked the night before.

He hardened instantly, aching to run his hands over that soft, warm skin, followed by his tongue. He'd never get enough of her.

He lay in bed and watched her sleep, wishing that he could wake up to that sight every morning. He wanted her in his bed—and his life—permanently.

But even after last night, he wasn't sure if that dream would ever come true. They'd come together feverishly, passionately, but there was an edge to Sophia's lovemaking that hadn't been there before. Almost as if she was preparing herself for the end.

He didn't want to think about it. It was Christmas. A day for wishes to come true.

If only Santa could give him Sophia, wrapped up in a bright red bow...

Or nothing at all. That would work, too.

The present in question stretched, rolling over onto her back. "Merry Christmas," she murmured, voice still drowsy.

"Right back atcha." He dropped a swift kiss on her lips. "Have you been a good girl this year?"

She smiled at him. "Why don't you tell me?"

"Hmm." He pretended to think. "That's a hard one."

She smacked him upside the head with a pillow. "Not that hard."

He glanced down at his lap. "Oh, baby, you have no idea."

Sophia laughed. "You're insatiable."

He whipped back the covers, ignoring her halfhearted protests. "I can see I've been a very good boy," he said. "Lookie what Santa left me."

"So I'm your present, eh?" She smiled at him, a very catlike grin. "Then what's my present?"

It was a bit earlier than he'd planned, but Ethan decided to roll with it anyway. "Come on out into the sitting room and I'll show you."

Sophia followed him out of the bedroom, wrapping a robe around herself. "You didn't have to get me anything," she said. "You being here is gift enough."

"Thank you, but I disagree." He walked over to the tabletop evergreen tree decorated with seashells and other nautical ornaments and pulled a little box out from beneath it. "I saw this and, well, I thought of you."

"When in the world did you have time to buy this?" She took the package gingerly, turning it over in her hand. "We were together the whole time."

"I have my ways." He waggled his eyebrows in a lame attempt to lessen the tension. Taking her hand, he tugged her down onto the couch.

She opened it carefully, taking so much time he had to sit on his hands to keep from ripping the paper off himself. Finally, she finished, tipping a velvet box into her palm. She looked up, eyes questioning.

"Open it," he urged. "Go on."

The hinged top flipped open easily, revealing the jewelry inside.

"It's a locally made bracelet," he said, mostly to fill the silence. "Handcrafted."

"And the design?" She turned it over, puzzling.

"A fish hook." He shoved a hand through his sleep-tousled hair. "Because, well, you've hooked me."

She looked up at that, her eyes suspiciously bright. "Ethan," she breathed.

"Ah, hell." He stood and began pacing the room. "I don't want this to be just a cruise ship affair," he said. "I don't want the magic to disappear once we step foot back in reality. I want this to be our reality, Sophia. I want you to be with me, forever."

She started to speak, but he stopped her. "I know this is sudden, and I'll understand if you want to have time to think about it. I just couldn't keep going on without putting all my cards on the table." He paused. "I love you, Sophia."

She slipped the bracelet on and stood in front of him. "I love you too," she said. "I think I've loved you for a very long time."

He pulled her into his arms, kissing her with all the love and desire he had inside him.

When they finally broke apart, she rested her head on his chest, arms wrapped around him. "This is going to change things at home," she said. "We can't expect everything to go smoothly. I have no idea how Samantha is going to react."

"Oh, I think she's got some idea," Ethan said, playing with her hair. "It shouldn't come as too much of a shock."

"Well, at least we have a little time to figure out how we're going to handle it." At his silence, she looked up. "What?"

"Uh, that's the other part of your Christmas present," he said. "Sam'll be at the next port of call."

"She's what?" Sophia gripped his shoulders. "What are you talking about?"

"Well, I got to thinking, Christmas is all about family, isn't it? I just thought you should have your family with you, at least for the rest of the holidays. She and lover boy will be joining us for the rest of the cruise."

Sophia threw her arms around him and hugged him. "Thank you," she whispered. "I wanted her here so much."

"I know." He smiled. "So did I, to tell the truth."

"Hey, you said lover boy is coming, too. Does that mean…"

He nodded. "Robert answered the call, and confessed he was proposing on Christmas morning. We set it up as a surprise to Sam, too. They can think of it as an early honeymoon."

"How wonderful."

"Besides, you've got a perfectly good room going to waste…"

Sophia laughed. "Good. I'm thrilled they're coming, but I'd rather not share this suite with anyone but you."

He smiled and kissed her again. They may have been hundreds of miles from everything familiar, but in Sophia's arms, he was truly home for Christmas.

About the Author

Kate Davies first tried her hand at romance at the young age of twelve. Sadly, that original science fiction love story is lost to the ages. But after many years meandering through such varied writing fields as fantasy, playwriting, poetry, and nonfiction, she's made her way home to romance.

Kate lives in the Pacific Northwest with her husband and kids. When not chasing the rugrats around the house, she loves to write sexy stories about strong, passionate men and women.

Learn more about Kate at www.kate-davies.com, or check out her blog at www.kate-davies.blogspot.com. Join her newsletter at http://groups.yahoo.com/group/katedaviesupdates/ to keep up to date with new releases, signings, and other news. She can be contacted at kate@kate-davies.com.

Look for these titles

Look What Santa Brought

Annmarie McKenna

Dedication

To everyone who wanted Scottie's story...

Chapter One

"Craaap."

The hushed, indignant tones of Scott Wyatt's quarry reached his ears and he wondered what she'd done. Stubbed her toe? Spilled her usual caramel latte? He smiled and sat back, relaxing into the rigid, corduroy-covered foam blocks someone decided would pass as a chair, and waited for her to join him at their little group's usual table. He'd have to look into getting new chairs, despite his sister's protestations that these fit the décor of his coffee shop.

He pressed a button on his watch. "Ten twenty-two," a nasally, female voice told him. Tara Patrick was late this morning, by just over twenty minutes. She'd never been late before. A frisson of anxiety skittered across his nerves, overriding the hard-on her voice always seemed to ignite.

"Come on, come on," she mumbled.

He nearly groaned. Her choice of words and his heightened state of libido didn't mesh. Scott imagined her teeth grinding together with her agitation.

A muffled cartoon ring-tone grew louder as it was drawn out of whatever hidey-hole it resided in. He'd heard it before. The song Tara had programmed onto her cell phone mirrored her normal personality. Fun and carefree. Lots of laughter.

Papers shuffled, cloth moved over cloth, a joint popped.

"Ouch. Son of a booger. Unh. Hello?" she said, her voice getting closer to him, the hello much stronger than her previous whispered mutterings.

Scott pursed his lips, hiding his grin and welcoming back the rush of blood to his groin where his cock hardened further. Sounded like Tara was having a rough day. In the two months he'd known her, he'd never noticed her usual happy-go-lucky self having a bad day.

Maybe he'd talk to Brianna and find out what was bothering the woman of his dreams. His sister and Tyler, her husband in heart if not on paper, would be here any minute.

Scott envied Brianna. She'd been lucky enough to find not just one man, but two. Tyler and Cole both loved and cherished her. Their relationship might seem strange to people who didn't know them, but the trio was what worked for them and their two children.

Scott was waiting for that one special woman in a million he could share that same sort of bond with. He more than wanted it, he needed it. Felt it was the one thing missing in his life.

And somehow he had a feeling Tara might be the one, despite the fact he knew she'd been dating another man. He ground his teeth together thinking about her with someone else.

To Bean Or Not To Bean, the coffee shop Scott owned, was their regular Tuesday/Thursday meeting place. Brianna, Tyler or Cole, and Tara met him here usually without fail at ten o'clock. It had quickly become a habit and they'd all gotten to be a close group.

Scott was ready to get closer.

He squirmed in his seat and tried to adjust himself. Any harder and his dick would be imprinted with the buttons of his fly.

"What the hell? I asked you to leave three days ago."

Scott tried to tune out her worried side of the conversation, which he easily picked out over the din of the entire cafe. Her voice attached itself to his ears like a magnet. Because of his blindness, his hearing had always been strong in his good ear. Especially having to compensate for the bad one. Now, thanks to revolutionary surgery he'd had to repair the damaged ear, his hearing was even more superior.

The door opened behind and to his left with a whoosh of cold, frosty air, tinkling the tiny overhead bell and swirling the robust aroma of freshly brewed coffee, peppermint and boughs of pine throughout the café. The espresso machine whirred, foaming up a fresh batch of frothy milk for the next customer's order. A muted version of "Have a Holly, Jolly Christmas" floated around the room. Somewhere to his right, fingers clacked incessantly across a laptop keyboard as if the owner's life depended on it. Cattycorner from him, loose change hit the floor followed by a "goddamn it".

"He's baaack," a whiny, high-pitched voice sung out.

The woman did not even attempt to be discreet. Or maybe she did and his overdeveloped sense of hearing just made it seem that way. Scott hung his head at the distraction.

"Who?" a second woman asked.

"Blond Adonis, six o'clock."

"Oh Lord, he's hot."

Scott snorted softly and grimaced behind his mug of café mocha. Since the two female voices emanated from his twelve o'clock and nobody sat behind him, he could only presume they were referring to him.

"Just a second," Tara's voice intruded. "Um, hello, you do know the blond Adonis is blind, right? Waggling your fingers at him isn't doing you a bit of good."

Scott nearly spewed his coffee across the room. He choked down what he could and coughed out the rest.

"Shit," he muttered, and grabbed the napkin from its nine o'clock position on the table and wiped at his now damp shirt.

"And what makes *you* such an expert?" the first woman's snotty voice retorted.

"Oh, I don't know, the fact he's wearing sunglasses inside? Or maybe it's the *seeing eye dog* sitting next to him?" Tara nearly shouted.

Scott bit his lip.

"Or maybe it's because I'm sleeping with him, and I can assure you, the man can't see a thing. But damn, what he can do with those hands." Tara made this little moaning sound and Scott nearly came in his jeans.

Holy fuck. She hadn't really just said that, had she? If she wanted to know what he could do with his hands, he'd show her. Right now.

"Well."

"Yeah, well," Tara shot back. "Please refrain from ogling my boyfriend."

Tara didn't know what she was doing talking like this. If she continued, she would find out exactly what he wanted to do with her.

"Sorry," she said and Scott wondered if she was talking to him or still to whoever was on the other end of the phone. He heard her sit across from him with a sigh. Her coffee cup clunked on the table, her bag thumped to the floor.

"Don't do this to me," Tara pleaded.

Scott sat forward and placed his coffee cup back on the foot and a half high table he'd pulled toward him until it just touched his knees. His heart pounded at the near panic he heard in Tara's voice.

"Eric, no."

Eric? What the fuck? Was she having trouble with her boyfriend? Senses above their normal high alert, he leaned forward and rested his elbows on his knees, not even attempting to hide the fact he was listening to her conversation. It took everything in him not to get up and demand she tell him what the problem with Eric was.

"So what am I supposed to do?"

Sweet Jesus. Whatever it was, he'd help. Scott fisted his shaking hands.

"And you can go to hell." Her voice wobbled and he heard the distinct click of a cell phone being slapped closed then dropped to the wooden tabletop.

Goddamn, what he wouldn't give to see her face right now.

"Hey, Scott," she said wearily.

Like a high school kid with his first crush, Scott jerked. His shin banged into the table, unsettling the coffee cup. The hot liquid sloshed out and landed on his knee, soaking through his jeans and probably burning his skin. He didn't care. The sound of his name coming off her lips was well worth a bruised shin and a burned kneecap.

"Whoa, bud, just me. Tara."

"I know...I," he cleared his throat, "I'm your boyfriend, huh?" he asked, changing the subject. He'd find out later what was bothering her.

"Damn." Tara chuckled. "Shoulda known you would hear that. Okay if I pet Kissy-Face?"

"Uh-huh." Scott nodded and heard her move toward him. He automatically reached for the five-year-old German Shepherd plopped at his side. He buried his hand in the scruff of the dog's neck. Kissy whimpered and lifted his big head to lick at Scott's wrist.

"You're such a good doggy, aren't you?" she cooed. "Yes, you're a good boy. You watchin' out for Scott, Kissy? Keepin' him safe?"

Tara's fingers met his and for a moment they tangled together. Scott locked his hand with hers and held tight. "So, I'm your boyfriend?"

"Yep. You don't mind, do you?" she teased.

"Absolutely—"

"Hey there, sorry we're late." Brianna bustled over, scrubbing the top of Scott's head and kissing him on the cheek.

Scott shrugged his annoying sister off and ran a hand through his close-cropped, easy-to-manage hair.

"Hi, Bri," Tara said.

The gush of air beside Scott told him Tara had stood. Her knees knocked into his leg, her coat brushed over his lap, causing increased pressure where he definitely didn't need any. He heard a loud smooch and a few light pats from the hug shared between two friends.

He wanted to be the huggee. When Tara seemed to be leaning a little too heavily into him, he raised his hand to her thigh and balanced her. His fingers itched to give a squeeze. He'd get bopped over the head for his efforts, no doubt.

"I just got here myself." Tara's weight shifted once more and Scott missed her toned legs pressed against his when she moved away from him again. "Tyler. Looking yummy as always."

"And you are looking more than a little disheveled today. What's up?" Tyler asked.

Scott's ears perked. Had the phone call made her disheveled?

"God, Ty, could you be more obtuse? Don't listen to him, honey, you look fine. Ty's just cranky because he didn't get any this morning," Bri whispered none too quietly.

"TMI, girlfriend. Did not need to know that." Tara's laugh made Scott's lungs seize.

He was more than used to Bri's frank language. And Ty's and Cole's. Everything was out in the open at the Masters' house. Unless his nieces were present, of course. When nine-year-old Lily and six-year-old Chloe came through in their normal whirlwind fashion, it was all lips sealed.

"But seriously, Tara, something is wrong. I can tell," Brianna continued

There was a heavy sigh across from him and Scott sat forward. "Anything we can help with?" he asked.

"It's Eric," Tara muttered, sounding more than resigned.

He knew it. What had the fucker done to her?

"What's he done now, Tara?" Brianna snarled.

"You want me to look into him?" Tyler growled.

What the hell? Scott fisted his hands in his lap. Why was everybody privy to this obviously bad situation but him?

"God, no," Tara practically yelped and Scott heard a coffee mug scratch across the table. He smelled the caramel and knew it was Tara's. Tyler was more of a straight black kind of guy and Brianna went for tea.

"I can't get him to leave, that's all. I've been staying at a friend's, but now her roomie's coming back and I can't stay there anymore. I am *not* going back to my apartment with him there, and since he put his name on the lease, I can't really throw him out."

"Oh, honey. Eric's a shit." Bri's sympathy did Scott in.

"What the fuck is going on with Eric?" he ground out. Enough of the run around. If this shit was messing with Tara, he damn well wanted to know about it.

Brianna chuckled, but over her Scott heard Tara's sharp intake of breath.

"Little brother, where have you been?" Tyler's voice grated on Scott's nerves.

Apparently he'd been somewhere with his head up his ass.

"Sorry, Scott, I thought you knew about me and Eric. We broke up a while back and he's having a, um...hard time letting go." Tara's words were laced with disgust.

Scott shook his head sharply. "Uh-huh. Didn't know. Never heard about it." His heart hammered and a muscle jumped in his jaw. For two months he'd been waiting for the perfect opportunity to make Tara his and she'd been fighting off the advances of another man. If he'd known, he would have stepped up to the plate sooner.

"The man's deranged," Brianna offered.

Tara snorted. "I just need to make him see there is no us anymore. I don't know, maybe if he saw me with someone else, he'd finally get the picture. Must be nice to have two men at your disposal, Bri." There was laughter in Tara's voice.

Tyler grunted, and Bri gave an overly dramatic sigh. "Aah, yes, it certainly is."

"Watch it, little one. Payback can be a bitch," Tyler warned.

That drew a snort from Bri. "Whatever."

"I'll do it," Scott said softly, breaking up the momentary jovial attitude.

"You'll do what?" Bri asked, sounding perplexed. Even Kissy whined in an almost *huh?* kind of way.

Scott lifted his head and turned in Tara's direction, making it clear he was speaking to her and only to her. If this was his golden opportunity, he sure as hell wasn't going to pass it up.

"I'll be the other man."

Chapter Two

Tara nearly swallowed her tongue. "Wha...what?" she gasped. Her hands shook with his announcement. She carefully set the mug on the table so no coffee would slosh out. If only he knew how much she wanted him to be the other man.

He'd been such a good friend. *And that's all he's offering right now, dummy. Friendship.* Tara dug her nails into her jeans and inhaled.

"Scottie, be serious, would you? This isn't a game," Brianna snapped.

Tara nodded, agreeing with her best friend.

"I am dead serious," Scott ground out, his face taut.

Tara's heart lurched. What would it feel like to be held in Scott's arms, to be cherished by...

She shook her head. Not possible. The man was richer than rich, and besides wanting to help a friend, he wouldn't want anything romantic. Not when he could have his pick of any woman in the country.

Gathering her errant thoughts, Tara cleared her throat. "That's sweet, Scott, really, but not needed, I assure you." *I'm lying, please see that I'm lying! I do need you.*

Scott slumped in his seat and crossed his arms over his chest. His face looked dejected. Why? She would have thought he'd be overjoyed with being let off the hook.

"Somebody needs to help," Scott demanded. "You see any other candidates around?"

Tara had to smile. The man was sulking, pure and simple.

"Jeez, Scottie, we didn't know you cared so much," Brianna teased, reaching across to slap Scott on the thigh.

He didn't take too well to that. His lip curled and he stood. Tara let her gaze move the length of his delicious body from his knees, to his firm thighs, over the decidedly large bulge at his fly, the smooth hardness of his abs beneath his tight-fitting T-shirt—

Tara did a double take and returned her gaze to his fly and the very noticeable bump he did nothing to even attempt to hide.

Her throat was suddenly parched.

"Whenever you twits decide how you want to handle this situation, let me know, would you? I was only trying to help," he grumbled.

Scott moved away, letting Kissy-Face lead him through the crowded café.

Damn. Why did that make her feel like a complete loser? She hadn't meant to hurt his feelings.

"Did he just call us twits?" Brianna asked.

"I believe he did, little one." Tyler wrapped a big hand around Brianna's neck and gave it a caressing squeeze.

Tara sighed. She'd never had that kind of attention before. She wanted it. Badly. Would Scott be like that? Would he lavish her with sweet little kisses like Tyler was doing on Bri's neck?

"Oh, get a room," she barked, coming out of her musings. Scott and she together would never work. Ridiculous to even contemplate it.

Brianna cleared her throat and pushed Tyler's roving lips away. "I'm sorry, Tara. You're right, we need to think about you. What can I do?"

Tara snorted and flopped back on the small couch. She covered her face with her hands and rolled her head back and forth. "I don't know," she groaned. "I have to find a place to live, so unless you know someone who needs a roommate, I—"

"Stay with us."

She jumped at Scott's deep voice behind her and twisted to look up at him. "What?" She laughed, willing her heart back into a normal rhythm. She hadn't even heard the man come back. He smelled so yummy. His belly was eye level and Tara longed to rub her cheek against it.

"I said, stay with me, us, I mean. Stay at the house."

House? From what she'd seen, they didn't live in a house. The place was huge in an over-exaggerated sort of way. No. She couldn't stay there. Not with him. The nearness would drive her batty.

"I can't do that, Scott."

"Why not?" Brianna asked, drawing Tara's attention. She leaned forward, excitement lighting her eyes. "It's perfect. Moving in with us would have to make Eric see you're no longer interested. Plus, you wouldn't have to go apartment hunting. She could stay there, right, Ty?" She elbowed Tyler in the ribs.

"Oof." He rubbed the offended body part with a grimace. "What the hell did you do that for?" Tyler grabbed Brianna's fingers and held them under his palm on his thigh. "Of course you're welcome to stay. There's no reason to become violent," he mumbled at Bri.

Tara smiled. She could see how pissed he was as his thumb traced a soothing path over Brianna's wrist.

She shook her head. "I can't."

"Why not?" Scott growled behind her.

She turned again but he'd already moved. Stooping over, he ran one set of fingers along the table's edge and the other searched for his seat.

"Two steps, Scott," Tara whispered.

He stopped moving and turned his head toward her, his gaze hidden behind the sunglasses. She wished she could see his eyes just once. In all the time she'd known him, she'd never seen them.

He stood tall and took two steps. After doing a ninety-degree turn, he sat without feeling for the seat.

Her heart pounded. She hadn't meant for him to hear her, but he had. What if she'd been wrong? What if he'd taken two steps and fallen on his ass? Her cheeks flamed.

Scott's smile lit up the café, making her tummy quiver. "Thanks." Kissy flopped to the floor beside him. "Now then. Why in the hell can't you take our offer? If you want to show this dickhead you mean business, let me help."

Stubborn bastard.

"I'll be in the way."

Scott and Tyler both snorted. Brianna rolled her eyes. "Whatever. Do you know how many rooms we have? Hell, you could choose whichever one you want and we'd probably never see you again."

"But you've got kids, and—"

"So?" Scott interrupted. "I live there too. They don't seem to mind me being there."

"Yeah, but—"

"Don't you dare say it's because I'm blind. I will throw you over my lap and paddle your ass if you do."

Tara cringed. That's exactly what she'd been thinking. His words made her breathe heavily, exciting her. What would it feel like to have his hands on her, first causing pain, then soothing the pain away?

Tyler laughed, Brianna smacked him. "Knock it off," she hissed.

"Must have seen something on her face, huh?" Scott lifted his mug to his lips.

Tara's face flamed. Had she been that obvious? She shifted, trying to ease the persistent tickle between her legs.

Brianna sighed. "I don't know why you'd want to live with these Neanderthals anyway." She smacked Tyler again. "Stop it," she said when he continued to chortle.

"Stay with us," Scott murmured soothingly.

Damn. He was making it so hard to say no. She hated being beholden to anybody though. If things didn't work out, she'd be without a place again. Ooh...she simmered just thinking about Eric lounging in her apartment as they spoke. Jackass.

Tensions had been building between them the last couple months. She wasn't even sure why. Her heart just hadn't been in it anymore. Had it ever? Had she ever really felt anything for him? Or had he merely been a crutch?

For what? she wondered.

Deep inside she had a sinking feeling she knew what. And he was sitting not three feet from her.

"Please?" he cajoled, oblivious to his sister and her husband as they argued about Tyler's lackluster attempt to keep a straight face.

"I've got it," Brianna suddenly shouted, making Tara jump in her seat.

The café grew silent with her more loud announcement as everyone wondered what it was she got. More than one head turned their way in curiosity. Great. Just what she needed.

"Oops, sorry, folks." Brianna raised her hands in surrender, her cheeks pink.

"Nice goin', sis."

"Scottie," she warned.

Tara smiled. She loved watching the two of them together. They had the easiest camaraderie and no matter how much they argued, it was done in love.

Not like the arguments she and Eric had. No, those were pretty much what he considered petty arguments. Tara didn't see them that way. He was stifling her, starting to tell her— guide her, he would say—what she could and couldn't do, who she could see, what she could wear.

Uh-uh. No way would she stand for that shit. And still, since she'd left, Eric hadn't gotten the premise of "leave me alone". A few times, she'd given in. Tried to see it from his point of view. Hell, maybe she was being unreasonable. When she was ready to walk away from a fight, put some distance between them before things got too bad, he pushed closer. Emotionally and physically, as if he just wasn't able to let it drop.

Always later she would find some tangible evidence of his apology. A gift, a note, a flower, something. But never the words. Never a "Hey, I'm sorry, let's make up". His attitude ran more toward the I-know-you'll-never-leave-me-so-get-over-this-and-move-on way of life. It was an attitude she'd facilitated by going along with him every time they argued instead of seeing the light and getting out of the relationship. It had started getting more than creepy.

Then she'd seen a documentary on a woman who lived with a man who acted the same way Eric did. Things had ended horrifically for the woman, but had made Tara open her eyes to what was happening in her own life.

The next day she'd walked out. Where did that leave her? Homeless and sitting in a café with Studalicious asking her to move in with him.

"No, seriously. I've got it. I know you, Tara. You don't want to move in because you think you'll owe us something and don't have anything to give."

Tara's cheeks heated. Her best friend had read her mind.

Brianna practically vibrated in her seat. "Decorate the house for us!" She bounced to the edge of her chair, clapping and humming with a huge smile on her face.

Lunatic. "What the hell are you talking about, Bri?"

"Yeah, Brianna, what *are* you talking about?" Scottie echoed.

Brianna grunted and slapped her thighs.

"Give her a minute, ladies and gentlemen, sometimes it takes her a while to check her excitement." Tyler turned his head as if he were speaking to the whole café.

Most everyone had gone back to their business, but a few gawkers chuckled at his announcement.

Brianna turned to him and snarled. It was really a sight to see, honestly. Her lip curled up and her eyebrows came together to form a unibrow above her nose.

"The party, Tyler. She can decorate for the party."

"Aah." He nodded. "Yes. She can. That is, if she wants to," he said, turning to look at her in question.

"No way." Tara shook her head vehemently.

"Why not?"

"Oh don't go gettin' all whiny on me, Brianna. Christmas is three days away. I can't decorate your house for a Christmas party in that amount of time."

"And again I say, why not?"

Jeesh, the woman was dense. "Have you seen your house?"

Tyler laughed outright. Scott snorted. Good. At least the men were in agreement with her.

"I have every faith in you, Tara," Scott urged softly.

Rats.

"Which is why you'll have to move in with us in order to work around the clock to finish it," Brianna crowed.

Tara opened her mouth to talk but Scott beat her to it.

"Now wait a minute," Scott demanded.

Take that, she thought. Let her brother set her straight.

"Tara will not move into our home and work every hour of the day. I won't allow it."

Tara slammed her mouth shut. She didn't know whether to be pissed because he was acting like Eric or pleased that he was thinking of her comfort.

"She'd be too exhausted to join the party if you made her work full-time."

"True," Brianna agreed.

"Hello." Tara waved, trying to get their attention. Not that Scott could see her, but still.

"But it solves the problem of her feeling like she would owe us something for living there," Brianna insisted.

"You're not going to trade a bed for her work, are you?"

Scott sounded so disgusted, Tara had to laugh. Tyler apparently felt the same way. He threw his head back and his body shook with loud laughter.

"No, you dolt. I was merely saying if she lived with us, she could spend more time working on the decorations and not have to worry about leaving at a certain time or... Never mind. My point is this. Tara can't stand to be a burden. To anybody. Of course I would pay her. Her work is fabulous."

"Okay then. It's settled. Have Max pick up her stuff," Scott said.

Oh for God's sake. "You do realize I am sitting right here and have not said yes to this plan?"

Both siblings turned to her.

"We were just trying to get you away from Eric. That is what you said you wanted, right?" Scott asked petulantly.

Now she'd hurt his feelings again, which was almost as bad as being beholden to someone.

"Besides, Tara," Brianna started, "think of all the people who'll see your stuff. You could give out your business cards, we could make a banner, hand out flyers, announce who you are."

Good Lord the woman could get excited.

Ugh. She had a point though. This project could be a real coup for Tara's business. Knowing Tyler and Cole, all sorts of high-society people would be there. Just thinking about how many projects she might drum up made her breath catch.

And, Scott had a point too. It would take her away from Eric and hopefully make him see once and for all that she was through with him.

"Oh, all right." She sighed, giving in to the conniving brother and sister.

Brianna started in on the clapping again. Tyler cringed and dropped his head back on the seat with a groan.

Scott's face lit up like a little boy who'd finally gotten his way.

Why that little… He'd played her from the get-go. Hurt feelings, her ass.

❄❄❄

Who did she think she was, running out on him like this? Look at her laughing and having a good time with some other man instead of being at home where she should be.

Nobody walked out on him. Nobody.

He needed to teach her a lesson. She belonged with him. They were perfect together. Two parts of a whole.

He'd thought she would see that the second she walked out on him. Tara couldn't cope without him. She needed him to keep her strong, to keep her from straying on the wrong path. Which was obviously what had happened by the looks of things.

Their time apart was that bitch Brianna's fault. He would have to do something about her. Get her influence away from his Tara.

Tara didn't need the distraction. Her mind should be focused on him.

Sick. Brianna was a depravity. Having two men. He smiled. Maybe they weren't real men at all if the two of them couldn't handle one bitch on their own.

Not like him with his Tara. She just needed a bit more guidance.

He turned and tucked his face into his coat collar. He'd passed her Civic on his way in. Maybe if he scared her a little, she'd see her error in leaving him and come back on her own. After all, she'd need his protection.

Chapter Three

Tara stared at the side of her car in horror. Who the hell would do something like this? Her leftover Danish fell from her numb fingers and a sick feeling lodged in her throat.

Damn. On top of her current problems, some dumbshit had chosen her little Honda Civic to key. The scratch went all the way through the paint and traveled from one bumper to the other. It would probably cost her a fortune to repair. Money she didn't have.

Tara turned around in the parking lot. She was alone. A shiver rent her body beneath her down parka that had nothing to do with the freezing temperatures. She felt like she was being watched.

She shook the feeling off and looked at the ugly line marring her once pretty blue car. Tara slapped her hand on the roof. What could she do? Call the cops and have them tell her there was nothing they could do. Call her insurance, which she could do from the apartment. Tell Scott what had happened.

As owner of To Bean, he'd want to know. She didn't want this to happen to anyone else either. At least he'd be able to get someone to keep an eye on things in the parking lot. The thought of seeing him again made her knees weak. The man was more than potent.

She trudged back through the slush left over from last week's snowstorm and ripped the door open, snarling when the bell tinkled overhead. Her Christmas cheer had flown the coop.

Tara stomped her booted feet on the welcome rug thingy and searched the café for Scott's familiar dirty blond head.

"Are you looking for someone?"

Tara turned at the employee's pleasant question and nodded.

"Scott Wyatt."

The girl's lip curled on one corner for a split second before she offered a semi-polite smile.

"I'm sorry," she said in the most dramatic way possible, her smile growing. "He's in a meeting, you'll have to come back later."

Tara shifted her weight onto one foot, barely refrained from tapping her toe in agitation and crossed her arms over her chest. She looked closely at the girl's nametag.

"That's interesting, Melody, since I just left him not five minutes ago and he never mentioned having a meeting to attend."

Melody's smile faltered, her eyes narrowed ever so slightly and when she spoke, it was through gritted teeth.

"He's in his office and asked not to be interrupted."

Okay. She could buy that, but not why the girl so obviously didn't want her to see Scott. Or why someone her age and apparent status in the company would be privy to what the owner wanted or didn't want.

She cocked her head. "Perhaps you could just tell him I'm here. I know he'll want to see me." At least, she prayed he did, just to tick little Miss Hot-For-the-Boss off.

Melody huffed and pursed her lips. She threw her rag down in the plastic bin filled with dirty dishes and marched over to a door behind the counter.

Whoa. Can you say *attitude*? She better hope she never did this shit with a real customer or she'd find herself out of work.

Tara followed. When Melody stopped suddenly, Tara ran into her. Melody turned. Her nostrils flared.

"You'll have to wait out here," she said in agitation.

Tara leaned in and gave a two-fingered salute. "No problem."

Smoothing her Christmas green apron, Melody faced the door. Without knocking, she opened it and stuck her head in.

Some meeting.

"Mr. Wyatt, this woman insists on seeing you."

Good Lord. Tara dropped her chin to her chest and counted. To two. Then she pushed her way past Melody, ignoring her spluttering.

"Scott, it's me."

Scott stood so quickly his chair tipped over.

"Tara? What's wrong?" Hand trailing the edge of the desk, he rounded it and came toward her.

His furniture was arranged in such a fashion that he had a clear path to the door. He crossed it faster than a sighted man would.

Tara stopped him with a hand on his arm. "I needed to talk to you and Melody here was gracious enough to show me in."

Scott turned to Melody. How he knew exactly where she was, Tara couldn't fathom. The things he could do, the things normal people took for granted, were nothing short of miraculous.

"Thank you, Melody. Can you shut the door on your way out?"

Tara resisted the urge to smirk. Dashing whatever crush Melody had on her boss wouldn't accomplish anything.

Melody threw a glare over her shoulder and left the room.

"I thought you'd left, Tara."

"I did." Seriously, the man was beautiful. "But I had a little problem with my car."

He reached in his pocket for his cell phone. "Did you need me to call a tow?"

"I wish," she muttered. "No, actually someone keyed it."

"What?"

"Yep. I wanted you to know so you could maybe have someone keep an eye on the parking lot in case the person does it again."

"Shit. Yeah. God, I'm sorry. Whatever it costs, I'll pay for it."

Take off the sunglasses. "That's not why I'm here, Scott."

He ran a hand through his hair, hardly mussing the short strands. She fisted her hands against wanting to touch it herself.

"No, I know, I just... Damn." He unerringly found her hands and held them.

The touch electrified her, tingling every nerve in her body.

He stepped closer and her breath caught.

A knock sounded at the door.

Before they could break apart, the door opened and Melody reappeared. Her quick intake of breath and wide eyes told Tara how surprised Melody was to find her holding hands with Scott. Then those pert lips of hers curved upward.

She looked straight at Tara. "This man is looking for you, I believe," Melody smirked before turning and closing the door with an unmistakable click.

"Tara," Eric whined.

How in the hell...

"I've been waiting for you, baby." Eric stomped in like he owned the place and jerked to a stop. "Who's this, Tara?" he snarled.

Tara tried to let go of Scott's hand. No sense bringing him into Eric's warped world. Scott held tighter, squeezing her fingers. In fact, he tugged, knocking her off balance so she fell into him, and wrapped his arm around her shoulders.

Eric growled. "What the fuck do you think you're doing?"

"Hugging my girlfriend. Can I help you?"

Oh. My. God. Tara's cheeks flamed.

"Yeah, you can get your hands off her. Tara belongs to me."

Tara literally felt steam come out of her ears. "*Belongs to you?* Are you crazy, Eric? I'm a person, nobody *owns* me."

Scott held tight to her when she tried to move away. She welcomed his calming effect since her senses were reeling.

"We belong together, Tara. That's all I meant, baby," he cajoled, his cheeks red as if he'd seen the error in his words.

Eric was more delusional than she originally thought.

Tara took a deep breath, glad Scott was close by. "I've told you we're through, Eric. It's time for you to move out of the apartment and on with your life. Find a woman you're better suited to."

Eric's eyes narrowed and a muscle jumped in his jaw. Tara found herself reaching across Scott's body and taking hold of his other hand.

"You don't mean that, baby."

"I do, Eric. Every word, every time I've said it." Here goes nothing. "I have a new boyfriend now." She patted Scott's chest and prayed he didn't give her away.

Eric's hands fisted at his sides and he took a tentative step forward.

Kissy-Face whined from his position near the desk and got up, ready to defend his owner.

"So what, you think you can just dump me and go off to fuck another guy? Do you know what that makes you?"

Total shock slammed into her, leaving her with the sensation she'd been slapped across the face. Her face drained of blood. Scott shoved her behind his back.

"I wouldn't go any further if I were you," he said in a deadly quiet tone.

"Or you'll what? Hit me with your cane? Not much a gimp can do."

Oh my God. Eric couldn't see that Scott was blind. He thought Scott walked with a cane. If Eric came after him, Scott wouldn't see it coming. How would he defend himself?

Scott stepped forward, halting Eric's attempt to do so too. Her ex stiffened and his Adam's apple bobbed as he swallowed. Tara wanted to pump her fist in the air.

How Scott acted like any other sighted man she didn't know. It was another one of those uncanny abilities she'd seen in him.

"This isn't over, Tara. You'll see. In a few days you'll see how much you miss me and come crying back into my arms." Eric waggled a finger at her.

Please. How had she missed this pissy side of him?

"No, Eric, I won't. Move out of the apartment."

"No. My name is on the lease. You think you can dump me like this, *you* move out."

Damn it. She squeezed the back of Scott's shirt in agitation. Good thing she'd accepted Brianna and Scott's offer of a room. She could start apartment hunting as soon as she got settled there. The added commission from this party would go a long way in securing rent somewhere at least.

"Fine," she grumbled, stepping around Scott. She loved that apartment. "I'll be by to pick up my stuff tomorrow."

Eric's face held a mixture of disgust and...excitement? What the fuck would he be excited about?

"Don't be there," she said flatly.

Eric didn't answer. He turned on his heel and marched out of Scott's office, slamming the door behind him.

Tara let out the breath she hadn't realized she was holding and slumped her shoulders. She hated that Scott had to be here for Eric's little display. Talk about embarrassing.

"I'm so sor..."

Scott's hand moved in a slow arc toward her face. She froze and wondered what he was doing. His wrist grazed her ear and pulled back until his palm cradled her cheek.

Her heart thudded. She rubbed her cheek on his hand.

"May I see what you look like?" he asked, throwing her for a loop.

She'd seen this done before on TV. A blind person's way of "seeing" was by touch. How could she not grant him this?

Tara nodded. Scott brought his other hand up. His thumbs and fingers wandered ever so gently over her forehead, her eyes and nose, her cheeks, her lips, and curved around her chin. It was the most exquisite and erotic thing she'd ever experienced.

The room was so silent she could hear both of their harsh breaths. Her belly somersaulted with tender emotion. She wanted more.

"You're beautiful, Tara," he rasped.

Her eyes welled up. God. In all the time she'd spent with Eric, he'd never said anything as profound as those three little words to her.

She sniffed and dropped her chin to her chest. Scott lifted it back up and wiped an escaping tear from her cheek as if he'd seen it there.

"I have to kiss you."

"Yes."

Why deny how she felt?

He leaned into her, his thumbs at the corners of her mouth, and melded his lips to hers.

The world shifted. She felt her arms slide around his waist and tilted her head to provide better access.

There was nothing tentative from that point on. He took control of her mouth, coaxing her to open and slipping his tongue inside. The sexual dance continued for several long moments. Scott shuffled closer, insinuating his thigh between her legs, and pressed against her mound.

She moaned. Tingles erupted in her clit. It wasn't enough. She rubbed herself on his leg.

One hand left her cheek and settled on a breast, the thumb flicking at her distended nipple. She squirmed in his hold, raking his back with her fingernails. His cock ground into her tummy.

And then he was gone. Releasing her and stepping back, leaving both of them fighting for air. Tara shook in the aftermath, both saddened it was over and angered that she wanted more. Now.

"I'm sorry, I didn't mean for it to go—"

Tara pounced on his apology and covered his red, swollen lips with two fingers. "Shush. That was the most incredible kiss. Thank you."

He kissed her fingers, sending a shiver down her spine. Damn the man was potent.

And she was falling for him. Hard.

Chapter Four

"Everything is beautiful."

Tara spun around from her spot at the kitchen sink where she'd been staring out into the middle of the night blackness.

"Jeez. You scared the crap out of me. What are you still doing up? It's..." What time was it? She looked at her watch.

"Twelve-thirty, I know." Scott smiled. "Sorry. I didn't mean to scare you."

She willed her heart to crawl back into her chest. How did one man have the right to look so good?

"Just out of curiosity, and excuse me if I sound stupid or am out of line, but how exactly do you know what I've done is beautiful?"

His smile widened, revealing perfect teeth. Teeth that had nibbled on her lip yesterday in his office. Teeth she wished would nibble on her— *Stop. Stop right there. Don't even go one inch further with that line of thinking. Bad.*

"Because I've heard the girls and Brianna squealing every time they discovered something new. And my mom told me so." He shrugged. "It must be true."

She'd met his mom earlier today. Lydia Wyatt was wonderful despite the number of years she'd been out of Scott and Brianna's life due to their father's duplicity.

If it had been her, Tara wasn't sure she would have coped as well meeting a mother she'd been told her whole life had run off and wouldn't be back.

Of course they'd been reunited now for ten years and according to Brianna, Lydia had more than made up for the time she'd been forced out of her children's lives.

"So how'd you do it?"

"Do what?" Tara tried to remember what they'd been talking about.

"Get all this together in one day." He stalked across the obstacle-free kitchen toward her. No, prowled was a better word. She imagined beneath those sunglasses, his eyes would be glowing. Like a werewolf from one of her favorite paranormal books, staking his mate.

She shrugged and licked her lips as he came to a stop directly in front of her. "Whenever I take on a new project I like to dive right in. And in this case, that's a good thing since Brianna didn't give me much time. When I finally left your office yesterday, I got a lot of planning done. Today I shopped and put most of it together."

Scott crossed his arms across his chest. The muscles in his forearms bulged, emphasizing what she already knew about her friend's brother. He worked out. A lot. And man did she want to see what the rest of him looked like.

Lord she was turning into a nympho. Best friends were not supposed to lust after younger brothers. Thank God she wasn't as old as Brianna because it would make the whole situation too weird to handle. As it stood, Tara was still three years older than him.

Did he care? Did he know?

"Do you know how old I am?" she blurted.

One of his eyebrows slowly rose.

Ground, just open up and swallow me whole, please. She covered her face with her hands. What did it matter? It's not like he could see her.

"Twenty-nine." His deep voice washed over her, making her entire body tingle in awareness. "Do you know how old *I* am?"

"I'm practically robbing the cradle," she grumbled, then jumped when he barked out in laughter.

"There's only three years separating us. I hardly think people will have you arrested for taking advantage."

"Who says it'll be me taking advantage?"

"Hmm. I don't know." He stepped cautiously forward.

Tara moved her foot at the last second when he would have stepped on her bare toes. He crowded her, forcing her back into the counter. She reached back and grasped the granite surface with both hands.

She should have kept her arms in front.

His rock hard abs brushed against her upper belly, his... She closed her eyes and sucked in a breath.

Oh, mama. She licked her suddenly dry lips.

"Maybe we could take advantage of each other," he murmured, leaning in and laying his lips on hers.

Damn man didn't even need to coax her. She melted into him, opening her mouth to his and sucking in his tongue. His hands cradled her face; she reached up and gripped his shoulders.

"I didn't mean for this to happen," he whispered, kissing around her face.

"Really?" Her breath came out in tiny pants. He moved down her neck and she tilted her head to give him better access.

"Hell no, I'm lying to you. I've wanted to do this since the first day I met you." He nudged the collar of her flannel shirt aside.

His lips feathered along her collarbone. Her nipples hardened.

"Why didn't you?"

"I'm blind."

"I can see that. What does that have to do with kissing me?"

He shrugged. His hands came up to caress her throat and he rested his forehead on hers.

"Most of the women I know only want the novelty of being with a blind man."

She pulled her head back and stared at him. He was serious. She swallowed and took a breath.

"Then you haven't been with the right kind of woman." How could any woman not see him for the smart, strong, absolutely gorgeous man he was? How had *she* not seen him for more than a friend?

"No? Maybe you know someone?"

She was crazy. Absolutely nuts.

And totally, one hundred percent sure of herself for the first time in her life.

"Maybe." The word rasped from her lips.

"Hmm." He nibbled the corner of her mouth again. It was the sweetest feeling in the world. A hundred times better than the rushed gropings in the dark with Eric. It felt...right. Perfect.

"Take off the sunglasses, Scott. Let me see you."

This time he pulled back. He trailed his hands down her arms and clasped his fingers with hers.

"Promise not to laugh?"

She snorted. Shit.

"Too late." He smiled, saving her from being totally embarrassed.

Scott sighed and whipped off the dark glasses she'd never seen him without.

His eyelids didn't quite open all the way, and his pupils strayed, having never been trained to focus. Now she could see him as a blind person. Covered up, he was just like everyone else.

"So?" He ran a hand through his hair, ruffling the short strands to make them look like he'd just climbed out of bed.

Ugh. Do. Not. Think. About. Him. In. Bed.

"You're very handsome."

The corners of his mouth twitched. "You're not just saying that, are you?"

Tara stretched up on her tiptoes to reach his mouth and kissed him. "No."

"Then can I put these back on?" he asked, holding up the shades.

"Why?" She hoped he didn't feel the need to hide behind them anymore.

He cocked his head. "I don't know. They're kind of a part of me after all these years. Kinda like wearing underwear."

She couldn't resist teasing him and gasped. "You wear underwear?"

His entire body froze. The fingers of the hand he still held her with tightened and he audibly gulped.

"You're not wearing panties?"

Now why did he have to make that sound so damn erotic?

She slid out of the confined space he had her trapped in. If she didn't get out of there now, she'd be jumping him in a minute. All this talk about her panties was making her wet.

"I'll never tell."

He followed her with his head, sliding the glasses back on his face. Scott turned and backed up to the counter she'd vacated to rest his hips against it. His arms went back across his chest. The pose was cocky, arrogant, full of himself.

She wanted every bit of it.

Instead she bid him goodnight and ran.

Chapter Five

Scott forced his fingers to unclench from where they held the car's door handle. He'd spent a sleepless night in hell last night after Tara had left him standing alone in the kitchen. Thinking about her in a room so close to his only added to the torture.

Had she finally gone to sleep or had she tossed and turned like he had?

This morning she'd sounded none the worse for wear. Talking to Brianna in an animated voice, she'd detailed her plans for the rest of the decorations. His nieces seemed to be in complete awe over some of her ideas.

Then she'd mentioned having to go back to her apartment to retrieve the rest of her things.

He grimaced, remembering how he'd reacted. Over his dead body would she do that without one of them with her. He'd felt the anger in Eric in his office two days ago. No way was she going to face him by herself. She'd done a bang up job trying to convince him, Brianna, Cole and Tyler she'd be fine because Eric would be at work and she'd be there alone.

None of them trusted Eric would miss this opportunity to confront her again.

Hell, Scott had his suspicions Eric was the person who'd keyed her car. Tyler was looking into it.

"Relax, man." Tyler chuckled next to him.

"Max could have brought me, you know?" Damn. This is exactly the type of situation that irked him the most about being blind. He couldn't help protect the people he loved. How could you defend against something you couldn't see?

He heard Tyler sigh. "Look. Brianna's told me some of the stuff Tara's been through with Eric. Max won't be able to do much if her ex starts some shit. Eric likely knows what I do for a living since Tara is friends with Bri. He's more likely to back off Tara if he's sees me over a limo driver."

"How the fuck did I not know this was happening?" Another thing Scott had replayed over and over in his head in the wee hours of the last couple nights.

"My guess would be Tara didn't want you to know."

"Why the hell not?" They were friends. Even if they'd only known each other a few months, he'd never given her a reason not to trust him.

"Well, I'd say it's as plain as the nose on your face, but since you can't see the looks she gives you..."

Scott twisted in his seat to face Tyler. "You mean, all the time I've known her, I've wanted her but didn't do anything about it, and *now* you're telling me this?"

Tyler laughed.

"This is not funny, Ty."

"Hey. Don't shoot the messenger. Brianna's told me that Tara doesn't think she's good enough for you."

"What?" How fucked up was that?

"Apparently Tara grew up pretty poor and has a hard time believing someone wealthy might desire her."

"Bullshit. Eric really did a fucking number on her brain, didn't he?"

"Sounds like he's one manipulative bastard. Thank God Tara saw through him and got the hell out before things got out of hand."

Scott wasn't so sure things hadn't already gotten out of hand.

"Did you find out anything about who keyed her car?"

"No, I'm trying to find out where he was when it happened, but other than the fact I know he wasn't at work, I'm at a dead end."

"We know where he was, Tyler. In my office, which puts him at the car at the right time."

"I know what you're thinking, Scott, and yes, I'd like nothing better than to pin this on him, but until I have concrete evidence I can't do anything. And neither can the police. They'll look at the car, and the fact that Eric and Tara have been dating and ask, 'Why would the man key his girlfriend's car?' There's nothing that says there's bad blood between the two of them, only her word. Let me do my job. We'll get him, I swear."

Scott barely refrained from growling in frustration, but he understood everything Tyler said.

The car slowed down and made a turn.

"Why did she have to drive herself?" Scott grumbled.

"Damn, you've got it bad for her."

Even if he didn't have it bad, he'd hate what Eric had done to her.

"And on that note, we're here."

Scott threw his door open and stepped out.

Slush oozed over the tops of both feet, drenching his tennis shoes in icy coldness. "Thanks for the warning."

"Shit, I'm sorry, man."

"Yes, I can hear how sorry you are."

Tyler grabbed Scott's hand, placed it at his elbow and led him out of the melting crap and onto the curb.

"Anytime you want to stop snickering would be good," Scott said.

"Tyler," Tara huffed.

"What? Idiot jumped out of the car before I could warn him. He's a little hot under the collar if you know what I mean."

"May I, Scott?"

"May you what?"

"Guide you."

Scott heard the smile in her voice.

"Where's Kissy-Face?" she asked.

"He's in the backseat." He gestured over his shoulder with his thumb and dropped Tyler's elbow. Scott reached out. "Give me your arm."

She did. Too bad it was covered in a thick down coat. He would have loved to feel her skin against his palm.

"What do I do?" she whispered.

"Walk. I'll follow. Tell me if there's something I need to step over." He smiled at her. "You make me trip and I'm taking you down with me."

She burst out laughing.

"I wouldn't laugh if I were you, Tara. He means it." Tyler grunted.

"Oh? Did big, bad Tyler get taken down?"

"Hell yeah," Scott said. "Bastard walked me right into a rock border along a path. Never said a word. I remember exactly what he said afterward too. 'I thought you'd step over it, dumbass.'"

"Who the hell doesn't pick up their feet?" Tyler snapped.

"Oh my God." Tara laughed so hard she had to stop moving. Scott's hand slipped off her arm when she bent at the waist.

A second later she sniffed, collected herself and put his hand back on her arm, patting it in what he hoped was sympathy. He sure as hell didn't get any from Brianna or her two lovers. He guessed they'd grown too used to him over the years. His nieces were the only ones who really cared anymore. And his mother. She coddled him like he was still six.

"You know, it's really not funny anymore. It happened right after I met you," Tyler reasoned.

"Some things are hard to forget."

"Okay, Scott, there are twelve steps in front of you."

He lifted an eyebrow. "You always go around counting steps?"

"Absolutely. Don't you?"

His other brow matched the first in height. "Every day."

"Sorry."

She sounded so disgruntled he had to laugh. He pulled her to him and squeezed her in a tight hug.

"I'm kidding, Tara."

"I'm not. I didn't even think, it's like you aren't really blind. I mean you do so much that's so normal, sometimes I forget. Especially when you don't have Kissy or the cane or—"

"Hey." He pulled back, separating them. "It's okay, Tara. I'm used to it. And I know you don't mean anything. Trust me, after twenty-six years, you're not going to hurt my feelings."

Scott leaned over and kissed her forehead. She sighed and sank into his chest, snuggling against him. It felt so good. So right. Perfect.

He wanted more. He wanted forever.

Tara twisted the key in the lock and shoved the door open. The smell hit her before she even took one step inside.

"Ugh. What *is* that?" She cautiously entered, expecting to be greeted by a dead cow. What she found was almost as bad. Her once adorable apartment had turned into a pigsty. Dirty dishes, clothes, papers. You name it, it was on the floor. And the couch. And the table.

"What? What's wrong?" Scott nudged Tara farther into the space which had once been considered a living room.

"Looks like good ole Eric needs a maid." Tyler cursed and spun a slow circle, taking everything in.

Tara couldn't move.

"Maybe he thought he already had one." Scott pulled her closer and pressed her back to his front. He rested his chin on the top of her head. "You okay?"

She nodded. What an ugly piece of work Eric had become. Thank God she'd gotten out when she did.

Shaking his head, Tyler put his hands on his hips and sighed.

"Why don't you get what you need and let's get out of here."

There was nothing else to do. It didn't look like Eric had done one thing since she'd left. What the hell was he even eating on for God's sake? He hadn't appeared disgusting when he'd cornered her in Scott's office the other day, so what was he doing?

"I'm not sure there's even anything I want to—"

"Tara? It's about time you came home." Eric strode down the hall, took one look at her with Scott and Tyler, and his face turned beet red. "What the fuck are they doing here?"

"You weren't supposed to be here, Eric."

Scott stiffened along her back.

"I damn well wasn't going to be anywhere else when my woman finally decided it was time to come back where she belongs. Maybe I should thank you two for bringing Tara back," he snarled, edging closer. "You can leave now."

Tyler moved between her and Eric, blocking her view. Scott tried to force her behind him.

Damn it, this was her fight.

"I'm not back," she yelled. "We're finished, if you haven't gotten that message through your thick skull over the last couple weeks." Tara stomped past all three men, leaving them staring at her back.

"Nothing like egging on a sleeping bear," Tyler muttered and moved to follow her down the hall.

She didn't look back. Stupid man. She could only wonder where she'd be right now if she'd stayed with him. Probably tied up in the closet. Tara shook with the thought and eyed the once tidy closet in a new light.

"I'm glad you got out of this, Tara." Tyler stopped in the bedroom doorway and leaned negligently against the frame.

She knew better. There wasn't a relaxed bone in his body. If the situation warranted it, he could spring into action in a millisecond. It was what he was trained to do. Tara had seen him do so a while back when someone had threatened one of their girls. Tyler in full fight mode was more than impressive.

Tara dropped her shoulders and looked around the room, wondering what she could salvage. What she even wanted to try and salvage. Was there anything left here of great importance to her? Most of her things she'd taken with her the first night.

There were some more clothes and a few momentos. Oh, and her mother's quilt. She rummaged in the mess of her closet and pulled out a box.

"I don't have much left to get." She knelt and started packing.

"That's good," Tyler said, distracted.

Tara lifted her gaze. "What's wrong?"

"Nothing. Just watching Eric with Scott. I don't trust the fucker."

Tara jumped to her feet. "What's he doing? I'll be damned if I let him do anything to Scott."

Tyler smiled and arched a brow. "Really? Eric is circling him and Scott's just following him around with whatever freaky sense he has that lets him know where someone is."

She smacked his arm. "Bring him back here with me. Poor guy's just standing there, being corrupted by the loser."

"I wouldn't let Scott hear you call him a poor guy."

"He doesn't scare me," she scoffed.

Tyler laughed and went to do her bidding, leaving her to search the disaster area for her things. When she heard the front door slam, Tara hurdled the box she'd withdrawn and dashed down the hallway. She practically slammed into Scott's back since she had to watch where she ran because of the crap Eric had strewn all over the floor.

Scott turned and caught her. "What's wrong?"

"Nothing. What happened out here?"

Tyler slapped his hands together as if removing dust from them. He sniffed. "Eh, nothin', just taking out the trash." He shrugged. "At least you can pack in peace now."

She eyed Tyler in suspicion. "What'd you do to him?"

"I swear I didn't do anything, though I would have loved to put my fist through his face."

"And his leaving had nothing to do with the fact you got right in his face and told him to leave Tara the fuck alone, or the fact you had your hand on your gun?" Scott said.

"How'd you... Damn psychic freak," Tyler muttered.

Tara gasped but Scott laughed, his fingers rubbing up and down her spine. It felt so good she leaned into it.

"I heard the snap of your holster pop, and he did squeak, 'my nose', when you bumped it."

"You're still a freaky bastard."

"So you tell me, almost daily."

"Nice exchange, boys. Now, if you'll excuse me, I'll get this packing done so we can get the hell out of this creepy place."

Chapter Six

Fucking bitch. She'd let them brainwash her. He slanted a look back at the apartment. How long did he have? A few minutes at least.

He stormed over to the shiny black BMW. It was Tyler's. He knew from the countless times he'd seen Brianna show up in it.

Damn it. He could have prevented this a long time ago. Nipped it in the bud. But no. He'd wanted her to trust him and so he'd let her keep a few friends and slowly weaned her from the rest. One by one he'd picked them off. He had seen the light at the end of the tunnel that was her alone, dependent on him. He'd been so fucking close.

Eric hadn't foreseen something like this happening. He kicked at a mound of snow and trailed his hand along the hood. With one last glance at the apartment, he slid underneath the front end where he'd be hidden from view.

His heart raced in excitement as he pulled his pocketknife from his jeans.

"If this doesn't scare you back where you belong, nothing will."

He found what he was looking for and cut through it.

A muffled sound from above startled him and he froze. Were they here already? He wiggled around, looking in every direction but saw nothing. On his way out he rapped his head on the undercarriage and bit back a curse.

Another noise reached his ears. This time louder. It sounded like it was coming from the car. Shit. He hadn't even thought to see if there was an occupant.

Kneeling at the front bumper, he slowly rose to peek through the windshield. Staring back at him was a huge German shepherd, tongue hanging out.

Eric stood. "Stupid dog." He rounded the hood and stooped at the driver's side window to see better. It had a contraption attached to it, some kind of harness. It was the same dog he'd seen Tara petting at that coffee shop the other day.

He jerked his head up to his apartment.

"Mother fucker. That son of a bitch is blind."

He smiled. Tara wouldn't date a blind man. She was using him to play hard to get. He patted the roof of the car. The dog barked again.

What he'd just done ought to fix everything. He'd have her back by morning. He started walking away and realized her car was parked a couple of spots away. Shit.

They hadn't come together. How would she be scared if she wasn't in the car with them? The weight of the knife in his palm gave him another idea.

Eric slithered over to her Civic and stabbed the knife into one tire and then another.

He nodded in satisfaction. Now she'd have to go with them.

❄❄❄

Scott reached over the seat and laid a hand on Kissy's head. "Should we stop for lunch?" God knew his stomach was rumbling.

"No," both Tara and Tyler snapped.

"That was rather emphatic."

"Lily's got a Christmas thing this afternoon," Tyler said, shifting in his seat.

106

"And I need to finish the decorations for tomorrow night. I can't *believe* that asshole slashed my tires."

Scott turned toward her. "I'm just glad it wasn't you he cut, sweetheart."

She sighed. He hated Eric for this.

"You've got to eat sometime," he said, changing the subject.

"Does it look like I don't eat?" She gasped. "Shit. What I meant is—"

"Settle down. I can feel that you're not lacking in eating."

Tyler laughed. "Way to go, bro."

"You saying I'm fat?"

Scott dropped his chin to his chest and rubbed his eyelids beneath the sunglasses. He was starting to get a killer headache.

"I'm just teasing, Scott."

Tyler couldn't stop laughing. Idiot. "You sure know how to... Fuck."

"Excuse me?" Tara's shocked voice whipped through the car.

Scott braced his hand on the dashboard. He knew by Tyler's tone something was wrong. He heard him fumble with his phone.

"Cole. Send Max to pick us up, would you? Yeah, at the corner of Kingston and Cooper in Creve Couer. What's up? The brakes are soft and getting softer."

"What?" Tara screeched in the back seat.

Scott held his hand out, offering it to her if she wanted something to hold. Or mangle. He recognized her panic.

"I'm pulling off now."

Thank God they were moving slow enough to do so. What if they'd been on the highway?

"I'm not sure, but they were fine when we got to her apartment and now they're not. I'll call Garner so he can go over it. He's the expert in cars."

They jerked to a stop.

"Is he saying what I think he's saying?" Tara whispered.

The wobble in her voice ripped at him. "If you think he's saying that maybe Eric fucked with our brake lines, then yes, he's saying what you think he's saying."

"I can't see Eric doing anything like this. He may be a total ass, but why would he want to hurt me? He thinks I'm coming back to him, for God's sake."

"Tell Lily I'll be there. I might be late, but I'll be there. Will do."

The phone snapped closed. "Max will be here soon."

The door opened and slammed shut.

"He's pissed," Tara murmured.

"What's he doing?"

"Popping the hood. I can't believe this is happening."

He didn't want to ask her the obvious, but if he didn't know, it would kill him. Tomorrow night was the annual Masters Christmas Party and Scott fully intended to be standing under the mistletoe with Tara bundled in his arms. He didn't want anything standing between them, especially not this dickhead.

"Has he ever been physical with you, Tara?"

Kissy whined from his spot next to Tara. "Shh, boy, it's okay," she consoled.

Was she deliberately avoiding answering him? Did that mean she'd felt Eric's rage? His hand fisted on the dash.

"No. I think it was headed in that direction, but he hadn't gone quite so far yet," she said honestly, with a hint of sadness. "He wasn't like this when I met him and it was just in the last few months he started getting...possessive, I guess."

He had to grit his teeth against jumping out of the car, hunting Eric down and killing him with his bare hands.

Tyler's door opened, letting in a rush of cold air. "Brake line's been cut."

Tara inhaled deeply behind Scott. "I'm moving out of the house," she said.

Scott spun around. "What the hell for?"

"Now's not a good time to make rash decisions. If he's gone to this extreme, there's no telling what he'll do next," Tyler explained.

"I don't want to put your family at risk."

"Absolutely not," Scott hissed. "The best thing for you to do is stay where you have protection. No one can help you if you're alone. No fucking way will I let him get to you, Tara. Besides," he added, wanting to give her every reason in the world to stay with them, "Brianna will be pissed if you don't finish her decorations."

"Ooh, I like it when Bri gets pissed." Tyler chortled.

Scott rolled his eyes.

"You would." Tara groaned and shifted in her seat. "How did this get to be such a mess?"

"Because Eric's a psycho, Tara. He needs some serious help, and not from you," Tyler pointed out. "If he's been kind of standing on the sidelines, waiting for you to come back to him, then I have a feeling seeing you with Scott has pushed him over the edge."

"Which wasn't my intention at all. I only wanted him to get the drift of us being over. Done. Kaput. God, what a disaster."

"Let's get through the party tomorrow night and then we can sit down and get a better grasp on the situation," Scott offered.

"Sounds good to me. I'll have Max drop me off and you guys can finish whatever needs to be done at the house. At least security's tight there, Eric won't be able to bother you," Tyler said.

He wouldn't bother them in person, but Scott doubted Eric would be far from Tara's mind the rest of the day. He wished he could offer more to make things right.

Chapter Seven

"Another late night?"

Tara's heart pounded. Milk sloshed out of the glass onto her hand when she slammed it down on the counter.

"You've got to stop doing that," she breathed. "What are you still doing up?"

Scott shrugged. "I heard you moving around and couldn't sleep knowing you were agitated."

She swallowed as he came nearer. He wore only silky black pajama pants and nothing else. His feet padded across the tile floor. She drew her attention up, trying hard to bypass the noticeable bulge below abs to die for. And if she didn't stop looking at him, she'd likely embarrass herself.

"Nice pants," she muttered. Her cheeks heated and she covered her mouth with her hand. "I didn't just say that out loud, did I?"

The corner of his lips lifted. "I believe you did." He raised his arms, holding his hands out to "feel" for her.

The fingertips of one hand brushed across the curve of her breast. She sucked in a breath. He paused for the longest of seconds, both of them frozen in place, their harsh breathing the only noise in the otherwise silent kitchen.

She wanted so badly for him to touch her again.

He did. His fingers curled and his knuckles grazed her hardened nipple. She moaned and dropped her head back. Exquisite tingles shot through her body, yet it wasn't enough.

Scott leaned into her, his fingers growing bolder on her breast. "I've wanted you since they day I met you," he whispered, tickling her lips with his.

"Really?" she squeaked. Tara closed her eyes in mortification.

"Mm-hm." He nibbled along her jaw, up to her ear.

"I think I have too. Wanted you, I mean." Babbling idiot.

"What are you wearing?"

"Umm…a tank top and boxer shorts."

"My favorite." He nuzzled his nose into her hair and his hand crept beneath the hem of her shirt. "If you don't want this, tell me now, because once I start, I don't think I'll be able to stop."

Not want this? Was he crazy? Couldn't he feel her heart pounding?

"Yes. Yes."

She felt his lips curve at her cheek and then he was there, touching her breast. Pinching and tugging at the nipple. His thigh pushed between her legs. Tara ground her aching pussy on the slippery fabric of his pants.

"Maybe we should—" She gasped when his other hand suddenly insinuated itself inside her boxers. His fingers slid between her folds, finding her wet and more than ready.

"Maybe we should what?" His tongue darted into her mouth, rubbing against hers.

Two could play this game. She cupped his thick erection through his pants and squeezed.

Scott groaned. He laid his forehead against hers and tilted his hips into her caress.

"Bed." His voice was guttural to say the least.

She smiled. "Exactly what I was about to say."

He pulled his hand from between her legs and lifted her. She wrapped her legs around his waist.

"Wait."

He froze with his hands grasping her butt. "What?"

Tara smoothed the wrinkle in his forehead. "I want these off." She slid the sunglasses from his face. "I don't want to make love to a man with his shades on."

He growled, took the glasses from her hand and tossed them on the counter. With determined steps, he carried her out of the kitchen, up the steps and into his bedroom without once pausing to get his bearings. He had her tank stripped off practically before her butt hit the bed.

Moonlight streamed through the open shutters, highlighting his beautiful body. He lowered his pants and kicked them off.

Glorious. Every inch of his body was absolutely stunning. And all hers.

Scott crawled onto the bed, feeling his way around her, laying her back and yanking her boxers down her legs. The speed at which he moved would be hilarious if she weren't feeling the same way.

"I can't wait," he panted.

She laughed and smoothed her palm over his cheek. "You don't have to," she said, spreading her thighs and cradling his hips. The tip of his penis nudged her entrance. Biting her lip, she arched her back.

"Shit." His head dropped to the bed beside hers.

"What?" *Don't stop*, she wanted to scream.

He scrambled away from her, leaving her stunned. "What are you... Oh."

Scott jerked open a bedside table and fumbled in its contents, coming up victorious with a condom. He ripped it open with his teeth, spit a bit of plastic out and rolled it on.

"I'm not sure what the hell made me think of this." He pounced on the bed like a kid seeing Santa come down the chimney and settled between her legs again. "But I don't want to hurt you. Ever."

She couldn't respond because suddenly he was touching her everywhere. It electrified her, heightening her senses. Tara closed her eyes and let the feeling wash over her.

She swallowed when the thick head of his cock pushed into her, filling and stretching her to the max.

"I'm not gonna last long, sweetheart." He pressed in all the way.

She'd never felt so full or so complete. They were a perfect fit in every way. He inserted a hand between their pelvises and pulled back the hood from her clit. Every thrust rubbed against the tight bundle of nerves, taking her closer and closer to orgasm.

It exploded, shattering over her entire body. She fought the aftermath of his relentless rocking along those nerves.

A few seconds later, he slammed into her pussy and held himself rigid. She felt every pulse of his climax shoot through him.

They lay there, sweating, breathing hard, and unable to move.

She loved it. Loved him, she admitted to herself.

When she awoke sometime later, they were spooned against each other, his arms wrapped protectively around her, his nose tucked into the crook of her shoulder. For the first time in her life she felt cherished.

Chapter Eight

"Everything turned out absolutely amazing, Tara. And did you hear that a certain beer mogul wants to use you for his annual summer bash?" Brianna fairly bounced in her excitement.

Scott squeezed Tara from behind. He hadn't let go of her the entire night. Or the entire day. Not since they'd dragged themselves from his bed just before noon. The man had more stamina than he knew what to do with.

She'd feel awkward except for the fact they'd been caught in bed together early this morning when Cole had brought Scott's glasses up from where he'd left them in the kitchen.

Nope, their whole affair was out in the open.

"I gave him your business card and he said he'd definitely be calling you in the near future."

Tara smiled. Brianna had been right when she'd said doing these decorations would generate business.

"He wouldn't be if it weren't for you," she said, taking her best friend's hand. "Thank you. For everything."

"I'm so excited for you, Tara."

She got another fierce hug from Scott.

"Uncle Scott, Uncle Scott."

Scott turned with her to the sound of his nieces' voices.

"You're underneath the mistletoe." Chloe giggled.

"Well you'd better give me a kiss then, Chlo." He released Tara long enough to bend over and offer his lips to Chloe who waited patiently, hands behind her back.

"Me too, Uncle Scott."

Scott swung in Lily's direction and offered a kiss for her too.

"They're very sweet," Tara said when they'd run off.

"Monsters."

"No, they're not. At least, not since I've been here."

Turning her in his arms, Scott tucked her head under his chin and rubbed her back. "Then I guess I'll have to get you to stay longer," he murmured. He tipped her face up with a thumb beneath her chin. "If we're standing under a mistletoe, how come you haven't kissed me yet?"

"You didn't ask."

"I love kissing you, woman, don't make me beg."

Tara laughed and took pity on him, laying her lips on his and opening for him. Their tongues danced and entwined together.

"Scott and Tara sitting in a tree. K-I-S-S-I-N-G."

Scott groaned and lunged with a roar for his squealing nieces. Tara laughed again. She hadn't felt this free in years. She loved his family. Loved him.

"Monsters, I tell you."

Tara chuckled. "I'm going to the bathroom. Be sure you take names of anyone who might want my services," she threw over her shoulder.

Scott growled. "I better be the only man on your services list, girl."

Lights twinkled in the hallway, strung high on the ceiling and draped around the huge Christmas tree adorning the entry foyer. She thought everything had turned out beautifully and according to the hubbub, the guests did too.

It was peaceful out. Empty of guests and music. Tara rolled her head on her shoulders and arched her back to relieve some of the tension. She reached for the bathroom doorknob. A sweaty palm covered her mouth and yanked backward, jerking her into a firm chest.

Her scream was drowned out by the hand. In a panic, she clawed at the bare arm and fingers pinching her lips. She kicked back with her heels, earning a grunt from her attacker. It was Eric, she could smell him.

"Be still," he hissed.

She wrenched her head from side to side trying to dislodge him. A high-pitched scream shattered her attempts to struggle. She froze, Eric froze. Both turned to Lily and Chloe who stood ten feet away, having come out from the party.

Chloe's red face stood out against her snowy white dress. Lily had one arm on her sister's.

"Go get Dad, Chloe."

Tara whimpered and gestured with her eyes for the nine-year-old to go back in with the people.

Chloe scrambled, slipping on the tile floor and screaming like a banshee. Tara's brain yelled, *good girl*, but her heart nearly exploded. If anything happened to anyone in this family, she'd never forgive herself.

Something sharp pricked the skin of her neck. Lily's eyes widened into huge round discs. Tara frantically grabbed at the hand holding the knife, kicking and bucking, anything to loosen him.

Eric held fast.

"We're going to walk out of here, Tara. You are mine. You don't belong here with these people."

"Mm-mm. Mm-mm." She stomped down on his foot.

"Bitch," he snarled, spittle shooting from his lips onto her cheek.

117

"Eric." The yell came from Tyler. He shoved Lily into the room where guests started spilling out.

"Where is she?"

Tara's knees buckled at the sound of Scott's angered, worried outcry from the opposite direction. She wanted to scream at him to stay back.

"Stay the fuck away, Wyatt. She's mine."

Tara stomped down again, grinding her high heel into his instep. Eric howled in pain. His arm loosened as he hopped on his good foot. Tara took advantage. She tore out of his hold and ran to Scott.

Eric followed when he realized what had happened. He slammed into both of them in a football tackle. Tara's head cracked on the floor. Stars exploded in her vision, threatening to make the whole world black. Scott and Eric struggled next to her, wrestling and grunting, but she couldn't seem to move.

Someone shouted. Strong hands pulled at her arm. She had the sensation she was being dragged but didn't know why.

Fingers slapped at her cheek and she heard her name being called over and over again. Tara tried to sit up. A wave of dizziness forced her back down.

"I've got him."

Tara heard another series of grunts and the meaty connection of a fist on bone.

Her head was splitting in half.

"Let go, Scott, we've got him."

Another thud of knuckles meeting flesh made her gag. The sickening crack of bone was followed by an anguished scream.

Eric stumbled into her blurry vision, holding his nose and crying out in pain. Blood seeped between his fingers. A pair of hands grabbed him and shoved him to the ground.

The crowd gathered around her. She didn't want the crowd around but she couldn't seem to think to tell them to get lost.

"Call an ambulance."

Tara sank into Scott's body as he lifted her into a sitting position. The move nearly cost her the bazillion or so meatballs she'd eaten at the party.

"Tara."

She couldn't keep her eyes open. They were so heavy.

"Give me a towel," Scott roared. "I'm sorry, sweetheart," he whispered when she flinched.

A thousand needles pricked her scalp.

The last thing she saw was Eric being hauled up and shoved out the door.

❄❄❄

Red and blue lights swirled through the cascading descent of a million snowflakes. It was so pretty. She smiled up at them.

"You'll be okay, Tara. They're pretty sure you have a nice little concussion though," Brianna said. She sounded worried.

She didn't care. Look at the beautiful scenery.

Scott invaded her vision, his mouth tight-lipped, his jaw working hard. She realized he was holding her hand and tightened her fingers on his. She was lying down and he was walking next to her, which could only mean she was on a stretcher.

Eric, the fight, her head hitting the floor. It all came back to her. She swallowed and shut her eyes against the dull throb. Soon the stretcher lifted and she found herself in the back of an ambulance. The doors remained open even after Scott climbed in. He sat next to her and held her hand with both of his.

Tiny bells chimed in the far-off distance. She gasped.

"Do you hear that?" she asked him.

"What's that sweetheart?"

"Bells." She stared off into the wintery Christmas Eve night. Was it possible?

No…

"I think your brain is rattling." His jaw ground down again.

"Or maybe it's him." She couldn't help smiling.

Scott sat up straighter. "Him?"

"Yeah, you know, the big guy in the red suit? Listen. Maybe you can hear the bells too."

He cocked his head, then shook it.

"Can't be."

"Why not?" she asked, indignant.

"Because he's already been here." He brought her hand to his lips and kissed her knuckles.

"Oh," she whispered. "How do you know that?"

"He brought me you."

About the Author

To learn more about Annmarie McKenna, please visit www.annmariemckenna.com. Send an email to annmarmck@yahoo.com or visit her blog—the one she tries to keep up with but doesn't always succeed at—www.annmariemckenna.blogspot.com. She'd love to hear from you!

Look for these titles

Love Me, Still

Maya Banks

Chapter One

Their father's familiar scent drifted to Cael and Riyu through the mountain pine. The two wolves raised their heads, sniffing the wind. The fur on their backs prickled and stood on end. Danger.

Simultaneously, they shifted to their human form. More of their pack shifted around them as they forged through the trees in the direction of Magnus' scent. Nude forms became clothed, a barrier to the cold and snow. Cael and Riyu conjured buckskins, boots, a shirt and a heavy fur.

Their worry was not only for their father but for their mate, Heather. She had gone with him this day along with Niko to the small mountain town below.

They sniffed again but couldn't detect the scent of Heather or Niko. Only their father. And his blood.

They put on a burst of speed, bounding into the clearing where their father struggled through the snow in his human form.

"Father!" Riyu cried out.

Cael and Riyu rushed to where the older man collapsed, blood smearing his face and chest. His wounds were ragged, and the flesh lay open in several places.

The two brothers looked at each other, fear churning in their gut. Where was Heather? Where was their mate?

"My sons," Magnus said, his voice low and weak.

"What happened, Father?" Cael demanded. "Where are Heather and Niko?"

Behind them, the rest of the pack gathered. Silent and worried. A high-pitched scream shattered the calm. Someone must have summoned their mother.

She shoved by them and gathered their father in her arms, rocking back and forth as tears streamed down her face. Magnus struggled against her, looking beyond her to his sons.

"Heather..."

They surged forward, their minds consumed with worry and fear that they had lost their mate as it appeared they would lose their father. His wounds were severe. They were mortal.

"You must tell us where to find her, Father," Riyu pleaded. "Tell us what happened. Who did this?"

"S-she betrayed us," Magnus said, his voice heavy with pain and sorrow.

Cael reared back. "What? What are you saying?" He moved closer to his father, gently pushing his mother away. "Father, Heather is our mate. She would never betray us."

Magnus coughed, blood bubbling from his mouth. "She did this. I think Niko is dead as well. We were ambushed. I was taken. I saw her at the clearing where they held me and Niko. I saw her hurting him as the others beat me. I heard her swear vengeance on the pack."

"No," Riyu denied, shaking his head. "She wouldn't. She loves us. Accepts what we are. She would not lead hunters to us."

Magnus' clear blue eyes, mirrors of his son's, opened wide and stared at the two brothers. "Look into my sight. See what I saw."

Cael and Riyu thrust into their father's mind. It was a wild, swirling vortex. Blurred images. Painful ones. They heard Heather laughing. Saw her dance in and out of Magnus' vision, a bitter smile on her beautiful face. *You will die.* She came closer, stepping in front of the men who were beating their father. *They will kill you.* Determination was etched in her features as she looked into their father's face. More images. Heather in the embrace of one of the hunters.

Riyu and Cael fell back, their hearts pounding, grief swelling in their chests. Betrayal, sharp and agonizing, sliced through Cael's body. God, no! How could she? Their father. A man who had adopted her as his own daughter when Cael and Riyu had taken her as mate. And now she had killed him. And one of their pack brethren.

"I'm sorry," Magnus whispered. More blood ran from his mouth in a fine stream. "I loved her, too. Like...like a daughter to me."

A tear rolled down the older man's cheek and Cael and Riyu's mother wrapped her arms around him, sobbing her grief into his chest.

As Magnus breathed his last, he slowly transformed into the beautiful, black wolf he was. Around them, the pack transformed and began howling their grief to the skies above.

A tear caught in Cael's eye but refused to fall. His breath snagged in his chest and remained there frozen. His father dead. Betrayed by Cael's mate. *His* mate. The human he'd brought into the pack. This was all his fault.

Beside him, Riyu's shoulders shook in silent mourning. Cael knew he not only mourned their father, but the loss of their mate. Traitorous bitch.

The wind shifted and Cael stiffened. Another scent, one all too familiar, one imprinted forever in his heart and mind, wafted through his nostrils.

The wolves stopped their howling and growled menacingly. They'd smelled her too. The traitor was returning to the pack.

❄❄❄

"Hush now, little one," Niko soothed as Heather whimpered in pain. "We're but a hundred yards from the pack. You're going to be fine now."

His arms tightened around her as he gently set her down on the ground. Her feet hit the snow and she stumbled a bit as she sought to steady herself. Her right leg refused to support her weight and buckled beneath her.

"Where are you going?" she whispered. "Why aren't you coming?"

He put a finger to her lips and tenderly brushed his other hand over her bruised cheek. "Your mates will care for you. That will be their top priority. I'm going after the hunters. Justice must be served for their crimes against our pack. I'll return when I've done my task."

"I don't know if I can make it," she said. Her strength was nearly gone. She was so weak.

"You are the strongest woman I know," Niko said, his voice warm and full of admiration.

He bent to kiss her on the forehead and soothed his hands over her battered body. "Go now. Your mates await. Thank you, little human, for saving me and Magnus. You sacrificed far too much. I will never forget this."

He transformed to wolf and bounded away, leaving her swaying in the snowdrift. She shivered as the snow crept up to her knees. Cael and Riyu would come for her. They would have smelled her by now.

Tears slid down her cheeks. Would they want her still? The hunters touch lay heavy on her skin. She felt used and dirty. Her flesh crawled as though their hands still pawed at her.

She lifted a trembling hand to her cheek, wincing when her fingers brushed across her swollen eye. She put one foot out, determined to meet her mates with dignity and pride.

She struggled through the snow. She could hear howling in the distance. A slow, mournful sound. Her blood froze in panic. Had Magnus not returned? Or were his injuries more severe than she and Niko had thought?

She quickened her pace, ignoring the pain rocketing through her body. She must reach her mates. They would care for her. Only them. They loved her. They would be furious at what had happened to her, but they'd never turn away from her.

Finally she broke into a clearing. The trees fell away and she stared across the snow-covered slope to see Cael and Riyu kneeling on the ground around their mother and a black wolf. Magnus.

Fear and grief swelled in her throat until she could barely breathe. She hurried forward, pushing herself even as her body screamed in protest. Her mates turned to look at her.

She stopped a few feet away, recoiling at the hatred and grief in their eyes. There was no welcome here. No rush to her aid, no caring in their expressions.

They stood, her two lovers, the men she loved more than life itself. She started forward again, but the cold look in Cael's eyes stopped her once more.

"You have some nerve coming here," he hissed. "Were you not satisfied until you saw the results of your betrayal?" He turned, sweeping a hand in the direction of the fallen wolf. "Take a good, hard look, Heather. See what you've done here."

"But I didn't..." she protested, throwing her hand out in a defensive gesture. The movement cost her. She swayed and sank to her knees, the cold moisture of the snow seeping into her torn clothing.

What did Cael mean? Why did he speak with such anger? Anger never before directed at her.

"You lie," Riyu spat. "You are damned by our father's own words and his sight. We saw and heard what you did."

"You were our mate," Cael said, agony creeping into his voice. "We loved you as no other. Put your needs above our own. Above our pack. And you betrayed us. How could you? Does it satisfy you to see one of the greatest wolfs in our bloodline lying on the ground lifeless? Does it make you feel good to know that our mother grieves for a mate she has run side by side with for a century?"

"Cael, no!" she burst out. "Please, you must listen to me. I love you. I would never betray you." She glanced at Riyu who stood, shoulders heaving with anger and emotion. "I love you," she said softly. "Why have you turned against me? Why do you believe I could do something so horrible?"

Lorna stood, her eyes blazing. She strode over to where Heather struggled to stand again. She raised her hand and slapped Heather across her bruised cheek. The crack rang out through the air.

"Don't you ever speak of love to me," her mates' mother screamed. "You have betrayed us all. You are as dead to us as Magnus is."

Heather's head snapped back, and she fell backward into the snow. The sky spun crazily above her, and she knew without a doubt, the world had gone mad. Maybe she had died back there. Maybe she hadn't survived the brutal attack on her.

"Niko," she whispered. She needed Niko. He knew. He would tell them what had happened.

"You dare speak the name of the noble warrior you murdered," Lorna hissed. "You aren't fit to speak his name."

Heather looked up to see her mates flank their mother. Cael slid an arm around her thin shoulders.

"Come away, Mother," he said in a low voice.

"Don't go!" Heather cried.

Only Riyu turned to look at her again. His eyes brimmed with pain and sorrow.

"We loved you, Heather. We would have done anything for you. We would have loved and cared for you forever. And you threw it all away for what? Why do you hate us so much? My father took you in as one of his own. He loved you like a daughter. You repaid him with treachery."

She watched as he turned his back on her and walked away. In the distance, her mates shifted to wolves. They hovered around Magnus' body before gripping his fur in their mouths to drag him away.

They were leaving her. Panic swelled and exploded inside her. She was badly hurt. She would die here without their aid. More than that, she'd die without their *love*.

"Don't go," she croaked as tears flooded her eyes and spilled down her cheeks. "I love you. I *need* you," she whispered.

Chapter Two

Heather awoke and tugged the heavy furs closer around her body. Then she waited. Hoping this would be a day she could wake without the overwhelming deluge of pain.

Grief soared through her, leaving her weak and limp against the makeshift bed. Her body still hadn't healed from the attack three weeks ago, but her soul had suffered the most damage. Irreparable damage.

A thump alerted her to John Quincy's presence in the old cabin. The front door opened, and a rush of cold air blew in before he quickly slammed it shut again.

She looked up from her pallet by the fireplace to see him hauling a small fir tree across the floor.

"Good morning, girl. You feeling better today?" the older man asked.

She nodded just as she did every morning, and he harumphed as he did every morning when he saw the lie in her eyes.

"What's that?" she asked as she struggled against the pain to sit up.

He quirked a bushy eyebrow at her. "What does it look like, a grizzly bear?"

She tried to smile but gave up. Smiling took too much effort.

He sighed. "It's a Christmas tree, girl. Thought it might cheer you up. I have a few baubles we can hang on it to make it pretty. We can even string some popping corn if you promise not to eat it all."

She did smile then. She loved Christmas. Had told him so during one of their long conversations on the cold nights in front of the fire.

"There, that's better," he said approvingly. "Smiling ain't so bad, now is it?"

She looked down, wondering for the hundredth time what she would have done if the old trapper hadn't come across her lying in the snow. Lying there wishing for death to come quickly so she could turn off the pain.

John Quincy set the tree in a corner and moved to the fire to warm his hands. After rubbing them together a few seconds, he turned his attention to her.

"Let me have a look at that leg I set. I reckon it might be time to take the splints off. You'll more than likely walk with a limp for a while, but in the end, you should be good as new."

She allowed him to pull back the covers, and he ran his gnarled hands over the sturdy splints he'd secured to the sides of her leg. As gruff as he looked, he was amazingly gentle.

"Well, what do you say, girl? Are you up to trying to walk on it?"

She bit her bottom lip then nodded.

"Let me get my knife," he said as he rose.

He went to the area of the cabin that served as the kitchen and rummaged around in the cabinet before returning with a sharp hunting knife. He cut the cloth surrounding the splints then gently eased the wood away from her leg.

"Move your foot around a bit," he encouraged. "Then we'll have you stand up and test it out."

She flexed her foot, wincing when her muscles protested the action.

"It'll hurt a little," he cautioned. "Nothing to worry about, though."

He curled his arms underneath her back and waist, and she put out her hand.

"You can't pick me up," she protested.

He chuckled. "Me, can't pick up a little bit of a thing like you? How do you think I got you here? Girl, I've hauled an eight hundred pound grizzly out of the woods to skin."

She found herself lifted as he stood to his full height.

"Now, I'm going to set you down nice and easy. Take most of your weight with your good leg. Try not to overdo it."

Her foot hit the floor, and she gritted her teeth as her various body parts protested her being upright. After three weeks of lying down, her body was weak and shaky. She'd barely even sat up each time she had to relieve herself.

John Quincy held her around the waist as she eased her bad leg down. Then she shifted her weight to both legs equally. Her knee buckled and he caught her before she crumbled to the floor.

He half carried her, half assisted her over to the small table and plopped her down in the chair.

"There now, you just sit there and get your bearings while I rustle us up some breakfast. Then you can supervise while I get the tree all decorated."

Tears filled her eyes as she looked at the grizzled old man. "Thank you, John Quincy. I can't ever hope to repay you for your kindness."

His expression softened. "Now, girl, don't go getting all teary-eyed on me. That pack of yours ought to be hunted down, shot and made into fur rugs for what they done to you."

She hung her head as John Quincy started puttering around the kitchen. She hadn't wanted him to know about the wolves at all, but he'd known of their existence a long time before Heather had ever set foot in these mountains. He'd known Magnus himself when he was younger. Called him friend.

Once she'd realized he knew of her wolves, she'd poured out the whole story to him, going through an entire box of tissue in the process. He'd jokingly told her he hoped he didn't catch cold this winter because she'd used his entire supply up and he wouldn't get more until the spring.

She looked back up at John Quincy. "Will it ever stop hurting?" she asked in a soft voice.

Kindness softened the wrinkles under his eyes. "It will, girl. In time. One day you'll wake up and not hurt as much as the day before. And the next will hurt less than that day. It takes time, but you're a survivor. More importantly you're a good, sweet girl. You don't deserve what happened to you, but I have no doubt it'll make you stronger."

❄❄❄

Cael trotted toward the spacious cabin that served as his and Riyu's quarters. He'd run along the ridge of the mountain until he'd panted for air. But still, the pain squeezing his chest wouldn't dissipate. He could deny it all he wanted but he missed her.

She'd betrayed them, murdered two of his pack, but he still ached for her. He longed to go back before it all had happened. To the nights she lay between him and Riyu, her silky hair splayed out over his shoulder as she slept in the shelter of his arms.

His nose curled as he began his transformation back to human. No matter how he tried, he couldn't rid himself of the

135

smell of the hunters that had lingered with her scent that final day. She had reeked of them.

As he conjured his clothing and started for the door to his cabin, the remembered scent, the foul odor, was replaced by a more familiar smell. One that he should not be smelling.

He yanked around to stare across the snow-covered ground. In the distance he heard a yip. Niko. It couldn't be. It simply couldn't be. He'd disappeared the day Cael's father had died. Believed dead at the hands of the hunters. And of his mate. Could he have escaped and only now made his way back to the pack?

He threw back his head and uttered a harsh call to Riyu. In seconds, his brother threw open the door and ran out.

"What is it?" he asked Cael.

"Do you smell him?"

Riyu sniffed cautiously at the air. His eyes widened in disbelief. "Niko?"

Another yip rent the air and suddenly, incredulously, Niko appeared over the top of a hill. His paws dug into the snow, ice particles flying in his wake as he pulled a sled behind him.

Cael and Riyu rushed forward to greet their pack mate, their joy at seeing him alive immense.

As Niko stopped a few yards away, he shook the snow from his fur then transformed. He strode toward Cael and Riyu, his arm out to greet them.

Cael stared at him in openmouthed wonder. He was *alive*. Niko grasped the arm that Cael had stuck out in stunned disbelief, as if Niko hadn't just come back from the dead.

"It's good to see you, Cael," Niko said. "Where is Heather?"

Cael's face hardened. "She's not here."

Relief flashed in Niko's eyes. "Good. I wouldn't want her to see what I've brought you. It would upset her too badly." He looked around. "Though I think your father would be interested in a little vengeance. Where is he?"

Riyu stepped forward, confusion creasing his brow. "Niko, we thought you were dead. How is it you come to us alive? How is it you know nothing of our father's death? And why would you ask us if Heather is here knowing what she did to us all?"

Niko's mouth dropped open. His tall, muscular body tightened as his lips turned down into a perplexed frown. He shook his muddy blond hair as if clearing the cobwebs.

"Magnus is dead? How did this happen? He was injured when he left Heather and me, but he should have easily survived such wounds. And why did you think me dead? Did Magnus and Heather not tell you I was hunting the hunters who ambushed us?"

Dread tightened Cael's abdomen. Something was wrong. Very, very wrong. Nausea curled in his stomach and he rubbed at his gut to try and alleviate the discomfort.

"Magnus died because Heather betrayed us to the hunters," Riyu said flatly. "Father told us everything."

Niko went white. "He *told* you that Heather betrayed us to the hunters? He actually said that?"

Cael nodded.

"Where is Heather?" Niko demanded. Suspicion entered his eyes, and they glittered dangerously.

"We left her behind as befitting someone who brought harm to the pack," Riyu gritted out.

In a flash, Niko transformed back to wolf and lunged for Riyu. Riyu had no choice but to shift as well. He'd never survive the wolf's attack in his human form.

Niko snarled and latched onto Riyu's throat, and they rolled over and over in a mass of writhing fur. Cael quickly transformed and jumped in to separate the two wolves. They were of equal strength and stamina. They would kill each other before giving quarter.

Finally, Cael managed to grab Niko by the scruff of the neck and toss him away. Cael stood between Niko and his brother and growled menacingly, a warning to both of them to back off.

Riyu transformed first then Niko changed back to human, a dangerous scowl darkening his face.

"You left her there in her condition?" Niko demanded. "You *left* her there after what she suffered?"

Cael shifted and shook his head. He was growing more confused by the moment. He jerked his head toward the sled as a low moan rose from the bundle.

He stalked over and yanked away the blanket to see two men lying there bound. He gave Niko a sharp look. "Who are they and why did you bring them here?"

Niko glared at him, his shoulders heaving with anger. "They are the hunters who attacked *your* mate. The hunters who ambushed us and killed Magnus. I brought them here thinking you would want to exact vengeance for harming what is yours. I can see I made a mistake."

Riyu edged closer, giving Niko a wary look. "What are you saying, Niko? I don't understand any of it. You act as though Heather is the victim in all of this. Our father wouldn't lie. We saw what he saw. We forged into his mind."

"You saw wrong," Niko said flatly.

Cael and Riyu exchanged horrified looks. Niko was resolute in his defense of Heather, and he'd been there. Could their father have been wrong? Or did Niko have a reason to lie?

"She reeked of the hunters," Cael said darkly.

Niko moved as though he'd attack again, and Cael growled a warning. Niko stood there flexing his hands in anger.

"I claim the right to take her as mate," Niko declared. "I'm going to find her, provided she's still alive. If it means banishment from the pack, so be it. I will never forgive myself for her being turned out when she endured so much to save me and your father."

Cael and Riyu's mouths dropped open.

"Over my dead body," Riyu bit out. "She's our mate."

Niko rounded on him, a ferocious snarl working out of his mouth. "You turned your mate out. You turned your back on her when she needed you most. I assured her you would care for her, that she would be your top priority. I will never forgive myself for not carrying her all the way back to the pack, but I was fast losing the scent of the hunters. I thought she would be safe with you, so I left her and chased after the hunters. Even so it took me weeks to track them. I will revenge Heather. You don't have to concern yourselves with the matter."

"Cael, Riyu, what goes on here?" their mother said behind them. "Niko? Niko!" she exclaimed with a sob. She burst past her sons and threw her arms around their pack mate.

"We thought you dead," she said as tears rolled down her cheeks. "Thank the gods you have returned safely to us."

Niko gently pulled Lorna away from him and took a step back. "I'm sorry, Lorna. I must go. I probably won't be back. I must go find Heather and make things right."

Both Cael and Riyu lunged for him. Their combined strength was no match for him, but still he gave one hell of a fight. Finally, they subdued him and held him to the ground.

Cael stood, dragging Niko up with him. He shoved him toward the cabin as Riyu and their befuddled mother followed behind.

Once inside, he pushed Niko down onto a chair and stood in front of him. "Tell us what happened. Everything. And don't leave one damned thing out. Especially anything having to do with my mate."

Niko stared angrily back at him. "You don't deserve her."

Cael leaned in, getting into Niko's face. "If you have something to tell me about Heather, say it before I tear you apart."

"Heather?" his mother said in a pained voice. "Cael, maybe we shouldn't be discussing Heather. I know how hard her betrayal has been for you and Riyu."

Niko turned to stare at Cael's mother. "Heather betrayed no one. It is your sons who have betrayed her."

Riyu tensed and flexed his hands into fists. "Spill whatever it is you have to say before I spill your blood."

"We were ambushed," Niko said in a weary voice. "Coming back from town with the supplies. Magnus and I were pulling the sleds and Heather walked between us. I don't know how they knew we were there but it wasn't because Heather betrayed us.

"I made her run and hide in the trees. I didn't want her caught in the fight. They darted Magnus. He took about two steps and collapsed. I tried to fight them off but there were three of them and only one of me, and the drugs they used prevented me from shifting to wolf."

"And Heather? Where was she in all of this?" Cael demanded. He remembered the images from his father's memories all too well.

"She came in like an avenging angel," Niko said in a haunted voice. "She wasn't going to leave us to die or worse. She challenged the hunters." He looked bleakly up at Cael. "I've never felt so helpless in my life. That tiny little thing stood between Magnus and the brutes who were beating on him. She dared them to do their worst, and by God, they did."

Cael's legs went weak. He swayed and had to stumble back to one of the chairs before he fell.

"What do you mean their worst?" Riyu asked hoarsely.

Niko eyed him straight on, pain glittering brightly in his golden eyes. "The worst. And she endured it so I would have time to escape and free Magnus. She taunted them with the fact that they would die. That her pack would hunt them down and kill them. That her *mates* would never allow this injustice to stand. How ironic is that?" he finished bitterly.

You will die. They will kill you.

Cael remembered the words from his father's visions. Could Magnus have been so heavily drugged that he imagined Heather taunting *him* when in fact she challenged the hunters?

Oh God. Have mercy. He deserved none.

A tear slipped down his cheek as Riyu and his mother sat in stunned silence.

Niko's voice broke into the heavy blanket of despair draped over them.

"I managed to free myself, but it was too late to save Heather from the horrors she faced. As she knew they would, they'd turned their attention solely on her, forgetting all about me and Magnus in the interim.

"She bought enough time that the drugs in my system wore off. I shifted and attacked. The men ran. I freed Magnus and sent him on to you to get help. I gathered Heather in my arms and carried her back. All the way I comforted her by telling her that her mates would care for her, that I would go hunt her attackers down and justice would be served. Had I known what awaited her here, I would have never let her go."

He raised condemning eyes to Cael, Riyu and even Lorna. "Never did I imagine my pack would turn their back on a woman who needed aid so badly. Someone we adopted as one of our own. I'm going to find her, and when I do, I'm going to spend the rest of my life making it up to her. I'll replace the mates who threw her away like yesterday's trash."

"Oh my God," Riyu said, agony inflected in every word. "Oh my God."

Lorna stood wringing her hands in front of her. "I struck her. I struck the girl who was my daughter."

Niko stood in disgust. He moved to the door, and Cael knew he was a second from shifting and loping into the night to find Heather.

"Niko, wait."

Niko turned to stare at him.

"You have every right to be angry. God only knows how I'll ever forgive myself. But she's our mate. It is Riyu and I who must set this to rights."

Niko's eyes flashed angrily. "You gave up that right when you turned your back on her. You are her mate no more, no matter that she wears your mark."

"She is ours," Riyu said, his voice tight with emotion. "We have wronged her more than the men who attacked her, but as the gods are my witness I will find a way to make it right. She will be avenged, and she will come back under our protection."

Niko stared between the two brothers as if measuring their determination. His shoulders slumped the tiniest bit in defeat. Then he raised his head in defiance.

"You don't know that she'll accept you. We don't know that she's alive. You left her alone to fend for herself in an unforgiving terrain. I'm going with you, because if we find her, and she refuses you, I'll do everything in my power to make her happy and protect her. Even if it means doing it from a distance. I will never allow what happened to her to happen again."

Cael listened to Niko's vow and felt a surge of pride at his pack mate's defense of Heather.

"We welcome you on our journey, Niko. But know this. I will do everything in my power to regain Heather's trust and her love. Even if it takes the rest of my life."

Chapter Three

Heather gathered her courage and her strength as she pulled on the buckskin trousers John Quincy had made for her. They were fur-lined, a fact she appreciated as she shivered in the morning cold. Even the fire blazing in the hearth did little warm her.

This morning she'd woken to blessed numbness. She felt odd, actually. Her face was tight and felt warm to the touch, and yet, she shivered endlessly amidst the heavy blankets of her pallet.

But she'd lain here, moving little in the last month. Her splint had been removed for a week, so there was no excuse for her not to start getting up and around.

A wave of dizziness assaulted her as she stood and tested shaky legs. She wavered and caught hold of a nearby chair to steady herself.

She looked longingly out the single window of the cabin at the snow-covered landscape. It had been so long since she'd breathed fresh air.

Without making the conscious decision to venture outside, she headed in the direction of the door. John Quincy was out checking his traps, but he'd be back soon, and it wouldn't hurt to stretch her legs just a bit.

At the door, she carefully pulled on her moccasins, the effort nearly exhausting her. It was odd, but she felt weaker today than in previous days. Her fingers shook as she secured the laces of her shoes.

Using the door to help support her, she eased outside, flinching as the cold air bristled over her body. As soon as she stepped into the snow, anguish poured into her heart, overflowing and ripping through her body.

The scenery was beautiful and horribly ugly. The last time she'd enjoyed a day such as this, a day where the sky was impossibly blue and the sun high overhead, had been a day where Cael and Riyu had played in the snow with her. Just hours before she'd gone into town with Niko and Magnus.

Tears slipped down her cheeks, and her body rippled with chills. She limped through the snow toward the cover of trees in the distance. Old habits died hard. Cael had taught her to always seek cover. Never stand in the open.

But she'd never see him or Riyu again. They'd left her, sure that she was the cause of their father's death. And maybe she was. If she'd intervened sooner. If she hadn't stood in the trees working the courage up to do the impossible. If she had just been braver and rushed to Magnus and Niko's aid.

But she had never betrayed them. She loved her pack. They were the only family she had.

For the first time, she realized she had no one. No one but an old trapper who could ill afford to be responsible for a young girl who couldn't care for herself. She had no where to go, no future to look forward to, no mates to keep her warm on the long cold nights.

Oh, Mama, how I miss you.

Tears gathered in her eyes. Her mother, gone so long now, still simmered in the vague memories of her childhood. If she closed her eyes and concentrated hard, she could conjure a memory from Christmas time. Her mother, decorating a small tree with homemade ornaments, her tender smile as she hugged little Heather to her bosom.

Another full body shiver skirted up her spine until her body was covered in goose bumps. She ignored the aching cold, the ache in her body and heart, and trudged further into the trees. Ahead she could see a steep drop off. Then she realized she was approaching a ridge.

Her eyes stung as she looked out over the vast mountainous region. Hundreds of feet below a river cut a path through the land. Were her wolves out there? Did they ever think of her? Or had their love died along with their father? And their faith in her.

A sob welled from her throat. It sounded harsh and ugly in the silence. She'd lost everything that mattered. How could she go on knowing what she'd never have again? Never hold in her arms.

Complete and utter despair wrapped around her, tightening her chest, squeezing until she wheezed for breath. What she wouldn't give to not feel. To be able to close her eyes and have blessed darkness descend.

She took a step toward the drop off, staring down into the ravine. It would be so easy to step off into nothing. Then she'd never feel again. She wouldn't hurt so much. She'd find the peace she so desperately needed.

❄❄❄

Cael pulled the heavy furs tighter around him as he, Niko and Riyu fanned out and trudged higher up the mountain. Their inability to shift and move faster frustrated him, but there was a human in the area. A trapper if he had to guess. They didn't want to startle him by coming up on him in wolf form. It was a good way to get themselves shot.

For a week, he and the others had scoured the area around their old encampment. They could detect no trace of Heather's scent. Then yesterday, when the wind had shifted and blew from the north, he had caught the faintest whiff of her.

They had charged up the mountain in the direction of the scent, anxious to find her.

Suddenly Riyu stopped ahead of Cael. He lifted his head and sniffed. A low growl emanated from his throat.

"What is it, Riyu?" Cael demanded as he surged through the snow.

Niko joined them and raised his head as well. "It's her. I smell her. Much stronger now. She isn't far."

Cael inhaled deeply and closed his eyes as the sweet smell of his mate drifted through his nostrils. Longing, regret, so much sadness swelled within him.

He shoved past Riyu and Niko, increasing his speed up the mountain slope. Her smell grew stronger, and his body tingled with the anticipation of seeing her, even as his palms sweated in the frigid air at the thought of what he would say to her. How he would gain her forgiveness.

Then he stopped. Riyu nearly ran into him from behind. A low sob carried to them on the wind. Cael looked in the direction of the sound, and there he saw her. Poised on the edge of a drop off. Heather.

She took a step closer and stared down into the abyss. Terror clutched at Cael's chest. Beside him, Riyu hissed in fear. She was going to fall.

Oh God. They'd never get to her in time.

In a flash, Cael transformed, lunging forward in the snow. He dug into the terrain, running as fast as his wolf shape would allow. Behind him, Riyu and Niko shifted and set out for Heather as well.

No! He couldn't lose her again.

Just when he thought she would step off the edge, she crumbled into the snow and lay still. His heart raced with relief, but still he flew the remaining distance, his need to touch her, to hold her, to reassure himself that she was okay was all consuming.

He reached her just seconds before Riyu and Niko. He gently nudged her with his snout, but she was unconscious. He nuzzled her cheek and licked at her skin, trying to get her to awaken.

She was burning up with fever.

Cael shifted then stared down at his mate. Tears stung his eyelids, threatening to unman him completely. She was so fragile looking. Pale, thin, so breakable. And she wasn't well.

"Is she alive?" Riyu asked in a rush of fear.

Cael nodded grimly. "She won't be for long if we don't get her out of the cold. She's burning up with fever."

"There's a cabin in the distance," Niko said pointing. "It could be where she's been staying."

Cael picked his precious bundle from the snow and hefted her into his arms. She had always been a tiny thing, but her lightness, even amidst the furs she wore, was alarming.

He pressed his lips to her hot forehead and closed his eyes as he followed Niko toward the cabin. *I love you, my heart. I'm so very sorry for how I have wronged you. Please come back to me. I cannot live without you.*

Riyu fell in beside him, looking anxiously over Heather's unconscious form. He reached out a hand to touch her cheek, and Cael could see tears in his brother's eyes.

"We failed her," Riyu croaked. "When she needed us the most, we turned our backs. How are we ever supposed to get past something like that?"

Cael shook his head grimly. He didn't have the words to offer comfort to his brother. Not when their mate was without.

Niko opened the door to the cabin and investigated before returning to Cael and Riyu to motion them in.

"She's been staying here. Her scent is everywhere, but there is also the scent of another. A male. I think he's the trapper we knew was close," Niko said as Cael shouldered his way in with Heather.

The fire had burned low, and Riyu set to work adding logs as Cael lowered Heather to the pallet of furs just a few feet away. He gently arranged the covers over her. He knew how cold-blooded she was. He and Riyu had delighted in keeping her warm during the winter.

He smoothed a hand over her blonde hair, enjoying the feel of her silken tresses between his fingers. Anger and remorse surged through his veins as he saw the faint shadows of the bruises on her face. She wore a scar, still puckered and angry above her eyebrow where one of the bastards had struck her, cutting the skin.

He'd seen her limp as she had stepped toward the edge of the cliff. Now, he moved the covers up so he could examine her limbs. There were marks and bruises on one leg from what looked to be a splint. The indentions fit. His hand curled in rage at what the hunters had done to his mate. But that wasn't the worst of it.

He turned his face away, no longer able to keep the emotion from welling in his throat. A tear slid down his cheek. His brother's hand slid over his shoulder, squeezing in comfort.

"Is she badly hurt?" Riyu asked anxiously.

"She was," Cael said grimly. "It looks as though the trapper cared for her. He probably saved her life." He stole a sideways glance at Niko who stood to the side, anger and concern creasing his features.

A click alerted them to the doorway. Cael whirled, ready to shift and attack in an instant. An older man dressed in furs stood in the doorway pointing a rifle at them.

"I'll thank you to get away from that little girl," he said gruffly. "And don't be trying to shift on me, because I'm thinking your hide would look good next to my fireplace."

Cael blinked. Had Heather told him about the pack? Not that she owed them any loyalty after they'd deserted her.

"She didn't tell me if that's what you're thinking," the man said as he moved closer. "Are you Magnus' boy?"

Cael nodded. "I'm one of them," he said calmly. He turned and gestured at Riyu. "This is my brother. Did you know our father?"

The man nodded. "Knew him a lot of years. I was sorry to hear of his passing. Now what the hell are you doing here, and why are you hanging over the girl?"

"She's our mate," Riyu spoke up.

The old man raised one brow. "Well, now, then where the hell were you when she needed you? When she was lying in the snow praying to die quickly? When she was in so much pain, and was dying on the inside of shame?" His eyes glittered menacingly, and he gripped the rifle tighter. "I've a good mind to fill both your hides full of lead."

Cael flinched at the description of Heather lying so close to death. Desperately needing her mates. He lowered his head, no longer able to look the older man in the eyes.

"Just tell me one thing. Why are you here now?" the man demanded.

Cael looked back up, steely determination gripping him. "We're here because she's our mate, and we want desperately to right the wrongs of the past."

The man relaxed his grip on the rifle before finally lowering it. "Well, now, why didn't you just say so?" He put his hand out to Cael. "Name's John Quincy Ledbetter. You can call me John Quincy. Most folks do." His gaze fell to where Heather lay. "Is she out? When I left this morning, she felt like she was taking a fever."

Cael took John Quincy's hand and shook it in return. "We found her outside," he replied. "She collapsed and we carried her in. She's burning up with fever."

John Quincy shook his head and scrubbed a hand over his beard. "I was afraid the mite had taken sick. It's been such a struggle for her these past weeks."

"You have our gratitude for helping her," Riyu said as he stepped forward to offer his hand.

"Well, someone had to, didn't they?" He looked pointedly at them, and shame crawled over Cael once more. Then his eyes flickered back over Heather, and Cael could see the concern simmering in the old man's stare.

John Quincy gestured for them to follow him outside. "There are things that need saying, but I don't want the girl to overhear us if she wakes."

Cael and Riyu walked to the door, but Niko stayed behind, his ambivalent glare following them.

"She's had a hard time, that girl," John Quincy said as he rounded on the brothers. He shook his finger at them. "You've got a long road ahead of you if she's going to recover properly. Not a night goes by she doesn't cry out with nightmares. And I can't get her to eat worth a damn. She's dying on the inside."

Cael closed his eyes and wondered how many more tears he'd shed before it was over with.

"There's something else you should know," the old man said quietly. "She lost a babe not long after I carried her to my cabin."

"Oh God!" Riyu cried out.

Cael lost the battle to keep the tears at bay.

"Now, now, I didn't tell you that to make you feel any worse," John Quincy chided. "And she doesn't even know. I don't think she realized she was carrying. I haven't told her. I only told you because she's been ailing ever since. I think that's why she's got the fever. I don't know nothing about women's troubles. I've done all I can to help her. If she's going to get better, you're going to have to take her somewhere she can get help."

"Home," Cael said softly. "We need to take her home to the pack. Our shaman could heal her."

"If she'll go," John Quincy pointed out.

"I won't give her a choice," Cael said simply. "If she's not well, as her mate, I can only do what is necessary to ensure her well being. Leaving her here is not an option."

John Quincy nodded in satisfaction. "I was hoping you'd say that. Fact is, that little girl needs someone to take care of her. She's seen far too much pain in her young lifetime."

"She'll never be without us again," Riyu vowed. "She'll never be without our protection. Even for a minute."

"Let's go back in before we freeze," John Quincy said. "I'll see about getting some grub on, and I'll make the girl some broth. She needs to eat."

Chapter Four

Cael stepped inside the door and froze when he saw a tawny colored wolf nuzzling Heather's cheek. Niko had shifted, and now focused his attention on Cael and Riyu's mate.

A challenging growl came from behind Cael as his brother got his first glimpse of the sight before them. Cael was no less pleased until he saw that Niko had managed to rouse Heather.

Her beautiful, blue eyes opened sleepily, the eyelids drooping as she dragged a hand over her face. She blinked in surprise to see the wolf so close to her.

"Niko," she whispered.

She reached out a hand and twisted her fingers in Niko's fur.

"Oh, Niko, it *is* you."

She threw her arms around the wolf's neck and sobbed into his coat. Cael's heart lurched as her heartbreaking cries filled the cabin.

Niko shifted, wrapping his arms around her and holding her against his chest. "Shhh, little one. Don't cry so. It's all right now."

Cael grit his teeth. Niko had not even conjured clothing yet.

"They left me, Niko," she said, her voice so small and so full of hurt. Each word seemed dragged from her, and she slumped wearily against Niko. "They don't want me anymore. They think I killed Magnus, and maybe I did, Niko. I shouldn't have taken so long to intervene. I was afraid. How can a coward be a worthy mate to the alphas?"

Cael turned away, no longer able to bear the pain of seeing his mate so distressed. So full of pain and betrayal. She blamed herself when she made the ultimate sacrifice for two of her pack. It wasn't she who was unworthy of the alpha. It was the alpha who was unworthy of her.

Niko continued to rock her back and forth, holding her tightly as he soothed her. Her head lolled back as she slipped into unconsciousness again.

Niko gently lowered her back to the pallet, quickly hiding his face from the others' view. But Cael had seen the tears shining in his pack mate's eyes. Who could possibly be unaffected by her grief?

When Niko finally looked back at Cael and Riyu, a dangerous fire burned brightly in his golden eyes. "We take her home to the pack. If any wolf so much as looks at her wrong, I will lay down a challenge. I will win. I will take her away from there."

Cael nodded. "That would be your right if she is not taken care of properly. But it won't happen, Niko. She is our mate. The woman of our hearts. We love her, and the pack will accept her or we will leave with her ourselves."

"You don't deserve her."

Cael nodded. "You are right. But she is ours."

Riyu moved over to the bed and knelt by Heather's side. He reached out a gentle hand and stroked her cheek. Then he bent over and pressed his lips to her forehead.

He remained there a long moment, his eyes closed. He smoothed back the tendrils of hair from her face before rising and moving away.

Cael moved forward as well. It had been a month since he'd held his mate in his arms. A month since he'd touched her, kissed her, felt her skin against his. He'd spent the last weeks dreaming of better times, when she lay between him and Riyu, sated from lovemaking.

His need was a physical ache. He wanted her with every piece of his soul. He wanted her all spread out before him, waiting to take him inside her body. He wanted her to wear the beautiful smile she wore only for him and Riyu. But after what had happened to her, and then the ultimate betrayal by her mates, she might not ever smile again. But he'd devote the rest of his life to trying to make it happen.

He lay down beside her and pulled her into his arms. He needed this contact. He wanted to be the one who kept her warm as she shivered with the fever.

As she melded to his body, he felt a sense of rightness he hadn't felt since that horrible day a month ago. He wrapped both arms tightly around her and held her close. Then he prayed to the gods that this beautiful, giving woman would find her way home to the men who loved her.

❄❄❄

Niko and Riyu ran ahead of the sled Cael pulled, scouting the area and communicating back with a series of yips and barks. Cael loped at a gentle pace, the straps to the sled between his teeth.

Behind him, Heather lay tucked amongst a pile of furs on the wooden sled. He chose his path carefully, not wanting to jostle her more than necessary.

He worried for his mate. She hadn't awoken again since yesterday morning when she'd sobbed in Niko's arms. Her fever had soared during the night as Cael had lain holding her. She had writhed and twisted restlessly, fought her demons while Cael helplessly looked on.

They'd left before dawn, loading Heather onto the sled and taking out. They were at least two days hard journey from their pack.

As they covered the miles, the sun moved from high overhead, sinking toward the horizon. When darkness fell, they stopped to rest, building up a fire in order to keep Heather warm.

Cael arranged the furs over the snow then bundled Heather among the thickest of them. Niko volunteered for the first watch and Cael and Riyu lay on either side of Heather, allowing their body heat to envelop her.

She twisted restlessly against them, and at one point began to cry. Her soft sounds of distress tore at Cael's heart. When she began to struggle, Cael summoned his courage and thrust into her mind.

The images he saw made *him* cry out. For the first time since he'd viewed the scene from his father's eyes did he see the reality of the situation. He watched as Heather put herself between Magnus and the hunters, unwilling to let them continue hurting him.

He felt every pang of fear, every wince of pain as they tore at her clothing, struck at her. He felt her shame when they violated her. Tears slid down his cheeks even as they fell down hers. He relived every moment with her, hating himself all the more for the way he'd betrayed her.

It wasn't until he heard Riyu's harsh breathing that he realized his brother had thrust into Heather's mind at the same moment he had. Riyu had been witness to all Cael had just experienced.

The two brothers exchanged sorrowful looks over Heather's body.

"She has every right to hate us," Riyu said in a low voice. "We failed her. Failed to protect her then turned away when she needed us most. We believed the worst in her when she had nothing but faith in us."

Cael nodded, unable to form the words that were trapped in his throat. What could he say when he condemned himself with every breath? He was utterly and completely unworthy of her love or faith.

❄❄❄

Had she gone through with it? Had she slipped over the side of the abyss? Was she even now passing to the next life? The world around her was a myriad of convoluted images, wild hallucinations and bizarre sounds.

One moment she felt as though the flames of hell licked at her skin, and the next, she was submerged into the icy depths of a snowdrift.

She heard voices. Familiar voices. There were times she swore Cael and Riyu were speaking to her, their love washing over her like a healing wind. Tears pricked her burning lids. She had no more tears to shed. And the dead didn't cry.

She slipped in and out of her hazy world. When she heard the voice of her mother-in law,-she cringed in fear. When she heard the yips and howls of her pack, tendrils of dread skirted up her chilled skin.

They hated her. Her mother-in-law's voice drew nearer. Heather opened her eyes, trying to see if she was real or a figment of Heather's imagination. When she saw the woman hovering over her, she whimpered in fear and shrank away.

The pack would exact justice for Heather's sins. Had they followed her into the hereafter, determined not to let her go unpunished?

Warm, soothing hands slid over her hot skin. Words of love whispered in her ear. A low moan escaped her. Death wasn't supposed to hurt so much. She wasn't supposed to *feel*.

"Heather, my love, please don't cry."

She blinked rapidly, trying to make sense of the voice. It was Cael's voice. Soft lips brushed across her brow. A hand smoothed back her damp hair.

"I'm afraid," she whimpered. "Death wasn't supposed to be so scary."

She hated herself for being such a coward. She was mate to the alphas and she couldn't even go on to the great beyond without shaming herself.

"You're not going to die, my heart. I won't let you."

"You hate me," she whispered. "Leave me in peace."

She shook her head from side to side. Why was Cael here? Then a sudden thought, alarming, flashed across her battered mind. Had Cael died too? Was that why she could hear him? The idea filled her with grief, more numbing than any she'd felt so far.

"Noooo," she cried. "You weren't supposed to die too."

Sobs welled in her chest and burst from her throat with tearing agony. Strong arms wrapped around her, joined by a second set. Familiar hands. Familiar scents.

"No one is dying, little love. You must come back to us."

"Riyu?"

"Yes, love, it's me. Riyu. I'm here. Cael's here."

"Am I dead?" she asked in a small voice.

She strained to hear their response, but their voices grew dim as the world faded around her. She slipped back into the comfort of unconsciousness.

Chapter Five

When Heather awoke again, it was to an awareness she hadn't experienced since the day she'd trekked into the snow at John Quincy's cabin. She looked around, expecting to see the familiar sight of the fireplace. The tree John Quincy had decorated for her.

Instead, what she saw brought an ache to her chest.

Cael and Riyu lay sprawled on the floor beside her bed, furs tangled at their legs. They only wore buckskins, their chests bare. A fire burned low just a few feet away.

She moved and nearly moaned with the effort. She'd never felt so weak. So sore. Her muscles protested as she tried to crawl to her feet.

She glanced around the cabin, recognizing it as the pack's winter lodging. What was she doing here? Fear and anguish swelled in her belly. How had she come to be back with the pack?

A vague memory of Niko in his wolf form at John Quincy's cabin. Had she dreamed it or had he somehow returned her to the pack? And how would Cael and Riyu react when they faced her again?

Fear-induced nausea swirled around in her stomach until she was swallowing convulsively against the urge to retch. Air. She needed air.

Carefully, she eased from the soft bed, testing weak legs before she took too many steps. The floor felt cold to her bare feet, and she looked around for her moccasins.

At the door, a few feet away, lay a pile of shoes. She eased her way over, careful not to wake her mates. Her mates. She closed her eyes against the sudden shard of pain that snaked through her body. They didn't consider her their mate any more.

With a sorrowful look in their direction, she eased her shoes onto her feet and reached for one of the furs hanging by the door.

She opened the door and quickly slipped out into the snow. She breathed deeply of the crisp air. The smell of smoke from the fires of the nearby cabins filtered through her nostrils. The morning sun was barely above the horizon, and a damp chill pervaded her body.

Still, she picked her way carefully across the snow. She was thirsty, and she knew there was a brook not far. As she approached, she saw it was crusted over with ice.

She bent down and picked up a rock to break through the surface. Water bubbled over the small opening and she cupped her hands, collecting the ice cold water.

She drank greedily, taking gulps and refilling her palms quickly.

"You should have awakened me, love. I would have gotten the water for you."

She nearly fell forward onto the ice in her surprise. Strong hands grasped her arms to steady her. She stared up at Cael who stood over her.

She flinched away from his touch, stumbling backward as she sought to stand. He put out his hands to help her but she warded them off, putting several feet of distance between them.

"What am I doing here?" she asked. "How did I get here?"

Behind him, Riyu approached, his gait wary as if he feared spooking her all the more. She took another protective step back. Her eyes darted back to Cael who stood there watching her, so much agony reflected in his eyes it made her wince.

"We went looking for you," Cael said. "We found you at John Quincy's cabin burning up with fever. We brought you home for our shaman to heal."

"It wasn't a dream," she murmured. "You were all real."

"Yes, love. We're real."

He hesitated and took a step forward. She immediately backed up unsure of what to do. What to say. What to *feel*. Why had they come for her?

"It breaks my heart that you look at me with fear in your eyes," he said in a ragged voice. "Even as I know I deserve your loathing. I would prefer hatred in your gaze. But not the fear."

"Cael—" She broke off and looked at Riyu who now stood beside his brother. Panic bubbled up. "Why did you come after me?"

She swayed a bit, and before she knew it, she was kneeling on the cold snow, bewildered at how she got there. Cael and Riyu were beside her in a second, picking her up with gentle hands.

She looked up at them in complete confusion. Across the snow, she heard a sharp cry. She followed the direction of the noise to see her mother-in-law hurrying toward them. Heather tensed and unwittingly shrank into Cael for protection.

Cael swung her into his arms, cradling her close. He strode back toward the cabin, meeting his mother half way.

"Not now, Mama," he said sharply as he shouldered past her.

Soon they were back in the warmth of the cabin. Cael set her down on the bed and removed her shoes, shaking the snow from them in the process.

"You're freezing," he said as he wrapped her in the furs. "You shouldn't be out so soon after your fever."

She gaped up at him, still unsure if she was living some bizarre dream. Just to be sure, she reached up and feathered her fingers over his jaw. He closed his eyes and nuzzled into her hand.

She yanked her hand back, palming it with her other hand. "What am I doing here?" she asked. "I don't understand."

Cael knelt on the floor in front of her, his eyes earnestly seeking hers. Behind him, Riyu entered the room and moved over to the bed. He sat down beside her, keeping a small distance between them. He seemed to want to move closer, fidgeting, reaching for her with his hand before pulling away again.

"Heather, Riyu and I...we have wronged you terribly. We went looking for you to beg your forgiveness, to bring you home, back to us."

He reached up to cup her cheek, his thumb smoothing over her jaw.

"You don't think I betrayed you?" she asked in a bewildered voice. What had changed? If she lived to be a hundred, she'd never forget the look of hatred in her mates' eyes that day.

"We were wrong," Riyu spoke up. "Niko told us what happened."

Heather's spirits plummeted. She pulled away from Cael. She bent her knees and wrapped her arms around her legs protectively, pulling them to her chest.

"If Niko hadn't come back and told you what really happened, would I be here now?" she asked.

An uncomfortable silence descended between them. Riyu made an agonized sound and moved to her side. He slipped his strong arms around her, hugging her to him.

She stiffened.

"Heather, even when we thought you had betrayed us, we loved you still. If you believe nothing else, believe that. I can't tell you how much it hurt—"

She yanked away from Riyu, her mind flooding with anger. She stumbled from the bed, putting as much distance between the two brothers as she could.

"Don't talk to me about hurt," she hissed through her teeth. "I did nothing to earn your mistrust. Nothing. I was abandoned by my mates, the two men who said they loved me, who vowed to cherish me always. You didn't even listen to me. You never gave me a chance."

Tears streamed down her cheeks as she let out the anger that had simmered below the surface for so many weeks. She felt near to bursting. Like she'd explode any second.

Cael got to his feet, his eyes somber. "We were wrong, Heather. I won't offer excuses. Our father was wrong. Our grief was raw, a terrible thing. We watched our father die, his last words condemning our mate, the woman we loved. It was a double blow. We reacted badly. We should have cared for you, listened to you, meted out justice for the wrongs that were done to you."

His voice choked as he said the last, his face graying with sadness.

"Yes. You should have," she whispered, the words catching as emotion nearly swelled her throat shut. "You should have believed in me."

She was close to losing all control as her grief overwhelmed her. She limped toward the door to the cabin, once again seeking to leave. Instead of going back for her moccasins, she thrust her feet into Riyu's heavy boots and trudged outside.

The cabin had been closing around her. She had to get out. The brisk air washed over her wet face, blowing the tears to tiny ice particles. But she ignored the cold and walked aimlessly toward the edge of the encampment.

Members of her pack stopped what they were doing to stare as she walked past. She hunched her shoulders forward, ignoring their scrutiny. Never before had she felt so keenly that she didn't belong. The lone human in a pack of wolves. She was an outsider, made so by the fact her mates had cast her aside.

Her leg ached. She hadn't exerted herself this much since the attack but she needed space. Needed to get away from the overwhelming urge to scream when she faced Cael and Riyu. She wanted to hit them. She wanted to make them bleed. She wanted to cry. She wanted things to be the way they'd been before.

But that would never happen.

She stumbled up to one of the smaller cabins and leaned heavily against the door. They weren't used for living, mainly for storage. Here, at least she could be warm. And alone.

As she reached for the handle, she registered a cry from the distance. She ignored it and shoved open the door. She walked in and stopped cold.

Her hand flew to her throat as a scream lodged there. Her mouth opened and closed but no sound would come out. There on the floor, bound hand and foot were the hunters.

She backed hurriedly from the cabin, falling as she stumbled over her bad leg, the big boots on her feet making her clumsy. She landed in the snow and still she struggled to get away. She crawled, lurching to her feet, prepared to run.

She hit a hard chest. Arms gripped her tight and a soothing voice crooned in her ear.

Niko.

She relaxed, all the fight going out of her. Niko had saved her before. He wouldn't allow anything bad to happen to her now. She slumped in his arms, and he gathered her close.

"Niko," she whispered.

"Hush, little one. It will be all right. I tried to stop you before you went in. You always were too inquisitive for your own good."

She smiled for the first time since the morning John Quincy had gotten her the Christmas tree. She wrapped her arms around Niko's neck and hugged tightly.

"Why are they here?" she asked in a ragged voice.

He kissed the top of her head. "I'm sorry you had to see them. We were too intent on finding you to deal swiftly with them. So they waited until we returned. Soon, justice will be met."

She shivered in his arms, mentally recoiling from the horrible memories the hunters conjured.

"Come with me," he said, urging her away. "You don't need to be here. I must speak with you anyway."

She raised her gaze curiously, searching his face for his intent. He regarded her solemnly, his golden eyes full of resolve.

She allowed him to guide her away. He moved slowly, taking care with her injured leg. As they neared the edge of the woods, he eased her down to sit on a large bolder. He squatted in front of her, taking her hands in his.

Regret flashed in his eyes. "I have much to apologize for, little one. I should have never left you that day. I should have delivered you safely to your mates."

"Oh, Niko," she whispered, her voice trembling. "It wasn't your fault. You saved me. You carried me back when all I really wanted to do was lay there and die."

"I want to take care of you, Heather. I know you don't love me, but in time you may come to care for me. I would be proud to call you mate. I would honor and protect you with my life. No one would ever hurt you again. If you aren't comfortable with the pack, we can leave. Start a new life somewhere else."

Chapter Six

Heather stared at the handsome warrior in astonishment. "Mate? I don't understand."

"I think you do," he said gently. He put out a hand and tucked a strand of hair behind her ear. "I would take you away from here if that is your wish. I only want for you to be happy. You sacrificed everything for me. I would see that you never want for anything."

Heather's heart clenched even as she looked sadly at him. His declaration was true and honorable. She had no doubt he'd do exactly as he promised. But he didn't love her. And was that so bad?

She looked down, her heart beating a little harder as she considered his proposal. Love was painful. It burned. It bled. It was the sharpest knife and the dullest blade. It carried the highest joys and the deepest sorrows. She was tired of feeling. Would being with a man without the burden of love be easier?

"What are you thinking?" he prompted.

"I don't know what I should do," she said honestly. "I hurt." The admission came painfully, a sharp burst, pulling from her chest.

"I know you do," he whispered. "And I'm so sorry."

He pulled her against his chest, rocking back and forth as he rubbed his hands up and down her back.

"Think about it," he said as he finally pulled away. "I won't leave you nor will I rescind my offer. Take as much time as you need. Let me know when you've reached your decision. I'll respect it no matter the outcome."

"Thank you," she said, reaching out to pull him closer to her. She kissed him lightly on the lips, a gesture of her affection. She'd done so before and never thought anything of it. But now it seemed inappropriate.

She pulled back and looked away.

"Come, little one," he said gently. "Let me return you to your cabin. You shouldn't be out in the cold. You need rest."

As they turned to walk back to the cabin, she looked up to see Cael and Riyu standing in the distance, watching her. Had they seen her kiss Niko? She pushed aside the guilt that plagued her, inserting anger in its stead. She had nothing to feel guilt over. Nothing at all.

As they drew closer to the two brothers, Cael stepped forward, wrapping an arm around Heather's shoulders and pulling her against his side.

"Thank you for seeing to our mate, Niko. We will care for her from here."

Niko nodded curtly and strode away, kicking up the snow with his boots.

Cael guided Heather into the warmth of the cabin. He could feel her trembling against him, though he wondered if it was just the cold.

Riyu followed behind, his stance awkward, his demeanor screaming helplessness. Cael understood that helplessness. Niko had offered Heather his protection. Had she accepted? Would she leave them to go with Niko now?

Cael couldn't blame her for wanting to go, for not wanting to stay with the men who had hurt her so badly. But he also knew he couldn't live without her. He would have to make his stand or risk losing her forever.

He guided Heather over to a chair in front of the fire. He eased her into the seat and tucked a fur over her lap. He eyed his brother over her head, silently communicating what he was about to do.

Riyu moved to Heather's other side. Together they would fight for their mate.

"Heather, we need to talk," Cael said as he pulled a chair at an angle to her.

Her blue eyes flashed at him, mirrored the hurt he knew she felt. He'd do anything to take the hurt away. To erase it. Make it never happen. But God, he couldn't. He couldn't change the past.

He slid his hand over her arm, enjoying the feel of her flesh underneath his fingers. "Do you love us, still?" he asked.

She tensed beneath his hand, and she looked away, but not before he saw the rim of moisture at her lids.

"We know you're angry and hurt, love," Riyu spoke up, his voice strained and edgy. "You have every right to be. But has your love for us died? Do we have any chance of making you love us again?"

Cael felt the tension in her, heard the stuttering of her breath as it tore from her chest.

"I never stopped loving you," she whispered. "It is you who lost your love and faith in me."

Cael's chest sliced open at her words, and his stomach rolled. "Oh no, my heart," he said as he gathered her into his arms. "Never. Not even when we thought the worst did our love vanish."

He held her close, whispering kisses through her hair. Her heart beat wildly against his chest. Riyu reached for her, his need to touch her reflected in his eyes. Cael relinquished her to his brother, but kept close as Riyu's arms folded around her.

"Can you ever forgive us?" Riyu asked hoarsely. "What we ask is no simple thing, but I beg it nonetheless. I can't live without you, my love. If it takes the rest of my life, I will live every day to make up for the way we have wronged you."

Heather was a mass of confusion. It was heaven to be back in their arms and the worst sort of hell. Niko's offer rested in the back of her mind, a safe haven from the pain and agony of the decision that she must make. It was the coward's way out, but she wasn't sure she had the strength to be courageous. Not anymore.

She allowed herself the exquisite comfort of Riyu's embrace for a few seconds longer before pulling away. She glanced between the two brothers, saw the fear and the anxiety in their eyes. They feared losing her. But hadn't they lost her already? Hadn't they been willing to go on without her? What if she had died when they'd left her?

Her eyes closed. She felt so weary. So torn. Never before had she faced a decision of this magnitude. One that had the power to affect the rest of her life in a way no other decision would. She could live out her life alone, denying herself the two men who claimed to love her, the two men she loved more than anything. Or she could take a chance, put herself into their keeping, something that before she would have done without thought or worry. But she didn't have that luxury now.

"I don't know," she whispered. "I just don't know."

Cael looked at her with bleak eyes. "It is all right, my heart. You must rest. Get better. We will care for you. Take the time you need to make your decision. But know this. We will always love you. We will always care for you. Never again will you be left alone."

She gazed up at him, wanting to believe him with all her heart, wanting to start over and forget the past. But it wasn't that easy. It never would be.

Slowly, she looked away, turning her stare into the flames of the fire. "The hunters," she whispered. "I don't want them here."

She wrapped her arms protectively over her chest, clutching at her arms as memories rolled over her.

Cael and Riyu both stiffened, and when she looked up at them, rage rolled off them in waves.

"It will be done," Cael said in a dangerously low voice. "You will never have to look upon them again."

She shivered at the intensity in his expression. He bent his head, hesitantly at first, and softly brushed his lips across hers.

It was a jolt to her system. She closed her eyes as a sense of homecoming hummed sweetly through her veins. When Cael pulled away, she felt bereft of his touch.

"Rest, my heart. Your mates will watch over you."

Cael moved away and Riyu bent to kiss her as well. His lips were hungrier than Cael's. More impatient and demanding. He nipped lightly at her bottom lip, tugging downward until she opened for him. Then his tongue swept in, tasting her, allowing her to taste him.

He raised his head, breaking the kiss. Her eyes followed him, feeling the same hunger she knew rolled within him. He reached out his hand and touched her swollen lips. "Rest now," he whispered.

Chapter Seven

Over the next few days, Cael and Riyu did everything in their power to make Heather smile again. They dragged a tree into their cabin, and with the help of their mother, decorated it until it sparkled from head to toe.

Christmas was but two days away, and normally, it would be a delightful time between Heather and her mates. Last year they had sledded down the hills, played in the snow, laughed and loved with a joy that still made her ache.

This year the atmosphere was tense, sorrowful and filled with so much regret that it made her uncomfortable.

Heather rested, concentrating on regaining her strength. Cael and Riyu bullied her into eating, and already she could feel the results of the nourishment.

But the nights. The nights made her ache. Her mates slept on the floor while she lay alone on the bed. She wanted them next to her but was too afraid to issue the invitation. So she huddled amongst the furs, mourning her loss.

Christmas Eve afternoon, the encampment was alive with holiday festivities. The joyous sounds of children scampering about, the adults laughing and jesting, they assaulted her ears as she limped through the snow.

She needed some time alone. She must make her decision. She couldn't go on like this, wanting, needing but so afraid.

She approached the edge of the woods and took refuge underneath the beautiful fir trees. She sank into the snow, leaning against the trunk, uncaring of the wetness bleeding into her clothing.

Quietness descended. Not even the stirring of wind could be heard. Then she heard the soft echo of a lullaby. She cocked her head, the melody eliciting a long buried memory. She knew this tune.

It curled around her. She could feel the tendrils of comfort. So odd and yet so pleasant. A soft glow sparked before her eyes. She blinked, thinking she was seeing things, but the light took shape.

The soft hum of the song grew louder. A woman appeared before Heather, her eyes alight with love, a soft smile showing tender on her face.

"Mama?" Heather whispered.

My precious daughter. How I ache for you.

Tears filled Heather's eyes. "I miss you, Mama."

I'm here, my angel. I'm always here.

Heather felt her mother's love envelop her like a hug. "What am I going to do, Mama? I hurt so much. I don't want to hurt anymore."

Oh my darling love, what a terrible time you've had. But you're strong. So much stronger than I ever was. Listen to your heart, Heather. Sometimes forgiveness is the hardest thing to give, but the most cherished thing to receive.

Forgiveness. Wasn't love all about being willing and able to forgive? Love wasn't perfect. No one was asking her to forget.

"I love them," Heather whispered. "So much. I don't want to live without them."

You are not living now, my angel. And you need to start. You have so much to give. So much life ahead of you. Just waiting for you to reach out and grasp it.

"I'm afraid."

Her mother's voice, so gentle and loving, soothed over her. *My darling, of course you are afraid. But in time, you will no longer fear. It will fade and each day will get easier. You'll see.*

"I love you, Mama. I wish..." How could she put into words that she wished her mother hadn't left her, that more than anything she wanted her here with her all the time.

I know. I know. I wish it could be so. But I'm never far away.

Heather felt her mother's presence grow lighter, and she opened her mouth to protest.

Merry Christmas, Heather. My wish for you is to live without regret.

"No, Mama. Don't *go.*"

But she was gone.

Heather lowered her head to her lap and wept. All the grief, the pain, the betrayal and the lost hope poured from her in a vicious torrent. But when her sobs quieted, she felt lighter than she had in weeks.

She stood to her feet, shaky from the expended emotion. In the distance she saw Niko striding toward her. She sucked in a breath, knowing what she had to do.

She waited until he approached her. He cocked his head to one side, studying her.

"You've made your choice," he said.

She nodded.

He reached out and took her hands. Then he leaned forward and pressed a kiss to her forehead. "I wish you happiness, little one. Know that I am never far away. If you ever need me, you have but to call."

She threw herself into his arms, her injured leg buckling underneath her. She hugged him tight. "Thank you, Niko. You are the truest friend I've ever known."

"Come. Let me help you back to your cabin. Your mates never should have let you wander this far."

She settled into his side and walked slowly beside him, his arm tight around her waist.

Chapter Eight

Cael watched as Niko approached with Heather. He'd been watching Heather ever since she'd retreated to the edge of the compound. He'd seen Niko approach her, then watched as they embraced. And now they returned. Together.

A knot tightened in his stomach. Panic seized him until he thought he might retch. She'd made her choice and it wasn't him and Riyu.

He closed his eyes against the horrible blackness spreading through his soul. Beside him, Riyu sucked in his breath.

Heather stopped a few feet in front of the brothers, and Niko squeezed her shoulders before turning to walk away. She stood there staring at them, her eyes awash with a multitude of misgivings.

"Can I talk to you?" she asked quietly. "Both of you."

Cael reached for her. He couldn't help himself. "Come inside where it's warm."

As he guided her inside, Riyu hovered close to her. Cael's pulse bounded. Did he have the right to ask her to stay when he'd been responsible for all the hurt she'd endured?

She stumbled a bit as she made her way to the chair in front of the fire. Riyu reached out and tucked his hand underneath her elbow. He eased her into the chair and tucked the furs around her.

Cael could smell the fear that radiated from his brother. Everything hinged on this moment. Their lives, their happiness.

When Heather was settled in, Cael moved to stand in front of the fire so he'd be in her line of vision. Riyu hunkered down beside her on the floor. To the side, the Christmas tree they'd decorated for her twinkled brightly with all the bits of bright paper they'd strung on it. He had a sudden urge to smash it.

She licked her lips nervously. Opened then closed her mouth. Her hand flew to her throat and massaged absently.

"Just say it," Cael said quietly.

Blue eyes shone back at him, so beautiful. Then she lowered her hands to her lap and looked down.

"I love you both so much," she whispered. "But I hurt. I'm so afraid. I don't want to be afraid anymore."

Cael closed his eyes even as Riyu let out a tortured moan.

"Niko offered to take me away from here if I wanted."

Cael flinched.

"I don't want to go," she added softly.

Both men surged to attention, their focus entirely on their mate.

"What do you want, love? Tell us. We'll do anything in our power to give it to you," Riyu said urgently.

She turned her gaze to Riyu and searched his face. Then she turned to Cael with the same questing look.

"I want your love. Your trust."

Cael sank to his knees in front of her. He gathered her hands in his, holding tight. "You've always had our love, my heart. And you'll never be without our trust again."

She reached forward, her first overt gesture of tenderness since before the attack. She stroked her fingertips over his jaw line. Then she turned and did the same gentle exploration of Riyu's cheek.

Riyu nuzzled into her hand, kissing her palm.

"I honestly don't know that I'll soon forget. At night when I close my eyes, the images are still there. Frightening and painful. But..." She stopped for a moment and swallowed. "But, I forgive you," she finally whispered.

Cael's heart soared. He felt curiously lightheaded and then he realized it was because he'd held his breath. He expelled it in one long rush.

"Do you still want me? Even after what happened? Do you love me, still?"

"Oh, Heather," Riyu said, his voice heavy with anguish. "I've never loved you more than at this moment. It shames me that you'd even have to ask if we still love you. It is because of us that you suffered so."

"Never again will you have cause to doubt our love," Cael vowed.

She slumped against the chair, looking so tired and so unbelievably fragile. But her eyes shone so brightly with her love. Unconditional love. Something they hadn't offered her.

He wanted to shout. To weep with the joy of receiving a second chance he didn't deserve. He and Riyu were so unworthy of the woman sitting before them.

Ever so gently, he cradled his arms around her, pulling her against his chest. Her heart beat erratically against his chest as she nuzzled further into his embrace.

"I love you," he whispered around the knot in his throat.

"I love you, too," she said.

Reluctantly, he relinquished his hold on her and allowed Riyu to move forward to pull her into his arms. He listened as Riyu reaffirmed his love for their mate, and in that moment experienced such a surge of rightness. As if finally, after so many weeks of turmoil, the world, at least for these few seconds was at peace.

"Will you take me to our bed?" she asked. "I'm so tired of sleeping alone."

"You'll never do it again," Riyu vowed as he bent to pick her up.

Cael followed his brother to the bed and watched as Riyu set her down. He moved forward, and the two of them slowly undressed her, baring her silky skin to their gaze. And to their touch.

When she was completely nude, they climbed into the bed with her, tucking her in between them. As they'd done so many nights in the past.

Chapter Nine

Heather awoke to a rough tongue licking her cheek. She pried one eye open to see a silver wolf nuzzling her face. She smiled and trailed her fingers through the thick fur. Cael.

She glanced over to see a slightly darker haired grey wolf staring at her. Riyu. The wolf bounced on his front legs, starting toward her then bounding briskly back toward the door.

Her wolves were playful this morning.

She threw back the covers and swung her feet over the side of the bed. She put her good leg down first and eased up. Cael pressed his muscled body against her knees to help support her. She reached down to scratch his ears in affection.

She dressed while her wolves paced impatiently. When she'd bundled herself up and put on her boots, they nudged her out the door into the snow.

A soft gasp of delight whispered past parted lips. Before her stood a shiny sled. Riyu and Cael pushed her in the direction of it and she climbed onto the seat and pulled the blankets up around her.

Her two wolves trotted around front and wiggled under the straps. They picked them up with their teeth and started off at a slow pace.

She sat back and let out a giggle of delight as they headed down the hill. The wind blew cold on her face. She closed her eyes, threw back her head and gloried in the moment. It was as if the last weeks hadn't happened. She was back with her wolves, laughing and playing. Enjoying life so close to nature.

They picked up speed, sailing her through snowdrifts and angling through the trees. She let out a squeal as they took a corner too fast. The sled tipped and she went tumbling into the snow, laughing like an idiot the entire time.

In a flash, her wolves transformed and stood over her in the snow, concern echoing in their eyes.

"Heather, are you okay?" Cael demanded as he bent to pick her up.

She retaliated by quickly forming a snowball in her hand and smashing it into his face. His look of surprise was priceless.

"What the...you little..."

She burst out laughing. Beside him Riyu grinned, his blue eyes flashing merrily.

"It's so good to hear you laugh again," Cael said hoarsely. "I'd take a thousand snowballs in the face just to hear that sound."

"In that case." She shoved another handful of snow but this time he ducked before she could clobber him with it.

She tensed, expecting him to retaliate, but instead, he bent and kissed her hungrily, his cold, wet lips fusing to her warmer ones. She melted, just like the ice on his face did.

"We should get you back," he said huskily. "You're going to freeze to death."

Riyu righted the sled and brushed the snow from the seat. Cael eased her onto the sled and arranged the furs around her again. Then he and Riyu picked up the leather straps and began pulling her back toward the camp.

She burrowed into the furs and stared up at the beautiful blue sky. Christmas Day. And it was perfect.

A good bit later, her mates pulled the sled into camp. Ahead she could see their pack, all assembled in the center of the compound.

Concern pushed her forward. She leaned, trying to see what could be the matter.

"Don't worry, love," Riyu said as he turned to look at her.

Both her mates stared at her, their love for her shining in their eyes.

"We have a surprise for you," Cael said as he bent down to pick her up.

Ahead she could hear the giggles of little children, the quiet whisperings of the women and the low rumble of men talking. Then they parted as Cael approached.

There, in the middle, stood a tall fir tree, decorated from top to bottom with cones, bright paper, handmade ornaments and an assortment of other trinkets.

Tears filled her eyes as she stared at her pack, all assembled, welcome in their faces. From behind several women, her mother-in-law stepped forward, her expression hesitant.

Cael gently set Heather on her feet as his mother approached. Heather blinked when Lorna put a gentle hand to Heather's cheek.

"My daughter. I'm so sorry for what was done to you by the hunters and by our pack. I can only hope that in time, you can forgive us."

She leaned forward and kissed Heather on both cheeks before stepping back.

Heather's throat threatened to close. "All is forgiven," she said hoarsely.

"Then come. Let us celebrate the holiday as a pack. As we always have, and the gods willing, always will."

She took Heather's hand in hers and pulled her toward the tree. Her pack swarmed forward, all bearing wrapped gifts with an assortment of ribbons and colored paper. They were placed under the tree.

Tables were set up, food and drink was brought out, and the more musically inclined of her pack pulled out their flutes and began playing merry tunes.

Heather stood back, humbled by the reception, her pack's willingness to admit wrong and embrace her once again. Two strong arms settled around her waist as Riyu and Cael flanked her.

"Merry Christmas, my heart," Cael murmured close to her ear.

She put her arms around their waists, pulling them closer to her. "Merry Christmas, my mates. I love you so dearly."

"And you are dear to us," Riyu returned.

They bent to kiss her but she stepped back and with a push, sent them both sprawling into the snow. She burst out laughing at their astonished expressions before leaping on the both of them.

They caught her, ever mindful of her wellbeing. She nuzzled their faces in an imitation of them in their wolf form. Then she rose up, staring into their eyes.

"Take me back to our cabin and make love to me," she said softly.

Two sets of crystal blue eyes stared back at her.

"It would be our fondest desire," Cael murmured as he closed his arms around her.

About the Author

To learn more about Maya, please visit www.mayabanks.com. Send an email to Maya at maya@mayabanks.com or join her Yahoo! group to join in the fun with other readers as well as Maya. http://groups.yahoo.com/group/writeminded_readers

Look for these titles

Miracle at Midnight

Stacia Wolf

Dedication

To the youngest members of my family: Dylen, Logan, and Duncan, my children's children, and to all my nieces and nephews. And to Solomon David, my nephew's son, whose early entrance into this world makes him all the more special. May all of you find your own miracles in your lives.

Prologue

"Enough!" Comtessa Amara de la Cortese shouted through a haze of anger at her advisors. Her deceased husband's advisors, in reality. "I no longer wish to discuss this ridiculous proposal."

"But—"

"I said enough!" She slammed her hand down on the massive desk. Although it made barely a sound, their slicing tongues ceased. "You don't care that I'm to be sacrificed on the marriage bed to keep your worthless hides safe."

Her head throbbed from the argument that had been roaring in her ears for hours now, ever since Comte Chavre DeLeon showed up with his marriage proposal. His honey-sweet words had veiled a threat—refuse and he would lay claim to her lands as her protector.

"I understand the risks. You've made that very clear—over and over. But now I need peace so I may think." She waved her hand in dismissal, then turned her back on them. They bickered amongst themselves as they shuffled out, leaving Amara alone.

Her maid entered, and Amara contained an urge to snap at her. Instead, she said, "I will eat in my rooms tonight. Let the kitchen know, then come help me out of this miserable dress."

She couldn't stand the idea of sitting at dinner and having all those prying eyes watching her. She needed some peace, but knew it would be fleeting. She longed to be free of this place, of the tall rock walls, of her duty to these people who didn't care whether she lived or died.

Her restlessness chased her all evening, and nearing midnight, she found herself on her balcony, listening to a light breeze rattle through the sleeping trees' branches. The icy chill bit through her opulent robes and nightgown, but her bitterness kept her blood heated, even as her stocking-clad feet protested being subjected to winter's deep freeze.

She should be in bed, warm and contented. But instead, she stood on the tiny balcony overlooking the deserted town center. Still no word from her brother, Ehren, who'd left nearly a year ago, promising to bring back her husband's killer. She didn't mourn her husband. He'd been older than her deceased father, and had shown little interest in her after receiving her dowry from Ehren.

In the harsh night of December 24th, 1507, in the large town of Dupois, France, Amara felt the coldness seep into her very bones. Raised by a remote, brutal widower father, Amara had learned quite young that those who cared, those who loved, were weak fools who could easily be destroyed. Now twenty-four years old, she ruled her dead husband's land with an iron fist, just as her brother ruled his own lands. Just that morning, she'd witnessed a beggar stealing food from the market. She'd called the soldiers, angry that anyone would steal from her.

When the man had been captured, he'd cried out to her, "You condemn my children to death!" Amara had covered her barren womb with her palm and replied, "Some do not deserve life." Then she'd walked away.

Restless, Amara stared out over the empty courtyard, as bereft as her heart. Her father had taught her that happiness was only achieved by power and domination. She'd learned not to show emotions or to feel anything. She'd been given one gift—her beauty. With long, dark hair the color of a raven's wing, pale skin and luminous green eyes, Amara had discovered the power of her looks on both men and women. A smile, a frown, a whispered endearment—they were all weapons she used well.

But the Comte seemed immune. He'd looked on her as a man would an inanimate object. He gave nothing away, which left her impotent to persuade him.

A movement below caught her attention. Someone skimmed through the shadows—no, two someones. Using the darkness as their cover, they moved carefully through the courtyard, heading to the stockade. The stockade wouldn't be heavily guarded. Instead, the soldiers manned the tall walls, to guard the village against the Comte's veiled threat.

Instantly, she realized the stealthy pair's goal. They were to rescue the thief. Stupid, foolish men. She'd exact a harsh price for their treachery, one that would set an example throughout the land. She waited in the shadows, still as a statue, the cold seeping even deeper into her, turning her outrage into strong contempt. Then when two became three, when hushed whispers marked their retreat, she stepped out of the darkness.

"Guards! Stop those men!"

In moments, soldiers poured into the square. Amara rushed down several flights of stairs and out to where the three men knelt in the dirty snow, torchlight illuminating their defeat. She stood in front of them and felt as if her father and brother watched her, judging her.

Her family had ruled for a half-century, and in that time they'd rarely shown mercy. These men, who defied her on such a sacred day, deserved no compassion.

But that was exactly what one asked for. The thief, she believed.

"Please, Comtesse, have mercy. My children—"

"How old are your children?" she asked.

"My daughter is twelve, my son ten. Their mother died long ago. Now they will be alone." His eyes held hope mingled with despair; tears left dirty tracks down his face.

But Amara felt nothing. He'd dared to steal from her and needed to be punished. She looked up at one of her soldiers. "Find these children. They will be sold to pay for this man's crimes." She only waited for his nod before turning away.

"Comtesse! May you be judged as harshly as you judge your own people!"

Amara didn't even break stride. The doomed thief's words meant nothing. She entered her chambers and shut the door, then closed her eyes, calming all her thoughts. No use letting some lawless man and his stupid curses upset her. She didn't write the laws of the land. "Thou shalt not steal" was a commandment of God. She only upheld it.

Is mercy not also one of God's traits?

The soft voice startled her. Her eyes flew open, and she looked wildly about her. "Who's there?"

I am who you refer to as Pere Noel. I prefer Nicholas.

A man stepped out of the shadows. He wore the robes of a priest and held an ornate staff. He was very old, his white hair streaming over his shoulders. Somehow, he glowed and didn't seem solid.

Pere Noel. Father Christmas. It couldn't be. She had to be dreaming.

"Who are you really and what do you want?"

You are very demanding. He watched her, his bright blue gaze never wavering. *I want you to answer me this question. What is your heart made of?*

He mocked her. This apparition in her own chambers mocked her. All the hurt and pain of her father's hatred, her brother's disdain, filled her. Amara replied, "My heart is of stone, to survive this world."

Pere Noel nodded, his eyes seemingly saddened. *So be it.*

He pointed his staff at her. *Comtessa Amara de la Cortese of Dupois, for your crimes against children, you have condemned yourself by your own words to a life of stone.*

Incredibly, the staff began to glow, and Amara felt herself grabbed by that light, frozen into place. She tried to cry out but she couldn't move, couldn't speak. The lights lifted her up, and she dangled, helpless.

I will grant you a boon. His eyes snapped at each word. *Every fifty years, the same length as your family's despotic reign, you will be granted two days to discover the answer to this question—what is the true meaning of love?*

Give me the correct answer, and your life will be your own. Give me the wrong answer and you will return to being a statue. You will have ten chances.

Then the light exploded, and Amara found herself outside, in the frigid cold, but she couldn't feel it. She knew where she was. In front of the little church, still under construction. And she understood several things at once.

She was made of stone, to match her heart.

She'd been cursed with a task—to find the true meaning of love.

And she'd been inscribed with the following words,

In tribute to those who have lost heart.

Then consciousness faded away.

Chapter One

Samantha Gamble couldn't sleep. The clock in her bedroom said eleven fifty-six, but she didn't feel tired at all. She couldn't remember being so sad at Christmas before. She missed her mom and her baby brother and their dog, Busby. But Mom had said she had to go. She'd told her all about fun stuff to do in New York at Christmastime. Sami didn't really care, she just wanted to stay home, but she'd heard her mom talking to her step-dad and knew she didn't have a choice. She rarely saw her dad, and usually she loved coming to New York, but Christmas was a time to be with family, and Daddy didn't feel like family any more.

She'd arrived in New York City this morning. Usually Daddy worked. As a doctor, he was pretty busy. But this year he promised to take time off and spend it just with her. Tomorrow he said he'd take her ice skating at Central Park, then they'd go see Santa at Macy's. Supposedly he was the best Santa around. Daddy hadn't been too excited about that, but he'd told her mother he'd take her. Sami's mom called Daddy a "big cynic", and although Sami wasn't supposed to hear, she'd listened as her mom told her dad to "lighten up and enjoy the holidays with your daughter".

She glanced toward her window that overlooked the church across the street and saw fat snowflakes falling. Some of her sadness faded. A white winter in New York City! And tomorrow she'd be skating in real snow. Her friends back home in Rhome, Texas, would be so jealous! It never snowed there.

Scooting out of bed, she ran to the window bench her daddy had put in just for her and crawled onto its princess- and fairy-covered fabric. She gazed outside, watching the snowflakes appear under the street lamp across the street. She followed them down to the ground, where they coated the three statues that adorned the open courtyard at the church. Sami loved the statues. One of them, a woman with flowing hair that stood next to the statue of Jesus, seemed to be reaching out to someone. Daddy said she didn't have a name, but he said her plaque read "In tribute to those who have lost heart" in French.

She pressed her nose against the glass and puffed on it, laughing when her breath fogged up the window. She wiped it away. Then a bright light flared outside, and Sami stared hard, trying to find where the light came from.

Her statue—it glowed bright as a headlight.

The light grew and flared, blinding her. She shielded her eyes and yelled, "Daddy!" before she remembered her door was shut and he probably couldn't hear her. Then the light died as swiftly as it had appeared—and with it, went her statue.

In its place stood a woman with long black hair and a fancy bathrobe. She looked like one of those Christmas angels her mother put on the tree every year, except her hair was messy and she didn't have wings. Then she yelled.

Sami opened her window by pushing the button and moving the latch, then giving it a hard heave upward—just like she'd learned last summer. Now she could hear what the statue said.

The woman stepped off the pedestal, her hair streaming about her. She stumbled, then turned back and picked something up, some sort of package. She didn't even open it, but whirled about instead, as if looking for someone. Then she yelled again. Sami could hear her clearly, but none of her words made sense. Then she heard one word she understood.

Jumping off the window bench, she ran to her door and jerked it open. "Daddy! Come quick! The statue's alive and she's yelling for you!"

"Nicholas! Where are you?" Amara couldn't believe she'd woken up alone on this, her last chance. Nine times she'd awakened and tried to escape this curse, and nine times she'd failed. This, the tenth time, she'd expected him to be there, to maybe give her a hint or a clue as to where to look. Instead, she was alone. She had only two days to discover what he wanted, or she'd become a statue again. And this time, it would be forever.

She whirled about again, and then it struck her. The church behind her, although old, wasn't the church from Dupois. And there were other statues. The street felt too close, the buildings surrounding her weren't right, either. Where was she?

She saw the bundle he always sent her. She snatched it up, but didn't open it. She needed some answers, and the bundle never contained those, although it probably had that horrible wafer she'd eaten the last few times. It granted her understanding of the language, since French had changed so much over the last few hundred years.

Heaven knew if she was still in France.

"Nicholas!" she yelled again. "What have you done? Where am I? You owe me answers! Nicholas!"

But she knew he wouldn't appear. Sometimes he'd be there when she woke up, and sometimes not. There were times she'd call out to him, out of fear, out of anger, out of need. But he never answered her summons. He appeared only when he chose to, never when she called. There was only one time she could be certain she'd see him. He would summon her back to the statue's base at the end of her time, at midnight on Christmas Day, and he'd ask her the same thing every time.

What is the true meaning of love?

And always she failed to satisfy him.

Yet still she called. Because maybe this time, the last time, would be different. Maybe something she'd done over the last nine times would have softened him to show her some mercy.

Then she remembered. She'd never shown kindness to another person. Very ironic she'd expect some now.

A movement caught her eye. A window across the street stood open, and a little girl pointed at her. Another figure appeared. A man. He leaned forward and looked right at her.

Amara stared. He was very handsome, with short dark hair, a style she'd not liked when she'd been "home", but had grown to appreciate during her last couple of awakenings. His face was long and lean. She couldn't see his eyes, but she imagined them to be chocolate, a delicacy she'd discovered about three awakenings ago.

She mentally shook herself. This wouldn't help her, standing here staring at some stranger. "Nicholas! How am I to learn this mercy that you spoke of if I never experience it myself?"

Shaking her head in frustration, she untied the silver cord wrapped around the cloth bundle and looked for the cursed wafer. She'd need the knowledge it brought her, but she hated the feeling it gave her. Like her bones were being shredded. And the pain—the last time she'd nearly passed out.

Re-tying up the bundle and setting it down, she put the wafer in her mouth and immediately tasted the bitterness. She couldn't stop now. This was her last chance; she needed to do the best she could.

She bit into the wafer and writhed in agony as the pain ripped through her.

This time, she did faint.

"Daddy!" Sami screamed as the woman tumbled to the ground. "She's hurt! Daddy, go help her!"

Nick Gamble looked at the woman, probably homeless and mentally disturbed, who moments before had been shouting at an invisible someone. "Honey, I'll call the police. They'll come help her."

"No, Daddy, you need to help her. She yelled for *you*. By the time police get here, she might be dead."

"She was calling for a Nicholas. Only your grandmother calls me that." Nick stared out the window. At this distance, he couldn't tell if she still breathed. "Baby, it's not our problem. We need to handle this the right way, by calling the police."

"She's not a bad person, she's a sick person. Isn't that what you're supposed to do? Help sick people?"

He saw the hope in her face, and a desperate belief that her parents could do anything. She seemed so young, so vulnerable. She'd grown up so much lately and had become almost a stranger to him. He longed to find a way to get closer to her.

He couldn't disappoint her.

"All right, I'll go look at her. Go grab my medical bag out of the hallway, and I'll get my shoes on. But you're to stay up here, with the door locked, understand?"

Sami nodded enthusiastically, and Nick sighed as he pushed away from the window. She raced off, and he reluctantly followed. He didn't mind helping people down on their luck, which was why he volunteered at a clinic. But spending any of his time off helping a mentally imbalanced person didn't seem like much of a vacation.

He glanced at his daughter as he left the apartment. She seemed too innocent for a six-year-old. Maybe in Texas they stayed younger longer. Not in New York. And she still believed in all that make-believe garbage. Like Santa Claus and the tooth fairy. He worried about how to teach her reality without bursting her bubble too cruelly.

In no time at all, Nick stood beside the fallen woman. From the window he'd noticed her long, dark hair, her pale skin, but up close he had to admit she was quite beautiful. Probably a model a bit high on something. Then he glanced up at the statue.

Or at the thin air where the statue had been. Nothing stood on the pedestal.

He remembered now that Sami had yelled something about the statue becoming a woman. No way that could be true. But he couldn't see any scratches or chips in the stone, something that would happen if someone had pried the heavy statue off its base.

"Daddy!"

He glanced up at Sami, who leaned out the window and pointed insistently at the woman. With a sigh, he knelt beside her in the thin layer of snow and felt her throat.

Yes, one strong pulse. And some very soft skin.

And two incredibly green eyes staring up at him.

He jerked his hand back. The woman didn't seem to react at all, just kept looking up at him. Then she felt around for something. He spied a cloth bundle a few feet from him. Reaching out, he grabbed it and handed it to her. She took it without a word, setting it beside her.

"How are you feeling? You passed out."

She glanced at him, watching his mouth as if fascinated. Then, insanely, she giggled. "Your lips don't match the words I hear." She possessed a strange accent that he couldn't quite place. Sounded European. It gave her voice a lilting quality. Then she touched her own mouth. "This is so strange."

Definitely high on something. He rocked back onto his heels, then stood up. "You don't seem frightened by your fainting spell, or about waking up with a total stranger beside you."

She shrugged and carefully sat up. "The fainting I knew might happen." She looked at him, as if seeing him for the very first time. "You don't look very frightening to me. Besides, I can't die." She frowned slightly. "I've seen you before. Ah, yes, the man in the window."

Nick frowned. In the lamplight, with her head tilted up at him, her eyes didn't seem dilated. Her skin hadn't been clammy and her pulse was steady. If she were drunk, then she also hid that well. But she could be coming down from an extended high.

"You should see a doctor, find out why you fainted." Code for "get some help". He almost asked her if she had a place to stay, so he could send her to a close-by shelter, but he didn't want to get involved.

"Isn't that what you do?"

"Why do you say that?"

She nodded at the bag. "I've seen those before. You're not the first one who thinks I'm a bit crazy." Her lips curved into an ironic smile. He wondered what she'd look like if her smile reached her eyes. She'd be stunning.

He frowned, pulling his thoughts back to the matter at hand. He couldn't let her beauty distract him from reality here. "I don't think you need me to diagnose what's really wrong with you right now, do you? It's either drugs or alcohol, or both."

Her brows lifted. He expected anger, or at least denial, but instead she laughed. "I wish those were my troubles. Those I could handle, but—"

"Are you an angel?"

Startled, Nick turned around and found his daughter standing not ten feet away. "I asked you to stay in the apartment. Go back to bed."

The woman ignored him, gazing instead at his little girl. She smiled, and this time it did reach her eyes. Yes, he'd been right. She was truly dazzling.

"No," she said, "I'm simply a woman who made some very bad choices, but I'm learning from them. Why do you think I might be an angel?"

"Because I saw you. One minute you're a statue, then poof!" Sami threw her hands up in the air, her eyes wide in excitement. "You're standing there."

Nick expected the woman to laugh, or perhaps to make fun of her. Instead she stared at Sami in wonder, then her eyes filled with delight. "You saw me? You honestly saw me?"

Sami nodded, rather vigorously, and the woman laughed and reached out to her. Before Nick could react, his daughter ran straight into her arms.

Horrified, he reached for Sami, but something held him back—almost like a hand on his shoulder, but nobody stood there.

The woman held Sami by her shoulders. Tears shimmered in her eyes. She whispered, "Once, a man stood right before me when I changed, and saw nothing. To him, the statue was still there, and I was merely a crazy woman. Yet you truly saw me. This must mean something. You must be the key to finding the answer. What's your name?"

"Sami." She looked in awe at the woman, as if she truly believed she were an angel.

"Sami. I like that name. I'm Amara de la Cortese, at your service." She seemed to curtsey while sitting, and Sami giggled.

Nick gritted his teeth. Enough was enough. "Listen, would you please let go of my—"

"Sami," Amara breathed, "Would you help me find the true meaning of love?"

Chapter Two

Amara sat gingerly on the edge of the bed with a sense of satisfaction. She could hear Nick Gamble moving about on the other side of the door. She imagined he still felt angry over how Sami had coerced him into letting Amara stay.

Amara relished the smile that came while thinking of Sami's pleas in her behalf. A statue couldn't smile, couldn't move, couldn't show emotion except for the very rare tear. A smile felt like a gift from heaven.

She couldn't describe herself as awake while imprisoned in stone, nor could she say she was exactly sleeping. It felt more like being in a constant state of almost-awake. Some things would penetrate her awareness, like a violent act or a poignant moment. She remembered a young man fighting a Nazi for the life of a child. She remembered a woman letting go of the memory of her dead husband at Amara's feet.

At first, she'd hated this not-really-awake state she'd traveled through the years in. But once, she'd spent several years wide awake. She'd seen everything around her, felt every raw emotion, every change in the weather, birds' claws in her flesh, bugs crawling about her.

And she'd nearly gone insane.

After the first few awakenings, she'd discovered that if she concentrated very hard, she could remember things that had happened around her during the past fifty years. It was almost like reading a book, or time-traveling. She'd learned that her disappearance had profoundly changed her brother, and he'd visited her "statue" nearly every day until his death from natural causes. He'd become a great, benevolent ruler, and his daily talks to her became precious memories.

She'd seen the ravages of war on her now-beloved France and watched as the world changed. Tools and weapons became more advanced and deadly, people became more sophisticated and complicated, the world became more crowded. Horses were replaced by bicycles and cars, daily conversations in person were made rare by the advent of telephones, and women became more empowered.

She wondered how the world had changed in the last fifty years, and if finding her answer on this, her last chance, would be easier or more difficult.

Then her spirits lifted. Sami had *seen* her. That beautiful little girl with the most expressive eyes she'd ever known gave Amara hope that somewhere close she'd find her answer.

And Sami somehow held the key.

But she couldn't bask in her hope. She had work to do. She needed to retrieve her memories, see if she could learn anything from the past.

Closing her eyes, she thought hard about herself as a statue, then thought about the square at home, about the surroundings.

And she saw the time flashing by. Fashions changed, familiar faces grew older, then disappeared. A face she remembered from before, the priest, looked at her in anger every day.

She could hear snippets of conversations. "The statue is cursed. It disappears, then reappears. No one is ever caught for the crime. It needs to go." Then a new man with the priest, also wearing a collar, gazed up at her with reverence. "I will give her a home."

Memories of darkness, jostling, then light. She could see that face, the young priest, and the church she'd woken up to. She now knew she'd been sent to the United States, to New York City. She'd been placed on a new base and turned toward the street as if to greet people. A bench and a young tree were placed near her.

Now the tree towered above her, and the bench had been replaced a few times. But the young priest had visited her almost daily. She watched him age, and still his eyes filled with reverence each time he looked at her.

The priest. Another key. Amara stretched back on the bed. In the morning, she'd visit him. Perhaps he'd know something to aid her quest.

She saw brief glimpses of Nick Gamble, first alone, then with a beautiful dark-haired woman, then with a baby. Samantha. She watched Sami grow up, watched that dark brown fuzz turn into becoming curls, then Sami and the woman disappeared, and only Nick walked by, his face dark and unapproachable.

Amara sat up. The depth of his unhappiness, apparent even in those fleeting glimpses, disturbed her. She almost felt like a voyeur.

She shook herself mentally. She didn't have time to worry about Nick Gamble. She touched the bed longingly. No time for sleep either.

Instead, she concentrated on her next steps. In the bundle were always scraps of fabric. Her memories had shown her today's fashions. The blue scrap was probably pants or a jacket. The red, a sweater. She chose a few pieces, laid them out on the bed, then placed her hands on them. They warmed, then grew.

When the heat stopped, she opened her eyes and found her first modern wardrobe.

It took her several minutes of struggling to get in the clothes. She'd never worn pants before. The bra and panties she knew, although the bra seemed lighter and tighter, and the panties mere snippets of fabric. And the white undershirt. But the pants felt funny and only fit right when the fasteners were in front. And the sweater was cut wrong. It showed too much of the undershirt.

A knock came at the door. Nick Gamble. Fascinating, unsmiling, suspicious Nick.

She opened the door, and he stood there with a tray. On it sat milk and slices of bread holding what looked like impossibly thin meat and cheese.

He stared at her, his gaze raking her up and down. She felt very naked dressed like this, in these form-fitting clothes.

"Where did you get those?"

She shrugged. "They were in the bundle, of course." She smiled and mentally sent him the message that she'd say no more on the subject. She glanced at the tray. That seemed to stop him from staring at her chest.

"I thought you might be hungry."

It had been fifty years since she'd last eaten, but appetite usually didn't trouble her. "Thank you." She reached for the tray, but he pushed past her and set it on the tiny nightstand. The room, although very small, was still bigger than the jail cells she'd put so many people in. To her, it felt like luxury.

Nick straightened up, then turned his somber face toward her. "Please don't make me regret letting you stay here. Sami's only six and very naïve. If you hurt her—"

"I could never hurt a child." She felt regret echoing from the past. She'd hurt many people before, some were children who'd lost their parents due to her tyranny. She could see now that she'd been a monster. She should be grateful to Nicholas for changing her, but maybe if she passed his test she could feel gratitude. Right now she struggled to feel nothing where he was concerned.

Nick stared at her for another long moment. "Do you really think you were a statue?"

She'd learned long ago not to discuss her unusual circumstances. "I'm not crazy, or dangerous. I'm just trying to get my life back on track."

His gaze dug into her, as if looking for all her secrets. It made her very uncomfortable.

"Do you have a newspaper I could read? I'm not tired."

He shook his head. "I get an online paper, but nothing paper."

"Online? What's that?"

He stared at her as if she'd sprouted two heads. "Online, as in on the computer."

Baffled, she shrugged, a gesture she'd picked up her last awakening. "I don't know what you mean."

"How can you..." His lips twisted into what she could only describe as a sneer. "Ah, this is part of your I-was-a-statue act. All right, I'll play along. Come along, I'll show you the computer." He nodded at the tray. "Bring your snack along."

She picked up the tray and followed him into the main living area, where a small desk held a flat metal case. He flipped it open, pushed a few buttons, and the flat glass that covered one half lit up blue. He watched it for a moment, then sat down and started pushing buttons on the other half at a rapid rate.

"By the way," he asked as his fingers danced over the buttons, "how did your cohorts get that statue off the base and moved so quickly?"

Amara didn't answer. She couldn't take her eyes off the glass. Images flew over it. Words, smiling faces, even tiny reindeer flying. She thought she heard bells. She set the tray down on the desk and moved closer.

"How did you do that?" she asked, both in wonder and fear. She'd witnessed a lot of changes—airplanes and flushing toilets being two of the strangest—but this! This had to be magic. She reached out to touch the strange glass, but he grabbed her wrist.

"No, never touch an LCD," he said, then studied her face. "Are you trying to convince me you know nothing about computers?"

Computer. She thought hard and could remember people walking past her saying something about them, but it made no sense. E-mail, IM, online shopping—it sounded more foreign to her than the language she now spoke.

Nick pushed a little plastic thing around, and Amara watched as a small arrow flew across the glass.

"I'm not buying your act. Here." He tapped a button on the plastic thing, and a picture popped up that said *New York Times*. He stood then and motioned for her to sit down. "This is the paper. The navigation bar is over here." He pushed the plastic thing, and the arrow on the glass moved.

She read "world", "US", "finance" and realized she had too much to learn. Even using this strange box overwhelmed her.

But this was her last chance, and learning as much as she could about the times she now lived in would probably help her succeed on her quest.

It certainly couldn't hurt.

Nick stood and watched her as she sat down in front of the glass and gingerly touched the plastic oval. It still felt warm from his touch. Her fingers tingled; she didn't know if it was from the thought of her fingers resting where his hand had so recently been or if the little arrow skittering across the glass petrified her.

She wrapped her fingers around the plastic thing, like she'd seen Nick do, and tried to understand what he'd done to make the page change. The New York Times had horrific headlines—ones about wars in countries she'd never heard of, about insurgents and terrorists, about shootings and other terrible acts. She wanted to cry. Nothing had gotten better in this world. If anything, they were worse.

She read through the list that Nick had indicated. She didn't know where to start or how to find what she needed.

Then she saw books and movies listed. She knew about those. A remarkable thing, movies. People on film forever, even after they were long gone. She'd seen an American movie, *Never Say Goodbye*. She still remembered how magnetic the actor, a Rock Hudson, had been. The person who'd taken her, a young wife missing her husband who was away for Christmas, had told her that movies showed the culture of the times.

So she'd look at the movies, and perhaps that would give her a glimpse into this strange new world.

She made the arrow glide over the word "Movies" and...

Nothing happened.

She could feel Nick Gamble watching her. He thought her a fraud or worse—someone who'd take advantage of his young daughter. She couldn't ask him for help. He considered her an enemy. One never begged for help from the enemy.

She waved the arrow over the word again. Still nothing.

Nick sighed and before she could even glance at him, his hand covered hers as he guided the oval thing. "I have to admit you're a great actress. Here." He made the arrow go over the word "Movies", then pressed down on her index finger.

The pictures changed, the words changed, and she stifled a screech. She glanced at Nick and found his face just inches from hers. His breath fanned her cheek, and her hand burned where his laid over it.

She understood what this feeling meant. Sexual attraction. She'd never truly experienced it before. She'd married for political gain, not love. Most men of her stature had been unattractive. And on each of her nine awakenings, although she'd met a few handsome men, she'd not felt this tug, this pull.

For an instant, she indulged herself, enjoying the sizzle where their flesh met, the way his warmth flooded her always-too-cold fingers, the feel of his arm brushing against hers. Then he spoke and she forced herself back into reality.

Reality being she'd be a statue forever if she didn't find Nicholas' answer.

"Just place the cursor over whatever you're interested in, until it turns into a hand. Then click this button."

She nodded, and he straightened up, breaking contact. She sucked in a deep breath, chose a movie title that sounded interesting and did what he'd said.

The image changed, and she smiled. Success!

She looked up at Nick, who'd withdrawn a few feet. His frown dug furrows between his eyes.

"Thank you."

He nodded. "I don't know what your game is, but there's no way in Hell that you were a statue. If it weren't for my daughter—" He shook his head. "I'll be watching you."

Then he left, heading to his bedroom, which was across from Sami's and in the opposite direction from hers. She noted that he didn't close his door.

No matter. The fact remained that she was here, and her time ticked away rapidly. So she'd make the best of it.

She started reading. And quickly became confused. Many of the movies were about alternate realities, or about people with super powers. Or movies where crazed things stalked and killed people. Was today's world really filled with these kinds of people? Or was this a way for people to escape from everyday chaos?

There were a few movies the reviewers called "chick flicks", so Amara studied those. Some of them, if she clicked in the right place, popped up with short pieces of the movie. These seemed more like what she'd expect. She learned about modern love and relationships.

Then the computer stopped working. She didn't know why, but nothing she chose would show, and an annoying message that made no sense to her wouldn't go away.

"You have too many screens open."

Amara jumped, and found Sami standing beside her. The little girl pointed at the bottom of the glass.

"See that? That means that your memory is all jumbled up. I did that before, when I was just learning how."

"Oh." Life for a six-year-old was much different than what Amara would have expected. And *her* memory seemed fine, so Sami must mean the computer. "How do I fix it?"

"Like this. You take the mouse and..." Sami took away the plastic thing, apparently a mouse, clicked a few times and everything went away. Amara breathed a sigh of relief. This computer thing was way over her head and told her way too much. She felt lost in a snowstorm of information and didn't know what to do next.

Then Sami did something remarkable and totally unexpected. She crawled onto Amara's lap while still retaining ownership of the mouse. "Did you find your answer?"

Amara shook her head. "You mean the true meaning of love? No, I didn't expect to. But I needed to know more about your times."

Sami cocked her head as she started clicking buttons on the mouse. "Isn't true love something that happens between a boy and a girl when they get older? Mom says she and Roger have true love."

Amara smiled. "No, I made that mistake the first time I guessed. He's not looking for a 'man-woman' thing."

Yes, she'd tried that. She'd guessed "a life-time commitment and devotion between two people". That, from listening to two lovers.

"A love where you'd sacrifice your own goals for another." That from a mother talking about her children.

"'A love where you would change anything or do anything for another." She'd found that from a brother who'd joined an army to free his family from poverty.

"A feeling that raises you up above the pettiness of the world." That from a nun.

"A love where you know you cannot live without the other." That from a young woman waiting for her beloved to come home from a war.

"Love is the process of extending yourself to one another." From a priest. She'd decided later he equated love with tithing.

"An intense feeling of desire and oneness with another." That she'd come up with on her own, after observing young couples defying their parents to be with the objects of their desires.

"Love is eternal and unconditional." That had been her last guess, and although she'd felt very strongly about it, it too had been wrong.

Eight guesses. Eight failures.

She didn't think about the ninth time. That time, she'd not guessed. Instead, she'd plunged herself into the ice-filled river, intent upon ending her torment. And instead found herself back in statue form and fully awake for several years. It had been true horror.

No, she wouldn't think about that. Instead, she concentrated on Sami, who apparently knew her way about this computer rather well. She'd already started up more pictures, this one showing a cartoon mouse.

"What is this?" she asked.

"Daddy set this up for me. It's a game site for kids from Disney."

She understood games. She didn't know what a "Disney" was. "So 'Disney' is the mouse?"

Sami giggled. "No, silly, that's Mickey Mouse." She looked at Amara. "Is it okay if I play? Daddy won't be awake for hours and hours, and I need something to do."

Amara nodded. And spent the next few hours getting to know Sami while the girl sat on her lap and played games. It felt good, having this little girl curled up against her, chattering away about all sorts of things.

Despite her deadline, despite the darkness facing her, Amara had never felt so happy in her life.

Chapter Three

"Tell me again why we're doing this," Nick grumbled.

Sami rolled her eyes as she tugged on one red mitten. "She wants to visit the priest, Daddy. And you said this is the only time he's not busy."

Nick sighed, glancing down the hallway where Amara had disappeared when he'd asked her about a coat. "She could go alone."

"Daddy..."

Nick contained a wince at Sami's whine. She'd become very attached to this strange woman. Too attached. Nick already regretted letting her stay.

Amara emerged, a fluffy white jacket with a fur-trimmed hood thankfully covering up her very distracting sweater.

"That was in your bundle?" he asked.

She smiled. "I'm a very good packer." She thrust out a pink-gloved hand to Sami. "Ready to go?" Sami slipped her tiny—and vulnerable—hand in hers.

Amara continued looking at Nick with a question in her eyes. "Sami asked me to go ice-skating with you. I hope that's okay."

Nick nearly moaned in frustration. He'd planned this time to get to know Sami better, to spend time only with her. Now a total stranger—a crazy stranger—just showed up and horned in on his time with his daughter.

212

But one look at Sami's hopeful eyes, and all he could do was nod his acceptance.

Sami squealed and Amara laughed. "You might not be so excited when you see how badly I skate. I've never tried before."

"Daddy can teach you. He taught me." She looked up at Nick with those Daddy-is-Superman eyes he loved to see, only this time he wanted to run away from them. He didn't want anything to do with the crazy statue lady, no matter how beautiful her eyes were or how her smile lifted him up somewhere he really didn't want to go.

Sami held him on the edge of an abyss with her gaze.

"Right, Daddy?"

And she shoved him right off the cliff. "Sure, honey."

❄❄❄

"You wanted to see a priest. We saw a priest."

Amara tamped down her growing impatience with Nick. He'd said that several times now, and she could only keep parroting the same thing. "That's not the right priest. They said Father Lattigan will be here soon."

Nick glanced at his watch again. "It's been a half an hour. We can come back later. Or Sami and I can go skating and you can stay."

"No, Daddy."

The office door opened, and an elderly priest entered. "I'm sorry for the wait," he said, turning around and carefully shutting the door. He nodded at Nick, then smiled at Sami. "We've had a bit of excitement around here. Seems one of our statues—" His gaze fell on Amara. His eyes widened.

"Oh, my." He sat in his chair heavily, his gaze never leaving her face.

"Hello, Father." Strange, his voice seemed so familiar to her. Comforting, like an old friend.

"Hello, child. Only you're not a child, are you?" His pale gray eyes regarded her with a mixture of sadness and excitement. "I knew the legend, of course, but I never thought I'd live to see it." He reached across his desk and squeezed her hand. "Yet here you are."

"Is this some joke?" Nick's voice showed his shock, and his anger. "I'm being set up, aren't I?"

Father Lattigan frowned at him. "Please. I'm a man of God. I have no need to play games." He turned his attention back to Amara. "I have so many questions for you."

His smile warmed her heart, and his belief in her plight made her so happy. She had two allies now. She glanced at Nick. And one very firm non-believer.

"I have questions for you. But Nick and Sami want to go skating. They've been very kind and patient."

"Then let them go, and we can each satisfy our curiosity."

Amara laughed. "But I want to go too. I've never skated before. You see," she said gently, "this is my last chance. And considering my lack of success in the past, I want to enjoy my last few hours of freedom."

"Your last chance? Then all the more reason to stay and see if I can help you."

Amara glanced at Sami. "Father, you are very kind. But you see, I think that getting to know Sami is the key. She's the first person to ever see me change."

"You saw that?" Father Lattigan looked at Sami in awe. "What a wonderful thing for you."

Sami didn't return his smile. "What happens to Amara if we don't help her?"

"But we will help her," he said. "Helping people is my life's work." He turned his attention to Nick. "Your father isn't as believing as you."

"And you seem all too eager to believe it yourself," Nick said.

"When I bought the statue, of knew of its 'habit' of disappearing. I know of the legend as well, that the statue is the Countess Amara de la Cortese, who disappeared one Christmas Eve, on the same night the statue appeared." He gazed at Amara, resting his chin on his steepled fingers. "So tell me what your quest consists of, and I'll try to help you while you enjoy life."

"I'm to answer one question. What is the true meaning of love?"

Father Lattigan's eyes widened in surprise. "That can mean so many things. And for each person, it could vary. I'll do a bit of research and when you come back, we'll discuss it. But I'm afraid, child, that the asker of that question is looking for something very deep and very personal—to you."

❋❋❋

"Amara! Look at me!"

Amara looked up at Sami, who did a two-legged spin, with her father standing a few short feet away. Then she grabbed his hand and did a one-legged spin.

Amara dropped her fight with the impossibly long strings on the skates they'd rented and clapped vigorously. "Good job, Sami!"

She looked at the strings balefully. She'd watched Nick tie his own, then Sami's, and thought she could do it, but she'd been very, very wrong. It had looked like a simple bow, but what to do with all the string?

She glanced around. The New York skyline loomed beyond the Central Park trees, fascinating Amara. She would never have believed buildings that tall could exist. And all the people.

She'd seen more people than had lived in her entire town just on the walk to Wollman Rink.

She turned her attention once more to the ice. There were quite a few people enjoying the crisp winter air, the pale sunshine. She hunted for Nick and Sami, and found the little girl several yards away practicing her spins. She didn't see Nick until he surged out of the rink to kneel next to her.

"Here, let me help you." Without waiting for a reply, he picked up one foot and rested it on his bent knee. He wrapped the long strings around her leg, made a complicated gesture which ended up with two loops, then stuffed the remainder of the strings in the top of her skate.

She stared at his handiwork as he swapped feet. "Thank you. You made it look so easy before, but I have to admit I would never have gotten it."

"I don't think I've ever met anyone over six who couldn't tie their own shoes." He glanced up at her, his dark brown gaze assessing. "You've almost convinced me that your fairy tale is true." He finished tying her skate, then stood up and held out his leather-encased hand. "Come on, let's get you out on the ice."

Tentatively, she placed her hand in his. He helped her up to her feet, then walked with her to the ice. He moved so well on those thin metal blades. Amara tried mimicking the way he walked and did quite well, she thought.

Until they stepped on the ice.

Then her feet went in opposite directions, and Amara found herself hanging onto Nick's arm to stay semi-upright, while her butt stuck out behind her.

Nick didn't miss a step but just kept gliding toward Sami. Amara held on for dear life. She looked up at Nick and discovered him smiling at her.

"Relax," he said. "What's the worst that could happen?"

Yes, what was the worst that could happen? She'd fall. Compared to being a statue, falling would be welcome. With a laugh, she pulled on his hand, straightening herself up a bit. "You're right. I'm going to enjoy this." She tried moving her feet the way he did and had some success. "Yes, I'm going to have fun." She smiled at Nick. "Just don't let go."

They reached Sami, and after a minute or two of practicing moving her feet, Amara let them lead her around the rink a few times. The wind nipped her cheeks, music flooded her ears, and she knew that one tiny misstep and she'd fall flat.

She loved it. It was life, and she loved it.

"Okay," she said after the third time around and only one fall. "I'm ready."

"Ready for what?" Sami asked.

"I want to spin, just like you did. Well, not like you did." She looked at Nick, whose dark hair had been ruffled by a soft breeze. "Spin me."

His eyes crinkled as he guided them carefully through the crowd. He seemed impossibly handsome. "Spin you?"

"Yes. I want to feel how it is to twirl without a care. So spin me."

His mouth quirked. "All right. Just do what I do with my feet, okay?"

She dropped Sami's hand and took the other hand he offered her. And while copying his movements, she gripped both his hands tightly, leaned back as instructed and hoped to heaven that he'd not let go.

They picked up speed and soon she felt like she flew over the ice. Her spirit soared and laughter burst out from her. Nick's hands were her only link to the earth and his smile the only gift she ever wanted as she twirled and twirled.

In five hundred years, she'd never felt so free.

Chapter Four

"So this is pizza?" Amara stared at the round pastry smothered in cheese with funny round slabs of meat all over it.

"You've never had pizza?"

She shook her head, aware of Sami and Nick watching her every move. They sat around Nick's tiny dining room table, the one window framing a beautiful sunset. They were all happily tired after a day of skating and "window-shopping". Amara had never thought staring through windows could be so much fun, but these weren't ordinary windows. These were Christmas windows. Sami said her mom told her these windows were magical.

Although a victim of magic herself, Amara didn't think the displays were enchanted, just a marvel of the modern world. But she still enjoyed them. The elves, the moving trains, the dancing children, they all made Sami laugh, so Amara laughed as well. She even got over seeing images of Saint Nicholas, or as the Americans called him, Santa Claus, everywhere. Of course, they displayed a happier and fatter version of her tormenter, so it became rather easy to pretend it wasn't him at all.

They'd stopped a few blocks from Nick's home and gotten a pizza for dinner. A New York style pizza, which apparently meant it was much better than ordinary pizzas Sami could get back home. Since Amara had nothing to compare it to, she let daughter and father joke around about toppings and whether things were truly "bigger in Texas".

Now, though, they expected her to eat this concoction, and with her hands, not with a fork or knife, something she'd used at special occasions when she'd been a Comtesse. She'd rather liked the fact eating utensils were widely used these days, but apparently not with pizza.

So she picked up a slice and bent it slightly down the middle, like Nick did, and took a bite. Hot cheese, thick, chewy bread and tangy sauce. She chewed carefully, trying not to singe her tongue.

"Very good." She took a sip of water. "And very hot."

A few more bites told her she didn't like the meat, called pepperoni, so Nick and Sami laughingly fought over the meat as she handed it to them.

"You have been so kind to me," Amara said. "I would like to make you a Buche de Noel."

"A what?" Nick asked.

Amara smiled. "A Christmas cake. Over the centuries, it took place of our yule log, which is what I grew up with. The last few awakenings, I've learned about this and would like to share it with you. It's a cake, spread with filling, rolled up and frosted and decorated to look like a log. In France, this is on everyone's table. I would like to share this with you."

"Weren't you like a pampered princess? And you know how to cook?" Nick asked.

"Please, I am French, we live for food." She lifted her chin in mock-indignation, and Sami laughed.

Nick frowned. "We have reservations at a local restaurant for a ham dinner. Pie's included. I hate to see you go to too much trouble."

"Oh, Daddy, this sounds much better than pie," Sami said, her small face lit with delight. "And Christmas dinner at a restaurant doesn't sound very Christmassy."

"I know how to cook ham," Amara said.

Nick looked from Amara to his daughter. Over the few years since the divorce, she'd become a stranger to him, with a whole other life. He'd wanted to connect with her so badly this trip, and despite the presence of this strange woman, he felt they'd become closer. Perhaps this dinner would help.

"I don't have any of the food here," he told them.

Amara smiled. "You have a market close by, no? I'll write down what we need, and we'll go shopping. It will only take a moment."

Frowning, Nick glanced out the window. "I'm afraid you have a previous date, Comtesse." He nodded toward the church. There, on the bench next to the now-missing statue, sat Father Lattigan.

❄❄❄

Amara sat quietly in the dark living room of Nick's apartment, the only sound that of the traffic outside. Hot tears stung her eyes.

She'd pinned so much hope on Father Lattigan, but he'd offered her little more than empty advice. "Listen to your heart, child. Love isn't ruled by logic or reason. It's ruled by the heart. When it comes time, look there for your answer."

But her heart still felt as if it were trapped in stone. Had she ever known true love? No. She'd been desired for her beauty and her family's power, but never truly for herself. She'd find no answers from inside.

At least she hadn't lost her temporary home. Nick had left it unlocked for her to return. She'd wondered, for a moment, if he'd use this chance to rid himself of the "crazy woman". Maybe, just maybe, he'd started to believe.

She heard some voices and a key being inserted into the entry door. Amara hastily wiped away an errant tear, stood up, straightened her sweater, planted her fingers in her back pockets as she'd seen Sami do and pasted a welcoming smile on her face.

Only, when she saw Nick and Sami happily chattering as they entered, the smile became genuine.

They'd seemed so distant to each other when she'd first met them. Now they truly enjoyed each other's company.

Nick caught Amara's gaze. "The good father any help?"

Amara shrugged. "It's up to me." She continued to smile, but knew she didn't hide her disappointment well.

Sami crossed to her, setting her bag near the kitchen. She took Amara's chilly hand. "It's okay. It's Christmas time. Miracles happen at Christmas, don't they?" She looked up at Nick, who nodded. Amara thought he hid his doubts well.

"You're right," she said, grinning at the little girl, so beautiful in her childish simplicity. "Let's make a cake, okay?"

❄❄❄

"No, we had no electricity. Or indoor plumbing. Or running water. I like all of that." Amara laughed. Sami giggled as she carefully stirred flour into some beaten egg whites.

Nick, sitting on a kitchen stool, watched his daughter's face as she and Amara worked on the Christmas cake. She seemed so happy, and what about Amara? With the weight of her future on her shoulders, she seemed as carefree as Sami.

Nick still couldn't wrap his head around the fact that she'd ever been a statue, that she came from five hundred years ago or that she needed to break a curse with such a ridiculous question. How hard could it be to define love?

Yet even as he thought it, he knew he'd never quite succeeded. The only love he'd ever been sure of came from his parents, now in Florida with his sister's family. Sami—well, he knew he loved her and, before this visit, thought she loved the idea of a daddy but not really *this* daddy. But when she'd hugged him this afternoon while traipsing through Manhattan, he'd felt her love emanating from her.

So he could sympathize with Amara's plight. He wanted to help her himself. Maybe go online and find some definitions of love?

Then he mentally shook himself. Was he starting to believe all of this? Sami believed, but she thought she'd seen something through tired eyes and a blanket of falling snow. The priest believed, but he'd bought into some French legend that had come with the statue. Nick didn't have any of that cluttering up his head.

Yet he'd let her in his house, near his daughter. A crazy woman or a cursed woman stood in his kitchen teaching his little girl how to make a Christmas log.

He nearly snorted. Maybe his cynicism had melted a tiny bit.

Amara spread the no-stick aluminum foil down on the cookie sheet and carefully poured the batter while Sami scraped the bowl. Small splatters of chocolate batter dotted the little girl's face and Amara's hands. Then Sami opened the oven door—the oven that rarely saw anything more than frozen pizzas—and slid the cake in.

Amara straightened up and smiled. "You're sure about the temperature?" she asked Nick for the tenth time.

He shook his head. "Now who's the cynic? That's what the recipe called out for."

They'd printed a half-dozen recipes off the Internet, and Amara had chosen one she considered fairly simple. But for a woman who'd grown up with wood ovens, the idea of his electric one seemed to fill her with doubt.

"Now we set the timer," Sami said very matter-of-factly.

"A timer?" Amara looked at her in confusion. "What's a timer?"

Nick smiled, stood up and punched the timer button on the stove. "What does the recipe say for how long to cook?" he asked.

Amara searched the print-out. He still marveled over her reading skills—if she were from France, how did she know English? Her explanation of a magical wafer seemed rather far-fetched.

But so did her very existence.

And the clothes. He'd seen that bundle. He'd lifted it himself. There could be no way that fat jacket, those jeans and sweater had been in that package that had been barely two inches thick and the size of a phone book. No way.

Then, where had it all come from?

He shook himself mentally. He was a doctor, damn it. He dealt in scientific facts. Nothing in his life had prepared him for any of this.

"Ten to twelve minutes," she said.

Nick set the timer for ten and sat back down.

He watched as the two of them started making something called marzipan. Amara looked up at him and her half-smile and the twinkle in her eyes made him forget that none of this could be real.

All he knew was that with one tiny smile his cares melted away.

❄❄❄

"Sami, hand me another plate, will you?" Nick glanced at his daughter, wearing an oversized apron, as the three of them served up Christmas breakfast at the local homeless shelter. He and his co-workers did this every year, and this year was no different. This year marked the first time he'd ever brought anyone with him, and they'd greeted Sami with welcoming smiles and "she's adorable", and Amara with questions in their eyes.

He'd had no answers for them.

Amara, despite her purported royal bloodline, pitched right in, pouring glass after glass of orange juice and doling out smiles to everyone. It didn't matter that very few returned the smile, she still beamed at them. Especially at the children. She would also hand them a tiny candy cane that the shelter had piles of.

Yet somehow she carried a aura of sadness. When the line died down a bit, he stepped around his daughter and leaned into her.

"Why so sad?" he asked, his voice barely a whisper.

She bowed her head. "These people—they remind me of the villagers under my rule. Sad, hollow eyes, without any hope. It reminds me of how cruel I'd truly been." She lifted glittering eyes to him. "I imprisoned a man for stealing food for his family on Christmas Eve. I threatened his children. Little children, who only wanted food."

"Amara..." He didn't know what to say. She'd not shown any hard-hearted tendencies around him.

"I was a monster." She grabbed another glass of juice, gave out another smile.

"Obviously you've changed a lot," he said. "Maybe that's the whole point of this. To change into a better person."

Although he could only see her profile now, he couldn't miss the tremble of her hands. "This change—how do you think it will help me when I'm frozen into stone?"

❄❄❄

Christmas carolers belted out a rock-beat version of "Silent Night" as Nick and Sami held hands, with Amara on Sami's other side. None of her anguish showed on her beautiful face, and she laughed with the crowd when children sporting antlers and large noses acted out "Rudolph, the Red-nosed Reindeer".

Then Santa appeared, doing a solo of "Santa Claus is Coming to Town" and Amara stopped smiling. She stared up above the singers, at the huge Christmas tree, and Nick wondered why. He'd noticed a similar reaction in her when they'd been admiring the window displays.

She called Nicholas, Daddy. She was calling for you. No, she hadn't. She'd been calling for—Saint Nick?

Was that who'd done this to her? A jolly old elf had turned her into a statue?

I threatened his children. Saint Nick's legend spoke of protecting the children. Had this been his way of stopping their suffering?

Oh gawd. He was starting to believe all of this.

They walked toward home, and Nick pondered all of it. Amara, Saint Nick, the statue, her predicament. Somehow, it all made sense. In a crazy, bizarre way, it did all fit together.

He wanted to talk to the priest again, ask him more about the legend. Somewhere in there might be a way to free Amara.

Chapter Five

"Was it good?" Amara looked around expectantly, and her childish need for approval caused Nick to laugh.

He swallowed a bite and said, "Yes, it was wonderful. Amazing what you can do with ham."

Amara shook her head. "I've never seen such a thing as a canned ham. Who would have thought? But I will miss the bone." She shook a fork at him. "Good soup with the bone."

Even as she said it, it struck her—she wouldn't be here tomorrow to have used that bone in soup. These last two days, they'd been wonderful, like an amazing gift. But she knew that in six hours, it would be over. She fingered the little necklace Sami had made her out of beads and given her that morning. Made with childish fingers, it was rough and crude, nothing like the jewels that had adorned her as Comtesse, but she found them more beautiful than anything that had ever touched her skin, because they came with love.

Her heart filled with warmth as she gazed at the little girl. Then she glanced at Nick, found him watching her. His eyes held questions, but also admiration. He was so handsome, and when he laughed, she felt her pulse jump. All day thoughts of kissing him flitted through her mind, and she determined right then and there that before midnight she'd steal a kiss. It would be something to cling to if she once again became stone.

The thought of kissing him brought heat and a smile to her face. He looked at her questioningly, and she could only smile larger.

"Who wants dessert?" She scooted away from the table, grabbing plates to clear as she went. Nick stood as well, picking up some items.

Once they entered the kitchen, he asked her, "What was that smile about?"

She shook her head. No way would she tell him what she wanted. "I'm happy. You and Sami—you make me happy."

He eyed her with doubt. "I'm not quite buying that, Comtesse. You're up to something." He finished scraping his plate and set it in the dishwasher. Another appliance she adored. "But it can wait until later. For now, let's get that dessert."

"Oh, no. I worked very hard on this after you two went to bed. Go sit down. I want to make an entrance."

With a faint protest, Nick let her shove him back into the dining room. Then Amara went to the fridge and pulled out the cake she'd hidden under a tent of aluminum foil. Peeling it off, she gazed at her creation.

It looked wonderful, just like a log, with marzipan mushrooms, leaves and holly berries. She grabbed the powdered sugar and placing some on her palm, blew on it gently, causing it to rain down over the cake like frost. Grinning happily, she picked up the platter and carried it into the dining room. She wanted to see the joy on their faces at what she'd done.

And when they ooh'ed and ahh'ed over the creation, it filled her with such warmth that all she could do was laugh.

❄❄❄

"Goodnight, sweetheart." Amara leaned over the sleeping Sami and, caressing her hair back off her cheek, kissed her. The little girl had fallen asleep while her father had read her one of the new books he'd gotten her for Christmas. She'd tried to stay awake until midnight, to find out what would happen to Amara, but she'd not come close.

It was almost eleven. A little over one hour.

Amara returned to the living room to find Nick sitting on the couch, watching her. She sat next to him.

"So, how does this work? Do you return and he magically appears?"

She nodded. "If I don't return, he calls me there, right at midnight. Then I give him my answer. If I fail, I return to being the statue. If I succeed—" Her smile felt weak. "I've never succeeded, so I don't know what would happen."

"Don't say 'if'. Say 'when'.'"

She didn't want to hope too hard. And she didn't want him to worry. "Whatever happens, it will be as it should be." She spread her hands. "I've had a wonderful two days, Nick. Thank you for that gift."

"You're welcome." He picked up one of her hands. "You gave me a gift as well. You gave me my daughter back." His face became somber. "We'd grown so far apart, and now, I feel we have a good shot at a real relationship.

"Thank you for that." His words were another blessing.

He smiled and Amara decided to take her one last gift from him.

With a swiftness born of nerves, she leaned in and pressed her lips to his. Then pulled back. Even in that brief touch, a shock wave entered her, and things inside her bubbled up. As if her life had finally come to fruition. She could only stare at him in wonder.

But Nick didn't waste any time staring. His hand cupped the back of her head and he pulled her to him.

And caught her lips in a searing kiss.

If she'd thought things bubbled before, now they boiled in ways she'd never experienced. She moved against him, pressing her body into his, wrapping her arms about him and soaking in everything she could. The roughness of his stubble against her face, the feel of his fingers in her hair, the smell of his skin.

All of it would be burned forever in her memories.

His tongue pressed past her lips, and she moaned. It felt exquisite, it felt like she'd waited just for this moment.

But when his hand traveled to her breast, she knew it had to end. She understood now that sex would be like a promise to him of a future, and she had no future to give him.

She pulled away and, with a small smile, stood. "Thank you. I'll cherish it forever." With that, she went into her room and shut the door.

Then she sat down and wrote Sami a note, telling her how their time spent together had meant so much. When she finished, she glanced at the little clock in her room.

Less than an hour to go.

Nick looked out the window at the empty statue base. Would she really end up back there at midnight, or was this all a far-fetched hoax?

He wouldn't know until after midnight, if even then.

"Daddy."

He whirled around and saw Sami standing there, rubbing one eye.

"Honey, what are you doing up? You should be in bed." He scooped her up and carried her back to her room.

"Where's Amara? She's still here, isn't she?"

He laid her back on her bed and pulled the covers over her. "Yes, sweetheart, she's in her room."

"I want her to stay."

Her words tore into Nick. How could he promise her anything when he didn't know himself what the truth was?

He thought of the kiss he'd shared with Amara. It had been incredible, bringing alive feelings he'd thought he'd long outgrown. But how could any of this be real? That empty base outside. How could she be who she claimed to be?

All his doubts raged forward as he struggled for an answer to Sami's demand.

"Honey, she can't stay. She'd not like a puppy we can simply adopt. If she's telling the truth, then she might become a statue. If she's not—well, then we need to get her some help."

Sami stared at her father. "Mom's right, you don't believe in nothing!"

Sami's anger shocked him. "Your mom said that to you?"

"She said that to Roger." Roger, her step-father. "And she was right. Amara's heart isn't stone. Yours is!"

"Sami..."

"Just go away!" Sami twisted away from him and, pulling the covers up, slid all the way under them. "I don't want to be here any more. I want to go home."

Nick sat there for a moment, wishing he knew what to say. But no brilliant answer came to him. One thing he did know.

If his heart had been made of stone, it wouldn't ache so much.

Sami waited until she heard her door shut, then dressed quickly. She didn't want to stay around and watch Amara turn into a statue again, and she didn't want to stay with her dad. He was hateful and mean. She'd go home. To Mom.

She knew how. She'd done it many times with her father. She'd catch a cab to the airport, then a plane home. She'd talked to her mother earlier, and she'd sounded like she would love Sami to come home, so she would.

She packed up her small backpack with a few pieces of clothing. She looked out the hallway then, after shutting her door silently, she crept to the front door. She could hear voices in Amara's room. While fighting tears, Sami left the apartment in search of a way home.

"Could you watch Sami for a few minutes? I want to go talk to Father Lattigan." Nick had looked outside and seen the priest sitting at the bench by the statue, as if waiting for the outcome to Amara's story.

Amara nodded as she glanced at the clock. All her clothes lay neatly folded on the bed, which was perfectly made. The room looked like nobody had ever stayed there. "Please don't be gone too long. I don't want her alone when I—"

She didn't finish, but he knew. One way or another Amara would be gone.

"I won't be long."

He closed the door and resisted an urge to look in on his daughter. Either she'd be awake and angry or sleeping with a broken heart. Either one he couldn't deal with right now. Right now, all he could hope was that between him and Father Lattigan, they could come up with a solution.

"So that's it? We just wait and see?" Nick's frustration boiled at the priest's answer to his question—how they could help Amara.

Father Lattigan nodded. "It's up to her now. The answer she needs is inside her."

231

Nick wanted to pound on something. "She's answered this question nine times. She's failed nine times. How is this time any different?"

"Eight times."

"Excuse me?"

"She answered eight times. Once she...refused to answer. And what's different this time is that she's met you. You and Sami. I believe that's changed her profoundly."

Nick remembered her kiss, how sweet and sexy and somehow innocent it had been. Those kisses had affected him deeply. Could they possibly have given Amara the answer?

"It seems like a hell of a gamble for her life."

"Nick!" Amara raced across the street, her dark hair flying about her.

"Amara. Where's Sami?"

"I hoped you knew. Oh, dear heaven, I'd hoped you knew. I went to say goodbye—her bed's empty, and her coat and backpack are gone."

I want to go home.

Fear clutched at him. "She's run away. She's six, she's alone in New York City. She's trying to go home." He felt panic envelop him as he thought about what could happen.

"I'll call the police. You two go look for her." Father Lattigan hurried toward the church.

Nick rushed to the street, Amara following. "We'll do better splitting up," she said.

"No. I don't want you out there alone."

"Nick, I can't be hurt. Trust me. I've tried."

She answered eight times. Once she...refused to answer.

Suicide? Had she become so despondent she'd tried to harm herself? He looked at her, this strong impossible woman. And knew that somehow she'd changed him forever.

"Go." And he took off running.

Amara ran down the deserted street. She'd covered a few blocks now, and no sight of the little girl. Fear propelled her forward. Fear, and love for Sami.

If anything happened to her...

She rounded a corner, and she saw something ahead about a block. A small figure. Could it be—?

Amara started running faster.

Sami wiped another tear from her face. The freezing cold nipped at her wet cheek. She hadn't found any taxis, she didn't know why. Usually all she had to do was go outside and she'd see one. But maybe on Christmas taxi drivers stayed home.

She was scared, and people kept looking at her with cold, hungry eyes. She wanted to go home. She wanted her Mom. Or Daddy. Or Amara.

A sound thundered at her as she walked past a dark alley. With a small scream, she rushed away from the sound and turned the corner.

Up ahead she saw a busier street. There had to be a cab there. She walked to stand under a street lamp and started watching for a taxi.

"Sami!" Turning, she saw someone walking toward her. A tall man hidden in shadows, heavier than her dad, walked straight toward her.

Never talk to strangers. Sami's mother's words reverberated in her head.

Run.

She turned and ran around the corner, then stopped in fear. Someone ran at her.

In a panic she turned and fled from both of them.

Right into the path of a car.

Chapter Six

"Sami!"

Amara watched in horror as the little girl hit the pavement. With a scream, she rushed to her.

She lay there, not moving. Amara reached for her. "Sami, no. Sami!"

"Don't touch her." A man grabbed her arm. With a shout, she pulled away.

"It's okay, I'm a police officer. I called for an ambulance."

"Nick." Amara knelt by Sami, by her still form. *Please don't die.* "She needs her father. Nick. He's looking for her." She gave a brief description of Nick. "He's a doctor. He can save her."

The officer turned and talked into something on his shoulder. "We'll try to find him," he said.

"Oh, Sami, please be okay." She stroked her head, all the while praying.

"Is your name Nick?"

Nick had just yelled for his daughter when a man called out to him. Turning, he saw a uniformed cop leaning out of his patrol car.

"Yeah. I'm looking for my daughter, Sami."

The cop nodded. "We've found her." He motioned for Nick to get in the car. When he'd done so, the cop said, "I have something to tell you."

And Nick knew. Without the officer saying a word, he knew that Sami had been hurt. He closed his eyes in agony as the cop's words confirmed his worst nightmare.

He opened his eyes, bracing himself for reality, hoping for a miracle. The siren and flashing lights seemed unreal. One block, two blocks, then an officer watching for them. Amara. And a small bundle lying in the street.

Sami.

"Sami! Oh God, baby." Nick flew to her side. She lay crumpled on the street, Amara's coat covering her. Instinctively his fingers went to her throat. A pulse, but thready.

He opened one of her eyes, and his heart crashed. The pupil was dilated. He covered the eye and removed his hand. The streetlight shown right into it, but no change.

Brain damage.

He closed his eyes, unable to stand the pain.

"Nick?" He felt Amara's hand on his arm. "Can you save her?"

He couldn't answer her. He couldn't talk. His little girl was gone. He couldn't help her. He couldn't save her.

In the end, all he could do was watch her die.

Watching Nick, Amara knew. Sami would die.

"No."

The little girl had become too precious to her. She couldn't let it happen. Maybe she could stop it.

"Nicholas!" She stood up, stepping away from Sami and her dad. "Nicholas! I know you can hear me. I want to bargain with you. Nicholas, do you hear me?" She sucked in a deep breath, ignoring the two officers and the driver who stared at her as if she were insane.

Why should I bargain with you? She felt him, heard his words in her mind, like a whisper.

"Because of her. Because of Sami. She's precious, don't you see?" Amara sobbed now. "She deserves a good life. So I'll give you my life for hers. My soul for hers. Take me, Nicholas! Let her live! Heal her, Nicholas!"

Do you love her that much, Amara, that you'll sacrifice yourself for her? After all, she's only one child. You might have won your freedom this time.

"I don't care!" She looked back at Sami, at Nick who stood now, watching her in shock. She turned around, and she could see Nicholas, his tall form cloaked in red, his face looking at her almost kindly. "I don't matter, don't you see? She matters. She's the one with the loving heart. She's the one with the bright future, who deserves a second chance." She felt wet heat on her cheeks. "Not me." She took a step forward. "I'll do whatever it takes, Nicholas. Please."

Yourself for her.

"Yes." She nodded, and when he nodded in return, she sobbed her relief. "Thank you, Nicholas. Thank you."

Then the saint disappeared, and she turned back to Sami. Nick stood there, staring at her. "What have you done? Amara, what did you just do?"

She took in his dark eyes, the angles of his face, his lips that she longed to taste again. This moment, she thought, would last her an eternity. Then she looked past him and what she saw made it all worthwhile.

"Nick, look."

He turned and she laughed at his stunned expression. Laughed, then ran.

Because Sami was sitting up.

"Daddy? What happened?"

Amara reached her, held out her arms to her, but Nick held her back.

"No, she might be hurt." With his free hand, he checked Sami out, looking in her eyes. They were fine, Amara knew.

"She's fine." Beyond Nick's arm, she smiled at the girl. "Aren't you?"

"The car hit me, didn't it? Amara, were you talking to Santa Claus?"

"You saw that?" Finally, Nick let her loose, and she grabbed hold of the little girl. "You saw him."

Nick wrapped himself around both of them, pulling the three of them into a tight ball. He kissed Sami fiercely, several times.

"No, not really," Sami said, her voice muffled by her dad's hug. "I heard him, and I knew who he was."

"I could feel something," Nick said. "It was like someone stood there, just out of sight."

Amara began to tingle, then she felt it—the tug, the pull. She knew her time had run out. "I have to leave now, Sami." She hugged the girl tighter.

"You're going to go tell Santa your answer now?"

Amara looked down at her and shook her head. "I gave it away, and you know what? I've never been happier. I want you to know, you've given me the best present ever. Because of you, I learned how to truly love." She could see her hands starting to fade. Before it was too late, she kissed Sami's forehead.

"Goodbye."

"No, Amara! Don't go!"

She turned her gaze to Nick, who watched her with a look bordering on despair. She could admit it now. She'd fallen in love with him.

Their gazes locked, and Amara told him everything in that one instant, without ever uttering a word. Unbidden, one hand reached for him. They touched, and for a moment, she felt that sizzle, that recognition that here, finally, she'd found the missing piece of her soul.

Then there was nothing.

"No!"

Nick grasped at Amara, but nothing stopped her from fading away. His body screamed at the loss, his heart pounded at the message she'd sent him.

She loved him.

He looked down at Sami, still clutched in his arms, and up at the cops, who looked as stunned as he felt. Then at his watch, whose glowing dial stated he had under ten minutes to do something, anything.

"Sami, honey, I have to run. Literally. Baby, stay with these kind officers, who'll bring you home. Okay?" He looked at the cops, and one nodded as if in a daze. Then the other officer shook himself, nodded at his car, with the lights flashing on the roof.

"I'll drive you."

"And I'm going too, Daddy."

He looked at Sami's stubborn little face, to the cop's, then nodded. "All right, let's go."

It took them only a moment to get to the church. Nick closed his eyes briefly at the sight. It hurt too damned much.

The statue stood there, on its pedestal, with arms reaching out, just as before.

Silently, he and Sami exited the car. As they approached, he lifted Sami up, who'd begun to cry. At the base stood Father Lattigan. He smiled at Sami, obviously relieved she was okay. He looked up at the statue, one tear silently traversing his weathered cheek.

"The inscription's changed," he said. "It reads, 'Amara—a loving heart who gave her life for another'. And she's smiling now."

Nick looked up, and what Father Lattigan said was true. The statue of Amara—his Amara—radiated with true joy, where before she'd been almost expressionless.

"Daddy," Sami breathed, "She's wearing my necklace."

The sight of Sami's little beads, now encased in stone, brought unspeakable sorrow to bear.

It had been true. All of it. Now, he'd lost her forever.

Sami reached out to the statue, and Nick took her closer until she could wrap her arms about her. Amara wore her original robes and stood in the same pose as before, but Nick could feel the changes. Because now a good chunk of his heart stood frozen in that statue.

Damned if he'd let her go without a fight.

"Nicholas!" If the stakes weren't so high, he'd feel like a fool, standing in the middle of New York City yelling at a ghost, a spirit. "I understand why you imprisoned her all those years ago. She said herself she was a bad person. But she's not now. She just sacrificed her last chance at freedom for a little girl she only met two days ago. She's changed. You got what you wanted. She grew a heart. Now you're going to freeze that loving, giving heart?"

He looked around him. Nothing. When Amara had spoken to the saint, Nick had felt *something*.

He looked at his daughter, who hugged Amara, tears coating her cheeks. A few minutes ago, she lay dying. Now, she walked and talked. A true Christmas miracle.

But Nick wanted more.

"You gave Amara only part of her deal. She bargained her life away, and you didn't deliver. Look at my little girl, Nicholas!

Look at her. She might be alive, but she's not healed. Because you took Amara away from her, she now has a broken heart."

"Daddy!" Sami lifted her eyes to Nick. "Daddy, you're yelling at Santa Claus."

Nick looked at Father Lattigan, then at the cop. The cop shrugged, but Father Lattigan said, "I would say that under the circumstances, yelling would be acceptable."

Nick looked up at Amara. Somewhere, a clock began to toll. Midnight.

Right then, Nick felt it. That same surety of someone standing near.

And what are you willing to sacrifice for Amara? Because I agree, she has changed and become very precious.

Nick closed his eyes in relief. Saint Nicholas had answered. There was still a chance. "I'd give my life to her." Opening his eyes, he saw Nicholas shimmering several feet away, his bright eyes expectant. "Whatever it will take to make her happy, I'll do it. She'll never spend another day not knowing love."

That is a very ambitious promise.

"And I mean every word of it. Will you accept?"

Nicholas smiled widely. *It's not up to me.* He looked past Nick.

Nick turned around. Kneeling on the statue's pedestal was Amara, holding Sami.

Amara, you have exceeded my every wish for you. There's a saying that actions speak louder than words, and your unselfish sacrifice of yourself for Sami tells me that you learned the true meaning of love.

To truly love someone means that you'd die for that person. There is no greater love than that.

Nicholas walked past the dumbstruck cop, nodded at Father Lattigan and stopped between Nick and Amara. He lifted his staff and it burst into light.

Amara de la Cortesse, I declare you free. Please, child, come away from the pedestal.

Amara, looking numb and obviously overwhelmed, didn't move for a moment, until the light flared brightly above her. Then she and Sami scurried off. Before their eyes, the statue returned, looking as it had for centuries.

A gift to you, Father Lattigan, for comforting this child with your presence.

The good father nodded as he stared at the statue. Nick noticed the beads were gone from this version. The originals hung around Amara's neck.

Child, this man is willing to devote his life to you. But you are free now, and as my Christmas gift to you I will grant you a life anywhere you wish to go. Name the place and I'll give you the tools to start a new life.

Amara looked at Nicholas as she assessed his words. *You are free now.* She'd waited several lifetimes to hear those words. But right now she longed to hear four other words spoken from another Nicholas.

Amara, I love you.

She felt Sami's hand tighten in hers. "Santa Claus, I always thought you were a nice person," the little girl said. "But you're very mean to Amara."

The apparition knelt down to eye-level with Sami. *My gift to children five hundred years ago was to remove Amara from them so she could do no harm. My gift to you this year is to let you see how love can transform even the coldest heart.*

"Sami, he was right to do what he did," Amara said. "I understand now. Not only did you save the children, but you gave me many more chances than I deserved to become someone better." Then she uttered the words she'd sworn for five hundred years she'd never say to him. "Thank you."

They felt so good, so right, that she couldn't contain a smile.

Never letting go of Sami's hand, Amara walked past Saint Nicholas until she stood in front of Nick. She captured his gaze with her own and didn't let go. "Nicholas, you asked me to choose a life. To live anywhere in the world I want."

She reached out, and immediately Nick grasped her hand. Recognition flared between them. She looked into his eyes and she didn't need to hear those words. She could read them, bannered across his face.

As she spoke, each word erased the pain and loneliness of the last five centuries. "I choose this. I choose here and now. Nicholas, give me what I've already found."

You are in charge of your own destiny now, child.

Amara didn't see Nicholas fade, she didn't hear his soft chuckle or witness his lingering gaze filled with warmth and approval as he left.

Because she was too busy engulfed in Nick's hug, in melting in his kiss, in Sami's fierce embrace about her waist.

"I love you," Nick whispered against her hair.

"I love you." Amara laughed, hugging him intensely, then she wrapped an arm about Sami. She felt a tear stream down her face and shouted, "Thank you, Nicholas! And merry Christmas!"

Nick kissed her again, and with a bark of laughter, he twirled the three of them until they all laughed with joy. Then with a smile of thanks to Father Lattigan and the officer, he said, "Let's go home."

"Home." Amara smiled at her new family. "I love the sound of that." She held onto Nick and Sami's hands and marched boldly into her new life, her new heart full to bursting.

Thank you, Nicholas, she whispered silently, *for everything.*

About the Author

To learn more about Stacia, please visit http://www.staciawolf.com. Send an email to stacia@staciawolf.com.

Look for these titles

Now Available

You'll Be the Death of Me
Pretend You Love Me

Second Chance
Christmas

Mackenzie McKade

Dedication

To my daughters who light up my life. Thank you for your support. I love you.

Chapter One

This was gonna be a helluva night.

Two large fans whirling above Lori Dayton did nothing to ease the sultry flush across her skin, or the increase of her pulse. One set of fiery blue eyes across the room was responsible for her sudden reaction and the instant tightening of her nipples. The man she'd dreamed of for the last four years moved determinedly from the entrance, straight across the dance floor, and past the wraparound bar, toward the poolroom situated at the far end of the establishment where she stood. He didn't speak to her nor did he approach. But he was close—too close.

Focus and forget about Dean Wilcox.

He had clearly forgotten about her.

She diverted her gaze from his hot glare, choosing instead to study the intricate pattern of the tinsel draping the limbs of the large Christmas tree stuck in the corner. It must have taken hours to separate and lay each silver strand precisely an inch apart.

In the distance, she heard the band begin to warm up and laughter rang. The scent of cigarettes mingled with a variety of perfumes and colognes. A beer bottle or glass crashed to the floor. The loud, brittle sound startled her, making Lori's heart lodge midway in her throat. Normal barroom noises, so why was she nervous?

"C'mon, sis, call your shot," Mitch, her partner and brother, impatiently encouraged. His eyes were fixed on the table as he chalked his stick. Will and Lance Carter had challenged them to a game of pool. She hadn't wanted to play, but Mitch never turned down a challenge.

Two local gals had their hungry gazes pinned on Mitch's muscular six-three frame like it was hunting season, and he was their quarry. They sat at a high-top table looking as if they wanted to slink across the room and wrap themselves around him. All three of her brothers were babe material—they had golden hair and eyes to match.

Women thought her brothers were hot, but as far as Lori was concerned, no man came close to the raw sensuality Dean Wilcox oozed. When the two gals who had been eyeing Mitch now ogled Dean, Lori realized she wasn't the only one who thought so.

"Earth to Lori." Mitch pulled her from her thoughts.

Focus.

Narrowing her eyes, she sized up the table. Pool stick in one fist, she dragged the other hand along the cool railing, moving slowly in search of the best shot. She fought not to look at Dean, not wanting to let him know he affected her, but she couldn't help raising her eyes to meet his.

With a condemning stare, he watched her. Only six feet away, he stood with his legs wedged apart, unyielding arms folded across his broad chest. His stance screamed that if she drew any closer to him he would still be miles away, still be untouchable.

Forget him.

"Eleven ball, corner pocket." It would be a stretch, but it appeared her best choice. Leaning forward, she lengthened her five-seven frame across the table. With a jerk of her head she tossed her long blonde hair over her shoulder, and then positioned her fingers—

Well fuck. Her eyes were focused on Dean's zipper, which was directly in line with the corner pocket. The impressive bulge revealed he was erect, hard. The muscles in her throat tightened as she swallowed. She knew that cock, knew its length and girth, the way it felt sliding between her thighs, filling her to—

Her heart began to pound. *What's the matter with me?* Lust—nothing more. *Remember the man hates you.*

To make the situation more uncomfortable, when she leaned farther down, her T-shirt gaped to give him a direct, unhindered view of her bare breasts—helluva time not to wear a bra.

Dean made no attempt to look away. Instead, his eyes darkened. His nostrils flared.

And just like that her concentration flew out the door. *Adios!* It was gone in a heartbeat.

Once again she found herself thinking of him. Her vaginal muscles clenched as she imagined his strong hands touching her breasts, stroking the ache inside her. Her panties dampened.

She licked her suddenly dry lips, blinked.

Focus.

It wasn't like he hadn't seen her breasts before. But each time she slipped the stick back and forth between the cradle of her thumb and forefinger, she thought of Dean buried deep and rocking inside her needy core.

Stop it.

With more force than she intended, she thrust her stick forward and struck the cue ball lower than anticipated.

In horror, she watched the spinning white ball rise from the felt, clear the rail, and nail Dean dead center of his groin.

They say cowboys don't cry...

Evidently, they do if hit squarely in the nuts. Then all bets are off. They crumble like a day-old cookie to their knees. At least that's what Dean did.

With a gut-wrenching "ugh", he folded over, cupping his jean-clad crotch. She caught a glimpse of his painful expression as his golden skin tone drained to a pasty white. Like a snowman in the middle of summer, he melted and dropped to his knees. His head followed, bowing low.

"Ouch," a choir of rowdy cowboys cried in unison, hugging their cocks. Then they began to laugh hysterically at their fallen friend.

Exactly what a man found funny about seeing another man getting his balls crushed Lori would never understand. Perhaps they were simply glad it was Dean and not one of them.

With a grin, Will retrieved the cue ball and positioned it behind the invisible boundary on the table. With ease, he stretched his tall frame over the ocean of green felt, then slid his pool stick through his fingers. "Mitch, your sister's been back, what—two hours? Already the men in Safford have to watch their gonads."

Lori restrained the urge to chuck the eight ball at *his* crotch. Instead, despite the warning in her head, she went to Dean's side.

Crouched down next to him, she inhaled the warm scent of Old Spice. A tremor visibly shook him. Her hand wavered awkwardly above his shoulder as she fought the need to touch him. "Anything I can do?"

He yanked his head up, tossing back locks of wavy, black hair from his face. Blue eyes watered with the effort it took for him to breathe. "Get away from me," he growled.

She flinched.

Those were the exact words he had spoken to her the last time she'd seen him. Funny they would be the first ones she heard returning home. With a weighted sigh, she rose to her feet.

So he hadn't forgiven her. Not quite what she had hoped their reunion would be after all this time.

As she retraced her steps, Lori chastised herself. She should have never accepted her mom's invitation to come home for Christmas. Four years hadn't made a dent in Dean's anger.

Time hadn't changed her either. She still loved him more than ever. She crammed her hand in the front pocket of her jeans. The minute he had walked into the bar tonight, Lori went into meltdown. If anything, the man had matured and gotten better-looking. The distance between San Diego, California and Safford, Arizona hadn't been far enough to chase him from her memory.

With leaden feet, she eased next to her brother. Mitch folded his brawny arm around her shoulders and squeezed.

"I'm going home," she whispered, choking back tears she swore she wouldn't shed. Tears that blurred the red, green and blue string of Christmas lights blinking above the bar.

It didn't look to be a promising holiday.

"Ahhh...sis. Don't let him ruin your night. It was an accident. It's Christmas Eve—let's celebrate." Mitch leaned down and kissed her forehead.

A tear rolled down her cheek.

"Ignore him," Mitch said. Her oldest brother was always there when she needed him. But at this moment she needed out of this place. "Visit the ladies' room and wipe those eyes." He looked away and watched the balls race across the pool table. The blue number two ball made a beeline for the center pocket and fell. "Damn." He turned his attention back to her. "When you get back, all this will be forgotten." He grabbed her nose and shook it like he had done since childhood.

Forgotten? Now didn't that sound simple?

Betrayal and guilt all washed away by taking a pee and wiping her eyes. Yeah, right. Mitch had quite a sense of humor. Clearly, Dean hadn't forgotten that rainy day and neither would Lori.

With a duck of her head, she slipped from beneath Mitch's arm and headed in the direction of the restroom. The Hillside Bar hadn't changed much. The rustic atmosphere screamed cowboy and there were a lot of them here tonight. She didn't even make it halfway to the bathroom before one of the men stopped her.

"Hey, pretty lady, how about a dance?" Rusty was a regular, had been since they graduated high school together.

Lori frowned. "Not now."

Strong fingers curled around her biceps. "Lori, I haven't held anything as pretty as you in such a long time." Rusty's copper gaze made a complete sweep from her boots to her eyes.

A sharp jerk of her arm and she freed herself. "It looks like your luck hasn't changed, Red." Red was the nickname she had called him in school because of his beautiful auburn hair.

With a single step forward, he crowded her personal space. "Ahhh... Honey, don't be that way."

She really hated being called honey. "Rusty, you're drunk."

He crinkled his nose in a way that highlighted the devilment in his eyes. If she was in the market for a cowboy, she would consider the one standing before her. They had been friends in school, even went out a time or two. But it was Dean who had captured her heart.

"And you're still gorgeous." He leaned in for a kiss. Someone grabbed his arm and pulled. A surprised grunt left his mouth as he flew backward and landed on his ass.

"Keep your hands off her," Dean growled, fists balled. His face was still a bit pale, but anger showed clearly in the creases of his forehead.

Rusty jumped to his feet. "What the fuck is your problem?"

Lori wedged herself between them. Ready to... What? Stop two men from fighting?

When pigs fly. She stepped aside.

Rusty glanced from Dean to Lori. He shook his head. "Man, I didn't know you two were still an item."

"We're not," Lori responded a little too quickly.

"That's right." Heat smoldered in Dean's eyes when they met hers. "We're not." He swept by her, brushing against her shoulder as he headed for the bathroom.

Lori couldn't breathe. What was wrong with her? It was a simple touch.

"You okay, Lori?" Rusty's concerned gaze searched her face.

Emotion burned behind her eyelids, but she kept her tears from falling. "Yeah."

"Wanna talk?" he asked. "Or how 'bout I buy you a beer? We could drink away our troubles together."

A false smile touched her lips. "Why the hell not? Make it a Long Island iced tea and it's a deal."

He grabbed her hand. "C'mon, sweet thang. Let's find a table."

Maneuvering around the crowded dance floor, they found a table next to the band and sat. A waitress wearing tight blue jeans, a low-cut sweater, boots and a red and white Santa hat walked up. Rusty gave her their order and she moved off with a sway to her hips.

Lori snatched up the napkin the woman left and wiped her eyes and nose.

Casually, Rusty leaned back in his chair, causing it to tilt on its back legs. "So, Lori, what'cha been up to?"

She sat on the edge of her seat. The damn man was going to fall he was perched so far back on his own chair. "Nothing much. I run the mixer for a band in San Diego, and I'm going to school."

"Still sing?"

"A little." Lori didn't like the gleam in his eyes as he started to rise. "Rusty, don't you do it."

But it was too late. He was already out of his chair and speaking to the lead singer. The man grinned and nodded. Then his voice echoed in the microphone, "We have a special treat for you. One of your own is going to sing for you tonight. Lori Dayton." He applauded.

She shook her head.

"C'mon, Lori." Rusty grasped her hand and pulled her resisting form out of the chair. A tight squeal escaped her lips as he picked her up and deposited her on the stage. His light laughter made her grin.

Damn man.

"What would you like to sing?" the band member asked.

"Oh, pick anything country."

He glanced over his shoulder. "Trisha Yearwood. 'How Do I Live'?"

Lori froze. *Any song, but that one.* She started to say something, but the piano player's fingers fell across the keys and the drummer played the slow beat with his sticks.

A breath filled her lungs. She held it, before releasing it slowly. Then her mouth opened and the words flowed.

It hurt to sing this particular song, because it hit too close to home. Day after day, she had asked herself how she would get through one night after the next without Dean. The days had been long, the nights longer, and lonely. She had learned to live without him. It hadn't been easy. But she had survived—barely.

And then the song got even more difficult.

As she scanned the crowd, her gaze locked onto Dean's. He stood by the door—he was leaving, no doubt. His black Stetson was tugged low. His shoulders were rigid, making his six-foot frame seem taller, larger than life at the back of the room.

Clearly he didn't want to talk to her and she respected that. But if he was going to just stand there, he would hear her true feelings expressed in a song. Once he had enjoyed listening to her sing and loved dancing naked beneath the stars as he held her tight. One more time she would sing just to him.

Everyone in the bar disappeared seconds before the chorus to the song approached. Raw emotions spilled from her mouth. Words from her heart tumbled out. She was unable to hold back the pain that had been trapped inside her for four years. In that space of time she didn't care if she opened her heart and revealed the truth.

It had been hell living without him.

When she finished singing and the last chord faded, he still hadn't left the bar. She barely heard the crowd's applause. His expression was unreadable. Still he continued to stare at her. Eyes turning misty, she broke contact and turned toward the steps leading off the stage. But once again she found herself dragged back to the microphone.

"Let's sing a duet." The lead singer grinned ear to ear. "'Pictures' by Sheryl Crow and Kid Rock," he said to his band. Before she could tell him no, the guitarist strummed his instrument and the man next to her began to sing in a low, slow cadence.

Okay. Fine. But this was the last one, even if she had to jump from the stage.

The moment was awkward as the lead singer's bedroom eyes caressed her. He pretended to croon only for her, a sexy grin on his face. She was lost with what to do with her hands hanging listlessly by her side. It had been a while since she played this flirtatious game for the audience.

Everything was an act.

He dipped his finger beneath her chin, then stroked her cheek. The backup singers sung a measure of *oh's*. Their harmony signaled her turn to sing. She stumbled on the first word, but quickly fell into the slow rhythm. Closing her eyes helped her to feel the music, her body moving with a gentle sway.

When her eyes opened, she saw Dean had moved closer. His hat was in his hands. He must have decided to stay.

Oh goodie.

Chapter Two

Nothing had changed.

Lori still heated Dean's blood like no other woman had. Mesmerized, he had been unable to break the link between them when she began to sing. Her voice was silky, sexy. Like always, she sang from the heart and tore at his, the words describing how he had felt these past four years.

Damn. You're a fool, Dean Wilcox, he thought when the song ended and his feet refused to carry him out of the bar.

Even after all she'd done, he couldn't resist the urge to take her in his arms, feel her body pressed to his. He wanted to kiss her so badly he was seeing red.

A soft growl rumbled in his chest as the lead singer stroked her with his lusty gaze, but then she opened her mouth and he was lost again.

Lord. The woman had a way of turning him every which way but loose. If it wasn't her voice wrapping him in ecstasy, it was her body. He closed his eyes and let her words caress him. The last time he had made love to her she had cried, soft tears rolling down her cheeks, as she'd whispered, "I love you."

His gaze rose to watch the sway of her body in rhythm with the music. He wanted her naked, moving against him like that. Even the remaining ache in his balls didn't stop his wayward thoughts. Thank God the cue ball had struck the area where his groin and thigh met, or he'd be one hurting puppy. The spaghetti straps of her shirt fell over each shoulder and he had the uncontrollable urge to shove the material farther, down to her waist to bare her breasts. Taut nipples pressed against the cotton called to him, begging him to stroke them with his tongue.

But that was never going to happen. There was too much history between them.

After high school, scholarships had paved Lori's way to San Diego to attend college. She was getting out of this little town. But not him. Dean worked for his ailing father on their cattle ranch.

The thought of being separated from Lori had torn Dean apart. But he knew his father was dying. His mother needed him. There had been no way he could leave and go with Lori. Nor did he want to squash her dreams of an education. So he put his plan to ask her to marry him on hold. He loved her enough to wait.

The song ended and she nearly dove off the stage into Rusty's open arms. Jealousy raised its head and sent fire up Dean's throat to smolder across his face. Rusty swung her around before her body slid down his and she stepped away. She picked up the drink from the table and took a long, healthy chug. Long Island iced teas were her favorite. If she drank them like that all night, she'd be under the table passed out in no time.

Rusty grabbed her hand and pulled. A giggle bubbled up from her chest, as she barely had time to set the glass down before he pulled her onto the dance floor. Now that wasn't gonna be easy—watching another man hold her in his arms.

Mitch sidled up beside Dean. "Hurt her, and I'll kill you." He leveled Dean with a steely glare, and then quietly walked away.

Message received loud and clear. There was no doubt in Dean's mind Mitch meant what he said, and Chris and Ty Dayton would be right there to help their brother. They watched over Lori like three grizzly bears.

In fact, it was Mitch who revealed Lori was two months pregnant four years ago. When Dean had confronted her, she grew defensive and informed him that she was unsure whether she would keep the baby.

He'd blown up—it was his child.

They'd fought.

He'd spoken harshly. She left hurt and angry, splashing through the puddles in her little sports car as she sped away.

The memory was so raw, like it happened only yesterday.

He closed his eyes. Pain and regret washed over him.

It had been dark and raining. The streets were slick. Lori's taillights swung sharply left then right, before fading around the corner. He stood for what seemed like forever, drenched and confused that she had refused his marriage proposal. He turned to go inside when he heard the crash of metal. Without a second thought, he jumped into his truck and roared down the road. High-pitched sirens and flashing lights followed not far behind.

But it was too late.

He brought his truck to a screeching halt and ran to the car as a fire truck roared up behind him.

Blood. Everywhere.

In moments, the paramedics were loading Lori into the ambulance.

Later at the hospital, when Mitch told him Lori lost the baby, Dean had gone crazy. This had been his fault. If he'd only handled the situation differently. If only she had loved him as deeply as he loved her.

When he finally pulled himself together, Lori was gone—without a goodbye, she had left for California.

Four years passed without a call or a letter. This was her first visit back home since that fateful day.

The song ended and Lori headed straight to her drink. She chugged the remaining liquid. It was clear to Dean what her plan was—the woman couldn't hold her liquor. With a satisfied male grin, Rusty flagged the waitress for another drink.

This little scene had disaster written all over it. And there was no way Dean would stand idly by and watch her walk out of this bar with Rusty tonight.

As Rusty hauled her onto the dance floor again, Dean intercepted them. "My turn."

"I don't think so." Lori's face was flushed.

"Don't argue with me, darlin'." He and Rusty exchanged a silent look of understanding. Dean pulled her out of Rusty's arms and into his.

The minute their bodies touched, it felt like Lori had never been gone. She fit perfectly against him. The ends of her hair brushed his hand at the small of her waist.

Her eyes were bright, the liquor starting to take hold. "Don't think you can boss me around."

She trembled beneath his touch, as she always did. The woman was so responsive. The slow rhythm of the music took hold of them and they shuffled across the floor.

When he wedged a leg between hers, pressing it to the vee of her thighs, she gasped. "I don't think this is a good idea."

His cock hardened, lengthening, knowing it was only a heartbeat from where heaven lay.

"Dean?"

He twirled her away from him, pulling her back into his arms to grind his hips to hers when they came together. His hand slipped lower to cup her ass, holding her tightly against his erection.

"Dean, don't do this." Her voice was a soft plea.

He couldn't help himself. Anger and guilt raced through him. He wanted to punish her—punish himself—for the child lost and the time that had separated them.

With a desperate cry, she pulled from his arms and ran for the door.

His eyes briefly closed on a weighted sigh.

God. It was happening all over again.

Then he reacted, pushing through the crowd to follow.

"Dean—"

He heard Mitch call his name before he bolted out the door in pursuit of the woman he still loved.

A chilly breeze struck Lori in the face as she stepped outside. It took her breath away. She gulped down a mouthful of air and tried to stop the tears. Arms folded around herself, she realized her coat hung on the back of a chair in the bar. Goose bumps prickled her skin. But there was no way she was going back in there.

The dim lights of the parking lot shrouded everything in shadows. She stumbled toward her Jeep. Her hands shook. She jabbed one into her pocket to retrieve her car keys, fumbling and dropping them after she set off the automatic unlock feature. She scooped them up quickly.

As she opened the door of her 1999 yellow Jeep, someone grabbed her arm and spun her around, slamming the door in the process.

Her heart stopped.

Dean.

Before she could speak, he sealed her mouth with his. The kiss was hungry, lacking tenderness. With little effort, he forced her lips apart and thrust his tongue inside. He plundered her mouth as if starving to taste every inch of her.

She wedged her hands between them and shoved, but his iron grip remained. She tried to fight him—

Then, like always, she dissolved into a puddle in his arms. He tasted bittersweet, of beer and a second chance. And he kissed her with a hunger she matched.

"Lori?" Mitch's presence broke Dean's kiss, but his mouth remained a breath away from hers. His breathing was labored. He still pinned her to the car with his firm body. If anything, he moved closer, pressing her tighter to him. Over his shoulder she saw Mitch's frown, her coat in his hand. The tension in her brother's jaw said he wasn't happy—not at all.

"I warned you." Menace coated Mitch's three words.

"Back off, Mitch." Dean's tone held the same threat. "This is between Lori and me." As he spoke, his lips moved across hers. Fire raged in his eyes. He wedged his body between her legs.

"Sis?" She heard Mitch's concern. He threw her coat on the hood of her car. Fists balled, his stance was rigid.

Crap. She crammed her keys into her pocket. No way did she want them to fight. "It's okay."

But would it really be?

"Are you sure?" Mitch asked. The vein in his throat ticked.

"Yes. Just give us a minute," she managed to say.

When Mitch pivoted and strolled toward the bar, Lori realized she was at Dean's mercy. A mercy he didn't show. Instead he took her mouth in another scorching kiss.

The cold was forgotten when his warm hands disappeared beneath her shirt and cupped her breasts. As he devoured her with his mouth and tongue, his fingers squeezed her nipples, causing her to gasp. He swallowed her cry and increased the pressure. Rays of sensation headed down south to tighten the already simmering burn in her belly.

She had to touch him.

With a yank, she pulled her hands free from between them and grasped his western shirt. Within seconds, she ripped apart the snaps and taut muscle was beneath her palms.

Their kiss suddenly broke. He stared at her without speaking. She didn't know whether his expression was of anger or passion. But an uncontrollable tremor shook him. He jerked his Stetson from his head and put it on the roof of the car.

"Naked," he choked. "Now."

He didn't wait for her response. Instead he smoothed his hands up her waist and lifted her shirt over her head. He stared at her breasts as he threw the garment to the side. Swirls of air played at her bare nipples, drawing them into painful nubs. Before she could respond, he knelt and tugged at one boot and then the other, leaving her knee-high nylons on. She braced her hands on his shoulders to keep her from falling.

Oh God. Oh God. Oh God.

She stood half-naked in the parking lot of the Hillside Bar. Rational thought told her she should stop Dean, but if she did, the moment could be lost forever. Selfishly, she wanted this night with Dean, needed to feel him buried deep inside her one more time. The entire bar could catch them this second and it wouldn't matter to her.

When he stood, their mouths clashed together. Again, he pressed her firmly against the car. She ignored the chill from the window against her back. His body covered hers like a second skin. He released a cry that wrapped around her heart. There was sadness to his quick, frantic movements. He slanted his head to take her one way and then another, acting as if he couldn't get close enough. His tongue swept her mouth, dueling with her tongue and stealing her breath.

Groans and moans filled her ears.

His? Hers?

With fumbling fingers he worked at unclasping her belt buckle. All the while, he continued to ravish her with his kiss. The hissing of her zipper falling sent a shiver up her back. The parking lot was gravelly beneath her nylon-covered feet. When her jeans dropped to her knees, her bare ass struck the cold car behind her, adding to the rage of sensations she was experiencing.

Then the kiss ended abruptly.

Dean pulled away from her.

"Lori." Shadows of indecision warred in the depths of his gaze.

No. Please don't stop. The thought was a cry in her mind.

A heartbeat ticked. He knelt again and pulled her panties down with her jeans. She raised one foot and then the other, stepping out of her clothing.

Trembling, she looked down at him. He stared at the small patch of hair covering her pussy, causing another rush of desire to anoint her thighs. Strong hands smoothed up her legs, over her hips, and rested at the curves of her waist.

Their eyes locked and held. His were so intense she could feel their heat, their desire.

With unsteady hands, he unfastened his belt and zipper, pushing down his briefs in the process. His cock sprang from its confines, arching toward his bellybutton. Pre-come graced the small slit at the crown.

"Dean." Her voice quivered. She licked her lips.

A deep rumble rose from his chest. Face shadowed by the dim lights, he looked feral, wild. He cupped her ass and raised her, parting her thighs with his body. There was no tender foreplay to their joining, just one violent thrust and he buried himself deep inside her. Then he stilled, holding himself tight against her cradle.

"Fuck." He forced the strained word through clenched teeth.

Her back arched. She cried out at the fullness—the sense of finally coming home.

Chapter Three

Dean fought the burn threatening to rush down his cock as he entered Lori with one thrust. Warm, wet and tighter than he remembered, the instant pleasure was so intense it was painful. He still hadn't recovered completely from the blow she'd given him to the balls, but there wasn't anything in this world that would stop him from taking her. She locked her ankles around his hips and drew him deeper, sending a shudder through his body. If he lost control, came before she did, Lori would know this moment meant more to him than anything in this world.

He had missed her so much. Only his anger—oh, who was he kidding—his hurt had helped him to survive without her. He was as guilty as she was for what had happened.

Moisture touched his eyes. He quickly bowed his head on her shoulder to hide his emotions.

Damn her for turning him into a bundle of raw nerves. Only when the strain against his erection eased could he begin to rock, gliding in and out between her slick core.

She gasped and moved against him.

"Fuck." It felt so good. Before he could say something damaging like "I love you", he took her mouth in another kiss. But this one was tender. He attempted to rein in his tormented feelings, tried to take hold of himself and the situation.

Dean just about had everything under control, until she cried. "More, Dean. Harder." Her desperate cries threw him over the edge and he lost it.

He tore his lips from hers. Air escaped from his lungs in a single gush.

Blood rushed to his groin. His balls slammed tight against his body. Grinding his teeth, he held on to his climax—barely.

As he withdrew, his cock hardened even more, making his toes curl in his boots. With a savage thrust, he buried himself deep into her warmth. Flames licked his moist skin.

Her inner muscles clamped down then rippled across him, lighting the fuse to his orgasm. He exploded. With one more grind of his hips against hers, he paused, unable to move as he came.

With a sudden jerk, she threw back her head and screamed, following him into the arms of heaven. A series of spasms made her twitch and writhe against him.

Damn. It drove him crazy when she did that.

A low, sated sigh brushed the damp hair at his neck and sent goose bumps across his arms.

In the afterglow, he held her, unwilling to release her. Not now. Not when his nightly dreams were finally coming true. But the sound of the bar door opening and the rise of voices yanked him back to reality.

He had just fucked Lori Dayton in the parking lot of the Hillside Bar.

Without a second thought, he let her slide down his body. His breathing was labored, rapid pants. He frantically started to gather her clothes. He threw her jeans at her. She flinched, catching them before they whacked her in the face.

Mitch was going to kill him. "Get dressed," Dean barked.

"My panties?" Panic touched her breathy words.

"Can't find them." He scrambled to locate her other boot. Then he opened the Jeep's door and threw them inside. When he glanced in Lori's direction, he saw that she had found her shirt. She finished slipping it over her head when Mitch and Will turned the corner, heading straight for them.

Dean pivoted, his back to them. He tucked his flaccid cock inside his pants and fastened the zipper. There was dead silence, but he finished snapping and tucking his shirt, before he clasping his belt. He steeled his shoulders, readying himself to face the music as he turned toward Mitch.

Mitch's jaw clenched. His gaze shot to Lori leaning casually against her car, but the rapid rise and fall of her chest revealed she was anything but calm. He leveled his hot glare on Dean—if looks could kill...

Mitch focused back on his sister's disheveled condition. Mussed hair and barefooted, except for her shredded nylons, she appeared like a woman who had just been thoroughly made love to. "Lori?"

"Yeah?" Her voice squeaked, but she straightened her backbone.

His frown deepened. "Everything okay?"

"Of course." She cleared her throat, working way too hard to appear casual, as she thrust a hip out and placed her palm against it.

He narrowed his eyes. "If you're heading home, you might want to turn your shirt right side out before Mom sees you."

Lori's eyes widened before she looked down and saw the seams showing.

Then Mitch bent down and retrieved something. Dean knew he was a dead man when Mitch rose with Lori's silky red panties hanging off one finger. "Lose something?" He shook his head. "Fucking in a fucking parking lot?"

Will chuckled. "C'mon, big brother. Looks like everything is okay out here."

Dean snatched the panties from Mitch's hand and stuffed them into his pocket.

"Make sure she gets home safely." Mitch's voice softened to a menacing level. "Don't forget what I said, Wilcox."

Fuck the man. Mitch could threaten all he wanted, but tonight Lori was his.

"She's going home with me tonight," Dean said before he realized it. With a swipe of his hand he retrieved his Stetson from the roof of the Jeep and placed it firmly on his head. Next he grabbed her jacket and threw it inside the car.

"Keys." He held out his palm, waiting on a needle's point to see if she would refuse him. A breath of relief filled his lungs when she dug in her jean pocket and placed them in his hand.

Mitch was still glaring at them when they got into Lori's Jeep and spun away.

No one spoke as they drove the back roads to Dean's ranch. Maybe it was because it was the first time since that fateful night that Lori had truly felt whole. Maybe it was because once again she had screwed up. Both of them had been so caught in the moment that neither had realized they hadn't used a condom. It was like a replay of a very bad movie.

It took everything she had to hold back the tears. He hadn't really wanted to marry her back then. He sure as hell wouldn't want to now.

For a moment she was lost to the memory of that night. Mitch had deceived her. Dean knew she was pregnant. Lori had no doubt that the proposal came as a result of her brother's none-too-gentle persuasion. It hurt that Dean hadn't loved her enough to ask her to marry him before he knew a child was involved. He hadn't even tried to stop her from going to San Diego.

Memories forced her eyes shut. Lori curled her fingers into fists, nails biting into her palms. She hadn't known what to do that night. She wanted the baby, but without a father what kind of life could she offer? And then the decision was taken from her. In a flash, her life spun wildly on its axis and left her with nothing, not the life growing inside her or the man she loved.

Dean glanced at her. "You okay?"

A tight breath squeezed her lungs. She opened her eyes, a false smile on her face. "Fine." She rolled down her tattered knee-high nylons and tossed them in the back of the Jeep.

He stared blindly into the dark, headlights leading the way. "I'm sorry."

Her heart stopped. "Sorry?"

"Darlin', I should have never taken you like that. You deserve better."

She wanted to laugh with relief. He wasn't apologizing for the sex, but where and how it happened.

Instead of making a right to his ranch, he turned left passing several homes lit with Christmas lights.

A moment of panic struck. Was he going to turn around and take her home? "Where are we going?"

"Watson's."

Her chest tightened. Watson's Wash Hot Wells was northwest of town, a party location, and the first place they had made love. Was it just a coincidence or did Dean still feel something for her?

With a glide of his hand over the steering wheel, he turned the Jeep into a sandy wash. A few hundred yards inward the dry riverbed gave way to large cottonwoods, salt cedar trees and tamarisk bushes—a variable oasis in the desert. Cacti and shrub grass grew sparsely, and then the two-person stone tub appeared. Vapors rose from the heated pool as its warmth met the cool air. A rush of saltwater flowed from the spill-pipe casing into the manmade heaven. At a hundred and one degrees, the inflow and outflow rates promoted a natural cleansing effect. The water was pure enough to drink with a slight saline taste. But that was not what drew partiers to this obscure place.

Carved in the cement where people entered the tub were the words, "NO SWIM SUITS". It was a favorite place for adventurous couples and the occasional nudist seeking to commune with nature.

The Jeep came to a stop and for a moment they both sat quietly, unmoving. Dean shifted the gear into park and killed the engine. Lori didn't wait for him to speak. She opened her door and slipped from the Jeep, shutting the door with a thud. A pebble dug into the bare sole of her foot as she moved toward the pool. The musky smell of desert shrubs and dust stirred by the breeze touched her nose.

The whine of the Jeep windows rolling down joined the splash of water. And then she heard Dean flip the radio on. The country version of "I Saw Momma Kissing Santa Claus" filled the night. A full moon hung in the dark sky, a scattering of stars joined to set the scene.

Nervous and chilled from the cool weather, she hugged her chest and brushed her palms rapidly over her arms. Behind her, she could hear the thump of one boot and then the next as Dean began to undress. When he passed her, heading for the stone steps of the pool, she scanned his luscious body. His youthful form had bulked with muscles that rippled beneath his skin. His ass was taut, driving her wild with the need to touch him.

With one foot on the upper step, the other on the lower one, he turned to face her. His cock jutted out from the nest of curly, black hair. She couldn't help staring. A chuckle of male satisfaction greeted her. "Are you coming?"

Oh yes.

Shadows fell across his face, but she could see his full lips. "Strip for me, darlin'." His voice was sensual, stroking her as effectively as his hands could.

Catching the rhythm of the Christmas music, she crossed her arms and grasped the hem of her shirt. She let her hips sway before she took one step closer to him. He smiled, his cock rewarding her with a jerk. It helped to ease the tension inside her. Slowly, she raised her shirt up, revealing her breasts, already heavy with need.

When she threw the shirt aside, he groaned, "You're killing me."

They had attempted this play before. Each time he had grown impatient, stripping her naked before she could complete the dance.

But not this time.

Easing into the warm water, the lower half of his body disappeared beneath the depths. He leaned casually against the cement and stone ridge, his arms stretched wide on the bank of the pool.

A breath caught in her throat. He was so damn sexy sitting there and watching her. When she raised her arms high above her head and stretched, her breasts rose invitingly. Cupping the sides of her neck, she lifted her hair. A cool breeze caressed her skin, feathering her hair across her shoulders. With a gentle shift of her feet, she undulated her hips in slow, sensual movements.

She reached for the button of her jeans and unfastened it, swaying her hips, dancing, as she eased her zipper down.

"Sonofabitch." Dean growled, a low, deep sound that made a shiver race up her back.

She laughed. Her thumbs slid beneath the band of her jeans and gradually began to drag them down her hips and legs.

When they fell around her ankles, he groaned, "Get your ass over here."

Elated with the break they had made, she wasted no time to oblige him. He still hadn't moved from where he sat, watching—waiting.

The rocky surface was cool beneath her feet as she climbed the stairs. The warm water was welcoming. She eased next to him, but found herself pulled into his lap. For a moment all he did was hold her. Inhaling, she breathed in Old Spice and rested her cheek against his chest.

Then his lips found hers.

Gentle and tender, he moved his mouth over hers. His tongue traced the seam of her lips and then thrust inside. She angled her head, deepening the kiss, and flicked her tongue against his.

When he released her to feather kisses down her throat, she arched, loving the feel of his mouth on her skin.

An owl screeched high above them. The hot water combined with the burn simmering through her veins made her twist so that she straddled him. She raised and impaled herself on his rock-hard cock.

"Fuck, woman. You're tight." He nipped her shoulder.

She leaned back and let the buoyancy of the water keep her afloat. He cupped and kneaded her breasts. With a slow, easy pace, she rode him. Eyes closed, she relished the moment until he pinched her nipples hard, forcing a gasp from her lips and her eyelids to rise.

Fire flickered in his eyes. "Dammit. I need more." He moved her off his lap. Her hair felt wet and heavy against her back. "Place your hands on the bank."

A breeze whipped around her as she stood, turned around and placed her palms on the gravelly surface. Before she could get cold, he spooned her from behind. His rigid cock slipped between her legs. He pressed his palm on her back and guided her forward. Then pushed his foot between hers and spread her legs wide.

He must have held his cock in his hand, because she felt it tease across her clit to her anus and then back again before he entered her.

With hard, fast thrusts, he began to fuck her. She had to lock her elbows to keep from falling forward. The water rippled around her thighs, then began to splash over the banks as he pounded in her time after time.

When his fingers found her clit the knot inside her belly tightened. "Dean."

He was breathing hard. Masculine moans and groans told her he was close. For that matter so was she. Every nerve in her body tensed. They had already tempted fate once tonight.

"Dean. No condom." Her warning came out breathy.

"Holy shit."

He jumped away from her like she burst into flames. The jolt almost sent her over the rocky ledge, but she caught herself just in time

"Not again."

She shot a glance over her shoulder. His words and the panic widening his eyes was a punch to her stomach.

A moment of sorrow struck hard. Her hands drifted to her side. Then anger flared.

Dammit. This isn't all my fault. Squaring her shoulders, she raised her chin and quickly moved toward the steps. "I'm out of here."

"Lori?" He grabbed her arm, but she jerked away.

"Just take me home," she snapped.

"Not on your life, darlin'." There was a snarl in his voice. "We have some talking to do and we're not leaving until things between us are settled." The determined look in his eyes was unwavering.

Chapter Four

In the distance, saguaros stood like sentries. The desert scenery was a shadowy backdrop in the moonlit night. Crickets chirped and the Jeep's radio belted out one country Christmas carol after another. Water continued to spill into the hot spring, a haze of steam wafting from its surface.

Both naked, Dean stood facing Lori. The waves they had previously churned inside the small pool were calm around their knees, but the turmoil inside him continued to rage. In the parking lot of the Hillside bar, he'd had unprotected sex with Lori. Without thinking past his cock, he was about to screw up once again.

She stopped on the top step of the stone tub and looked defiantly down at him. "We don't have anything to say to each other." She moved briskly down the steps. When her feet touched the sandy ground, she headed toward the Jeep. He followed behind her, stopping when his warm flesh met the chilly air.

Fuck. It was cold. He stubbed his toe on the rocky surface. Pain splintered through his foot.

Tree branches swayed, their leaves rustling in the breeze. The strong aroma of greasewoods almost overwhelmed the soft scent of the woman running away from him. He couldn't let her go—not this time.

A sudden pain burrowing into the bottom of his foot made him jump and then crow hop. He reached down and dug out the pebble embedded in his instep as Lori reached the Jeep.

With a quick spin on the balls of her feet, she faced him. "Let's just forget about tonight." Angry tears swam in her eyes. Water beaded and rolled down her exposed body. Lips trembling, a shiver shook her. "I'm leaving tomorrow."

She bent over and retrieved her jeans. Her movements were sharp and clipped. With a wiggle, she struggled to get them over her wet hips.

"Just forget I was ever here." With a swipe of her hand, she grabbed her T-shirt off the ground and shook the sand out of it. Buried beneath the shirt now over her head, she grumbled, "Merry Christmas, Dean."

Her wet hair immediately dampened the cloth and made the material almost transparent, outlining her taut nipples.

Reaching for his jeans, he heard the Jeep door moan as she yanked open the driver's door and climbed inside. He hopped on one foot trying to get to her and simultaneously put his damn pants on. Jeans up one leg, he caught the door before she closed it.

Dean leaned over her and snatched the keys from the ignition. She wasn't going anywhere, especially without him.

Lori leveled him with a heated glare. "Give me the keys."

With his body, he jarred the door open. He raised his unclothed leg and crammed it into his pants, pulling them over his hips. She lunged for the keys. He jerked his hand and held the keys high above his head, barely escaping her grasp.

"Get out. I'll drive." Still holding the keys away from her with his free hand, he eased his semi-erect cock into his jeans. There was no way he could fasten his pants with one hand as she lunged for the keys once more.

"The hell you will." A flush reddened her face. She clenched the steering wheel so tight her knuckles whitened. Looking straight ahead, she said, "Give. Me. The. Keys."

"Fuck, Lori." He gripped her chin and forced her fiery gaze to meet his. "I'm freezing my ass off, but you'll hear me out before this night is over." He trembled with the effort it took to set aside his pride. He released her chin, afraid if he touched her he couldn't continue. He inhaled a breath of courage.

"I loved you." Air escaped his lungs in a single gush. She stared at him, unmoving. He waited for a reply that didn't come.

Exasperated, he crammed the keys in his pocket.

"Dammit, woman!" He closed his eyes, trying to hold onto his mettle. His jaw clenched and released.

This wasn't how he wanted this night to go.

"I still do." Resignation softened his voice. "I always have."

Dean couldn't read her expression. She didn't move or say anything.

Not a good sign.

Rapidly, he brushed his fingers through his hair. He'd already shelved his dignity. He might as well ask the burning question that had been on his mind for the last four years.

"Why?" He paused, choking on the single word. With a gulp, he swallowed his sentiment. "Why wouldn't you marry me?"

Hands still clutching the steering wheel, she raised her chin slightly. "I didn't want to force you into marrying me because of the baby."

His broken laughter met her reply. "Darlin', I've wanted to marry you since we were in high school and nothing's changed."

Color seeped from her face, leaving her pale. "Then why didn't you ask me?" Big tears fell down her cheeks. "Why did you wait until Mitch coerced you?"

"Ahhh... Darlin'." With his fingertips, Dean wiped the tears from her cheeks. Crouching low, he came eye to eye with her. "Mitch didn't coerce me. He felt I had a right to know about my child." He placed a palm on her thigh, and then slid it to cover her belly. "You carried my son or daughter."

Her face crumbled into a mass of agonizing emotion. "I'm sorry," she sobbed. Her head bowed so it leaned against the steering wheel as she wept.

Gently, Dean pried her fingers off the wheel and turned her body so he could wedge himself between her thighs. He kneeled, wrapping his arms around her waist, his head pressed to her chest. Her gut-wrenching cries tore at his heart. She was hurting and there was nothing he could do.

She hiccupped, the involuntary contraction making her gulp down more air. "You didn't even try to stop me from going to San Diego." Her heart beat rapidly against his ear. Her cries shook them both.

He raised his head to look at her. "I didn't want to be the one to take away your dreams, Lori. I was willing to wait until you finished school." He warred with the tears stinging behind his eyelids. "Then the accident... You left without a word. No goodbye. Nothing."

Memories of that day drove him to his feet. He turned away from her, trying to hold onto his control. His dad had died shortly after Lori left. His mom had passed a year later.

He had been so alone.

So many times he had dialed Lori's number at the dorm. Listened to her answer and then he would hang up. Childish— yes—but it was the only thing that kept him from losing his mind.

"Oh God," she gasped. "This is all my fault."

He spun around, sand squeezing through his toes as he pulled her from the Jeep and held her at arm's length. "This isn't your fault." With his finger beneath her chin, he raised her lips to meet his. Raining soft kisses across her face, he said, "If I hadn't been so stubborn. If I hadn't pushed you away that night…"

"I desperately wanted our child." She clutched her hands to her heart. "I just didn't know how I would raise him without you."

"Darlin', that would have never happened." He pressed his lips to her forehead.

"But it's too late. Look what I've done." She buried her face into his chest, weaving her arms around his neck.

Tears of loss and regret ran down his skin. His arms tightened around her. "It was an accident. The truck ran into you."

Her sorrow continued to fall. He recognized the guilt eating at her, because he felt the same ugliness gnawing at his belly. They had been such fools.

With a swipe of his arm beneath her knees, he cradled her to his chest. "You're freezing. I'm taking you home with me."

She sniffled. "Dean, it's Christmas morning. It's what, one a.m.? My mom is expecting me."

"Well, darlin', she's gonna have to wait, because I've spent the last Christmas away from you that I'm willing to."

Hastily, he rounded the Jeep and braced her against the vehicle to open the door. With a quick kiss, he placed her on the passenger seat and shut the door before heading back to the driver's side. On the way, he picked up his Stetson and placed it squarely on his head. He reached for his shirt and boots and threw them in the back of the Jeep as he climbed in. With a grunt, he pressed his back against the seat and reached into his jeans to retrieve the keys. Within seconds, the Jeep hummed to life, the scent of the heater filling the confines.

Except for the radio and heater, silence filled the Jeep. Lori leaned against the door, staring out in the darkness.

Dean still loved her.

Although she was thrilled, the moment felt surreal, almost unreal. Night after night, she had dreamed of him holding their child, both lost to her. With a heavy sigh, she placed her palm on her stomach. A habit she had developed over the past four years.

She startled when he clasped his hand over hers. "Let it go, sweetheart." He gave her a tentative smile, which she returned.

He was right. They had been given a second chance.

The dirt road to his home was bumpy, tossing them about as they passed through the wrought iron entrance of Wilcox Cattle Ranch. Headlights led their way to the four-bedroom Spanish-style house she'd been in a million times.

It was Dean's home now. Did he have roommates?

When his parents had passed on, she had wanted to come to him, but feared what his reception would have been. Had he needed her?

The fading of the radio and engine dying put her a little on edge. She didn't know what to expect. All her insecurities vanished when he opened the door, climbed out and moved quickly around the vehicle to open her door. In a heartbeat, she was in his arms.

"C'mon." He released her, setting her on her feet, but kept a tight hold on her hand.

After he unlocked the door, he stepped aside to let her enter. It was dark and quiet. Unlike her parents' home that was aglow with Christmas decorations. A flick of his finger against a switch and light flooded the room with cedar walls and tile flooring. He hadn't put a tree by the fireplace like his mom always had. Nothing hung from the mantel—no stockings or

Christmas cards. In fact, she wouldn't even know it was Christmas by the looks of his home.

Dean seemed to guess what she was thinking. "Didn't seem necessary for only me." He took off his hat, running his fingers through his hair before he hung the Stetson on a coat rack.

He lived alone.

The sad moment passed as he took her once again into his embrace and kissed her. "God, I've missed you," he whispered in her ear. Then he ran his palms up and down her arms. "You're freezing." A devilish grin and a twinkle in his eyes flashed. "Let's take a shower."

Like two kids hand in hand, they bounded through the living room, down the hall, until they came to the master bedroom.

Lori had never been in his parents' bedroom. It was big and spacious. The scent of Old Spice was stronger here. A hand-carved, four-poster bed of pine dominated the room. Dean had once told Lori his father made the bed especially for his mother. She didn't get to see much more than the bed. With a jerk, he led her into a large bathroom equipped with a bathtub and a shower, dual sinks and a toilet closed off to the side.

Since Dean wasn't wearing a shirt and his pants were still unzipped, he was undressed in no time. Naked, he padded to the shower stall. The glass door squeaked as he reached in and turned the faucet on. Then he glanced over his shoulder. "Shy?"

A playful grin creased her lips. She ripped her shirt off over her head and tossed it on the counter. Her fingers felt numb fumbling with the button at her jeans, but soon she was naked.

Steam began to rise above the shower, fogging the mirrors. One after the other they stepped inside. "Ahhh..." she groaned. Warm water rushed over her body. "This is heavenly."

From behind, his form cupped hers. Strong, callused hands cradled her breasts as his rigid cock slipped between her thighs. She leaned back and let the water caress her while Dean took care of the rest.

Kneading and fondling, he rolled her nipples between his fingers. When he pinched the nubs, a delicious ache raced through them releasing a flood of moisture to anoint her thighs.

"I've dreamed of you in here with me." His voice was deep and sensual, smoothing over her now heated skin. He reached for a squirt of the liquid soap hanging from the wall and began to lather her body.

It felt too good to be true.

A tremor of disbelief clawed her spine. She turned in his arms. "Dean, is this real? I won't wake up at any moment and you'll be gone?" Lori had experienced this way too many times.

"It's real, darlin'."

"But I live in San Diego. Go to school there—"

"Shhh..." He started to place a soapy finger against her lips, but stopped just in time. "We'll work things out. But for now I need to be in you."

Locked in his arms, he guided her until her back struck the cold glass surface. Then he placed his palms beneath her ass and lifted her, moving her up the shower wall. Her legs parted and he nestled between them. She locked her ankles together, pulling him closer to her aching flesh. When he entered her, she gasped at the exquisite fullness. He was hard and thick, thrusting in and out of her slick pussy.

His glare was hot and needy. His mouth slightly parted. "Damn, woman," he grunted.

As the pace increased, she could swear he grew larger, driving so deep she could feel him bounce off the wall of her womb. Inner muscles clamped down on him in attempt to keep him right where he belonged—inside her forever.

"I can't believe how hot you are." A hint of a smile touched his mouth. "So fucking hot," he groaned. His tongue wet his lips. He swallowed hard.

With a coarse growl, he slammed into her hard, sending spasms deep inside her to splinter. She cried out, refusing to lose it so quickly.

"Let it go, darlin'."

His encouragement was all she needed to push her over the edge. With the next thrust, he threw her into heaven. Every muscle tensed. A burst of heat suffused her body. The water, small pellets against her skin, did nothing to quench the fire as one after another, spasms racked her body. She writhed against him. Unmercifully, he ground his hips, wringing every last sensation from her soul.

A quiver shook him. He buried his head against her shoulder, fighting his climax.

Dammit. She'd forgotten the condom, but evidently he hadn't. He stood unmoving, his fingers buried into her ass. Then he released her and let her soap-slick body ease down his.

"Let's finish up." His voice sounded strained. His eyes darkened with desire.

Lori used some kind of herbal shampoo and quickly washed her hair as he did the same. They took turns rinsing off, sharing kisses in between. The faucet whined when Dean turned it off and opened the shower door to reach for a couple of towels. He handed one to Lori and she began to towel dry her long, blonde hair. He did the same before using his towel to dry her body. He touched and looked at her as if she was a precious gem.

"Gorgeous." He breathed the word.

She greeted him with a nervous giggle. "And you're crazy."

He ran the towel over his wet body. "Crazy about you."

When he jerked her to him, she released a squeal of surprise that turned to laughter. Before she knew it, she was cradled in his arms and he was headed to the big bed.

Gently, he laid her down upon the patchwork quilt and then moved towards one of the nightstands next to the bed. The drawer creaked as he slid it open and extracted a condom. His hesitant gaze rose to meet hers. "Do we use it or not?"

An array of emotions filtered through her. Her pulse leaped and tears filled her eyes. Could all her Christmas wishes be coming true? She shook her head, sending cool, wet hair sliding across her shoulders.

As he tossed the small package over his shoulders, a feral expression flared across his face. With predatory steps, he moved toward the bed.

Through shuttered eyelids he gazed at her. "Mine," he growled. "All mine." His muscular body covered hers, his hand parting her thighs, and he moved between them.

Without a second thought, he entered her. Filling her so thoroughly a tear fell from the corner of her eye.

Not once did he close his eyes. With an expertise she didn't know he possessed, he worked her body and soul into an ecstasy high. With each glide of his chest across her sensitive nipples they felt like they were going to explode with delight. The tightening low in her belly wrapped around every nerve ending to tease and tantalize and drive her wild. When she arched her back and let her orgasm take her away, he joined her, filling her with his warm seed.

The moment was serene. Their bodies convulsed as one, writhing against each other to get closer. His soft moans and groans mingled with hers. It was a perfect point in time that she would always cherish.

As the flame inside her cooled, she lay in his arms. He smoothed his palm up her thigh to rest upon her abdomen. And that's how Lori fell asleep—locked in the arms of the man she loved.

Chapter Five

Lori's eyes opened and closed quickly. Sunlight spilled through the parted curtains, flooding the bedroom. Blindly, she patted the area next to her seeking Dean, but the sheets were cool. The only thing that remained was his spicy aftershave. She loved Old Spice.

Funny, how quickly she'd almost forgotten about life in Safford. Unlike city life, there were cattle, horses and ranch hands to feed. There were no lazy mornings for someone like Dean Wilcox.

Still Lori was a little disappointed. Night after night she'd dreamed of waking up in his arms, his bed. With a grin of pure satisfaction on her face, she snuggled deeper into the comforter. In the process, she slid her hand beneath a pillow catching her finger on something that caused her to go no farther. She inched her sleepy eyes open and raised her hand before her face. A red ribbon was tied around one of her fingers. With her other hand, she reached for the loose end of the bow and pulled. A gasp caught midway up her throat. The brightest diamond she'd ever seen and it was sitting on the ring finger of her left hand.

Wait. She'd seen this ring before. It had been Dean's mother's wedding ring and now it was hers. Happiness bubbled up inside her. She threw the quilt off of her naked body, but couldn't quite make it out of bed before taking one more look at the glittering ring. She was admiring it when Dean walked through the door. He snatched his cowboy hat off his head, his wavy black hair damp against his forehead. His boots thumped across the floor as he approached the nightstand and laid his hat on it.

His smile went from ear to ear. "I see you've already opened your Christmas present." One snap and then another popped as he started to remove his blue denim shirt. His white undershirt followed until she feasted on his muscular chest.

"It's beautiful, Dean."

The sound of his buckle and belt being undone made her squirm beneath his warm gaze.

"You're beautiful."

She scooted toward the headboard to rest on her forearms. With a coy grin, she asked, "What are you doing?"

He sat on the edge of the bed and pulled his boots off. Pushing to his feet, he reached for the waistband of his jeans and dragged them down his legs. His cock jerked alive as it rose from its cotton confines.

"You didn't give me my Christmas present." Naked, his rock-hard erection jutted out from between his thighs.

A frown pulled her brows together. "But I didn't get you anything."

"Darlin', you've given me the best Christmas gift ever—your love." He crawled on the bed toward her. "Now I'm gonna seal the deal by taking your body over and over again."

Heartfelt laughter squeezed from her chest. Happily, she fell back against the fluffy pillow.

He kneeled at her feet. "Now open up for me, darlin'. I'm hungry."

Damn the man was sexy. His blue gaze followed her legs as she bent them. With a slow glide, she exposed herself.

"Nice." A devilish glint in his eyes met hers before he wedged his hands beneath her ass to raise her hips. Then his mouth touched her folds. She startled.

"Dean," she cried.

The sensation was like nothing she'd ever felt as his warm breath and tongue caressed her folds.

No one had ever gone down on her before, not even Dean. He licked a circle around her clit, then made a path along her slit before dipping inside to taste her. Her fingers clenched the bedding.

"Oh God."

Amazingly she was already on the verge of losing it. Every inch of her body screamed for more. When his tongue circled her clit, she grasped his head and pulled him closer. His soft groans echoed through her sex, sending her heart to lunge in her throat. She couldn't help the rise of her hips as he penetrated her deep, sucking and nipping at her flesh. When his tongue flicked over her swollen bud, she bucked beneath him and released a scream. Spasm after spasm washed through her.

Her cries released the animal in him and he began to devour her with such vehemence she thought she'd die. "Dean. Oh God. Dean." Pleasure so intense racked her body. She bucked again and he held her pinned to the bed, continuing his assault. "No more. God, no more."

From between her thighs, he gazed at her. "Good?"

"Amazing. I never knew—"

Male pride teased his lips into a smile. "I'm your first?"

Tears filled her eyes. She nodded.

A low rumble rose from his chest as he moved up her body. Without pause, he savagely captured her mouth. Surprise widened her eyes as she tasted herself on his tongue when he swept past her lips. It was strange and exciting. And she liked it. His kiss was passionate. His tongue caressed every inch of her mouth in a heated declaration of possession.

At the same time he entered her body, filling her completely with his cock. Tucked tightly inside her, he began to rock. Each slow movement was controlled and meant to dominate and force her surrender. But she needed no coercion, she willingly surrendered.

Muscles tensed beneath her palms. With long strokes she caressed his back, dragging her fingernails across his taut skin. He smelled spicy and all male. His heart beat rapidly matching the rhythm of hers. Their breathing was labored and a light sheen of perspiration coated them.

"Come for me, Lori," he cried, before he threw back his head and a deep, satisfying groan pushed from between his lips.

As he released his seed, she tumbled over the precipice, joining him. Sensation splintered into colorful facets behind her eyelids before it rushed hot and unrestrained throughout her body. She shook from the intensity of her orgasm, holding onto Dean to keep herself from drowning in the pleasure. And then a peace like she had never known wrapped around her.

Lori was finally home.

The quiet moment was lost when Dean said, "We need to go." He released her and rose from the bed.

Confusion furrowed her brows. "Go? Where?"

Jeans in hand, he began to dress. "Your mom called. She's threatened to tan my hide if I don't have you home within the hour."

"She scares you?" Lori chuckled, rising.

"No." He went to the closet and picked out a clean western shirt. "But I've tangled with those three big brothers of yours before." He shoved his arms through the sleeves. "Best to give them what they want now, because after we're married you're mine."

Married? That had such a sweet ring to it. She couldn't resist going to Dean and snaking her arms around his neck.

"What?" he asked, as he folded her into his embrace.

"I love you." She perched on tiptoes and kissed him lightly.

His face softened with tender emotion. "You don't know how long I've waited to hear you say that again." He slanted his lips over hers. "Don't ever leave me, Lori."

"Never," she whispered and meant it with every beat of her heart. "Now let's go show my family just what we've been up to."

He raised a brow, a smile teasing the corner of his mouth.

"Not that," she huffed, swatting his shoulder. "This." She raised her hand to show off her ring.

"Mrs. Dean Wilcox." There was pride in his grin and the gleam in his eyes.

She snuggled closer to him. "I like the sound of that."

"You better, because I'll give you a week before I drag you down the aisle."

With a startled jerk, she pulled out of his arms. "A week?"

His expression went stern. "Darlin', I've already waited a lifetime, don't make me wait any longer."

One step had her back in his arms. His hands griped her bare ass. She danced her fingertips up his shirt until she cupped his face. "I thought after we visited my family, we'd hightail it to Las Vegas. A week is too long to wait."

He raised her off her feet and spun her around. She threw back her head and allowed her happiness to show in her laughter. Lori could think of nothing more precious than two people exchanging vows on this special day.

Because their second chance at love was truly the ultimate Christmas gift.

About the Author

To learn more about Mackenzie McKade, please visit www.mackenziemckade.com. Send an email to Mackenzie at Mackenzie@mackenziemckade.com or visit the Wicked Writers' group to join in the fun with Mackenzie and other authors and readers! http://groups.yahoo.com/group/wicked_writers/

Look for these titles

Now Available

Six Feet Under
Fallon's Revenge
Beginnings: A Warrior's Witch
Bound for the Holidays
Lisa's Gift
Take Me
Lost But Not Forgotten

Discover the Talons Series

5 STEAMY NEW PARANORMAL ROMANCES
TO HOOK YOU IN

Kiss Me Deadly, by Shannon Stacey
King of Prey, by Mandy M. Roth
Firebird, by Jaycee Clark
Caged Desire, by Sydney Somers
Seize the Hunter, by Michelle M. Pillow

AVAILABLE IN EBOOK—COMING SOON IN PRINT!

WWW.SAMHAINPUBLISHING.COM

GET IT NOW

MyBookStoreAndMore.com
GREAT EBOOKS, GREAT DEALS . . . AND MORE!

Don't wait to run to the bookstore down the street, or
waste time shopping online at one of the "big boys." Now,
all your favorite Samhain authors are all in one place—at
MyBookStoreAndMore.com. Stop by today and discover
great deals on Samhain—and a whole lot more!

Discover eBooks!

THE FASTEST WAY TO GET THE HOTTEST NAMES

Get your favorite authors on your favorite reader, long before they're
out in print! Ebooks from Samhain go wherever you go, and work with
whatever you carry—Palm, PDF, Mobi, and more.

WWW.SAMHAINPUBLISHING.COM